THE GALLERY OF
LOST SPECIES

THE GALLERY OF
LOST SPECIES

NINA BERKHOUT

Thomas Dunne Books
St. Martin's Press
New York

THOMAS DUNNE BOOKS.
An imprint of St. Martin's Press.

THE GALLERY OF LOST SPECIES. Copyright © 2015 by Nina Berkhout. All rights reserved. Printed in the United States of America. For information, address St. Martin's Press, 175 Fifth Avenue, New York, N.Y. 10010.

www.thomasdunnebooks.com
www.stmartins.com

Page 22: Stanza from poem "Spring Morning" by A. A. Milne. Source: Library and Archives Canada / *When We Were Very Young* / AMICUS 8963009 / p. 34

Page 301–302: Excerpts from chapter "In which Piglet meets a Heffalump" by A. A. Milne. Source: Library and Archives Canada / *Winnie the Pooh* / AMICUS 970184 / Chapter V

Page 312: Heuvelmans quote is from *Cryptozoology*, Volume 7, 1988

Page 312: Heuvelmans quote is from Bernard Heuvelmans, *On the Track of Unknown Animals* (Paladin Press, 1970), p. 17

Designed by Alysia Shewchuk

Library of Congress Cataloging-in-Publication Data

Names: Berkhout, Nina, 1975– author.
Title: The gallery of lost species : a novel / Nina Berkhout.
Description: First U.S. edition. | New York : Thomas Dunne Books / St. Martin's Press, 2016. | 2015 | "First published in Canada by House of Anansi Press Inc. 2015"—Title page verso.
Identifiers: LCCN 2015049801 | ISBN 9781250085078 (hardcover) | ISBN 9781250085085 (e-book)
Subjects: LCSH: Self-actualization (Psychology)—Fiction. | Man-woman relationships—Fiction. | Sisters—Fiction. | BISAC: FICTION / Literary. | FICTION / Family Life.
Classification: LCC PR9199.4.B475 G34 2016 | DDC 813/.6—dc23
LC record available at http://lccn.loc.gov/2015049801

Our books may be purchased in bulk for promotional, educational, or business use. Please contact your local bookseller or the Macmillan Corporate and Premium Sales Department at 1-800-221-7945, extension 5442, or by e-mail at MacmillanSpecialMarkets@macmillan.com.

First published in Canada by House of Anansi Press Inc

First U.S. Edition: May 2016

10 9 8 7 6 5 4 3 2 1

For R.
and for my sister, Nadine

Real magic can never be made by offering up someone else's liver. You must tear out your own, and not expect to get it back.

— Peter S. Beagle, *The Last Unicorn*

crypto·zo·ology *noun* the search for and study of animals whose existence or survival is disputed or unsubstantiated, such as the Loch Ness monster and the sasquatch [Etymology: literally "study of hidden animals" from Greek *kryptos* (hidden) + *zoos* (animals) + *logos* (study)].

— *Canadian Oxford Dictionary*

THE GALLERY OF
LOST SPECIES

WHEN I WAS THIRTEEN, I saw a unicorn.

It happened the summer my father piled us into the wood-panelled station wagon and drove for a week straight to get to the Rockies.

We stayed in a motel off the highway near an old CP Rail town called Field. I looked the place up on a map recently and was surprised to see it was still there. Even back then it felt abandoned, as if everyone had left long ago.

My father planned the holiday a good year in advance, enticing my mother with brochures from the Automobile Association and buying gear he couldn't afford from the Mountain Equipment Co-op. He was no avid outdoorsman, he was a painter. But like so many family men, something in him craved that rugged, solitary landscape. This meant that every few years my sister and I wound up canoeing lakes in the backwoods of Manitoba or trekking along logging roads in northern Ontario while our friends went to Marineland, Disneyland, or the beach.

Driving across the country, my father went on about art and nature, addressing us in the rear-view mirror. He enjoyed preaching to us about the aesthetic beauty of the Great Canadian Wilderness. The day trips he planned revolved around Group of Seven haunts, culminating in a visit to Lake O'Hara, the subject of some of J. E. H. Mac-Donald's better-known canvases.

We travelled by bus for this portion of our trip. It was the only way to reach the lake unless we hiked the eleven kilometres in, uphill on a gravel road. My mother opted to visit the Château Lake Louise that day. She forfeited her spot on the bus at the last minute, so it was just us: me, my father, and my sister, Viv.

I was glad my mother wasn't coming. She'd be in a bad mood and slow us down. She joined us on a few excursions, digging up wildflowers she later pressed or suntanning on picnic tables, massaging the olive oil meant for salads onto her antennae-like arms and legs while we walked along the riverbank. But mostly we'd drop her off in Banff so she could shop, or she stayed in the room watching soaps until we picked her up for supper.

I remember my mother clearly on that trip. Flipping through *Paris Match* magazines, legs stretched carelessly across my father's lap as he drove through never-ending wheat fields, golden and rippling like her hair. Her complexion was flawless. She was forever seeking the holy grail of creams that would "youngify" her skin. Behind Jackie O sunglasses, her eyes — large and cold like reflecting moons — scanned the countryside in search of amusement. Or, like a teenager, she'd paint her toenails fire-engine red on the dashboard, dangling her feet out the window as she smoked cigarette after cigarette, half-heartedly partaking in I Spy or counting crows when we grew restless.

She baited us with made-up things in the scenery. I hunted for smouldering scarecrows and Zeppelins out the back window until Viv cursed, "Christ on a stick get real, Constance!" and she reached back with her free arm to slap my sister.

From the time we could talk, our mother made us call her Constance and our father Henry. North American children don't respect parents with no identity, she'd say. After that trip, Viv called her the Con, but never in front of our father. And never to her face.

WHEN WE ARRIVED at Lake O'Hara, we climbed a lush mountainside and stopped to rest by a waterfall partway up the trail. My father pulled a Thermos from his knapsack as I perched beside him on a boulder, scouring the valley for my mother until he told me she was out of visual range. Then a mote formed at the edge of my vision, a white fleck on green that caused the hairs to rise along my spine.

I jumped up, hollering, "Uuunniiiicooooorrrn!" over the turbulent cascades.

Viv was scrambling up a rock slide and missed it.

My father put his tin cup down, got up from his foam pad, and raised a hand to his forehead to form a visor against the sun. He squinted in the direction I was pointing then brought the binoculars, which hung around his neck, to his eyes, and pulled them away then back again, focusing and refocusing. He took his time examining the animal resting on the slope, eating grass. Then he turned to me and said, "By gosh you're right. It's a unicorn, Edith."

This was probably the last of my innocent imagination as I left childhood behind. It didn't occur to me that a male grown-up was unlikely to see this enchanted creature. I wasn't familiar enough with legends and my convictions stemmed from longing more than logic.

It would be years before I understood the unicorn was only a goat. But my father always encouraged us to use our imaginations.

"Do you have a story?" he'd ask me each night at bed-time. The story could be about anything—a leprechaun, an ant, a sidewalk crack, or a sound. "If at the end of your day you haven't got a story, your day has been wasted."

"I have a story for you."

"Tell me," he'd say.

ONE

ONE

My sister was a child beauty queen. Whenever she'd win another ten-pound crown, our mother would regurgitate the epic tale of Viv's first pageant as though it were a feat comparable to conquering Everest. Constance was eight months pregnant with me—*eight months!*—when she snuck her blue Chevy Malibu out of the garage and drove her three-year-old daughter all the way to the Kingston pageant and back, through a freak blizzard, without winter tires.

Arriving at the local Legion, she yanked a half-asleep Vivienne from her snowsuit. Opening her umbrella against the squall, she got out of the car and ran around to the trunk to extract a tutu obtained at Goodwill, which she'd refashioned the week prior.

Diving into the back seat, she groomed Viv in record time, painting her face and costuming her. She used a butane curling iron and an Avon travel kit bought from a neighbour for the occasion. The kit was made up of a wing for brushes and applicators, and three drawers containing six eye pencils and one liquid eyeliner, three lip pencils, forty-six eyeshadows, thirty lip glosses, six press powders, one mascara, three lipsticks, and four nail polishes.

With seconds to spare, Constance ushered my sister through the stale-smelling pool hall to the registration table. She pinned a number onto the stiff netting of Viv's skirt and shoved her onto the makeshift stage, reminding her to wink at the judges.

Over the next few hours, Vivienne competed against girls with names like Isis, Aurora, Mercedes, and Trinity. The panel was tickled by her uncompetitive, laissez-faire attitude. With her crystal-embellished outfit, her spell-binding eyes and pouty lips, she was awarded the highest honour — the Mini Supreme Queen crown — along with five hundred dollars, a Red Lobster voucher, and a hot pink double-column trophy standing twice her height.

As the story goes, I kicked so hard when Viv won that my mother thought she'd deliver me on the Precious Cutie-Pie pageant floor. She sped home before my father arrived from work, hastily spreading Viv's loot across the dining room table. Thanks to our selfless mother's adventurous spirit, my sister's fate was sealed on that tempestuous day.

Moreover, Constance was unashamed to admit to living vicariously through Vivienne. "I did *not* have such opportunities, *ma fille!*" she'd exclaim in her sophisticated accent as she considered my sister's prizes.

When she was younger, our mother dreamt of becoming a celebrity. She left France for *les États* without looking back. In New York, she endured the drudgery of au pair work, and saved every cent she earned for her intended move to Hollywood. Then she met our father.

Fresh off the Greyhound from rural Ontario, he painted

Hopper knock-offs in an unheated loft, took night classes at the Art Students' League, and worked as a cleaner during the day. Modelling for extra cash, Constance was intrigued by this unconventional man who sketched her hundreds of times in their first weeks together, or so she said.

Nulla Dies Sine Linea. No Day Without a Line. That was the League's motto. And Henry Walker fed Constance Moreau plenty of lines, reciting Leonard Cohen to her through the night, promising her the moon. But he got to New York too late, studying in a place whose importance was dwindling. Influential artists had been replaced by untalented kids with hefty allowances, and my sister and I ended up being named after the songstress and the star our mother never became: Vivien Leigh, the manic actress who died of TB, and Édith Piaf, who also perished in a rundown way.

After two years in New York, Constance was ready to move on. Henry's paintings weren't selling and nobody would take his work for barter anymore. He couldn't make the rent or pay for classes.

My mother bought herself a one-way ticket home to her Paris *banlieue*, settling back in with her parents. Soon after she found a job at a cosmetics counter, the morning sickness began. Her mother insisted she send a telegram to *l'homme* and return to him at once. Henry wrote back, proposing.

Constance wanted to live in Montreal because she'd read *The Tin Flute*. But in the mid-eighties, the Quebec economy was unstable and the separatist movement was intensifying. Raising a family in such a volatile political climate wouldn't be safe, my father said. They settled in the nation's capital instead, an hour away from the farm where Henry grew up, like Constance, as an only child. After his parents had died, the property had been repossessed by the Crown.

In Ottawa, my father got a job as a janitor in the public service. They purchased a house in Mechanicsville, a blue-collar neighbourhood consisting of small brick houses occupied by rail yard workers and riff-raff, bordered by the river, the Transitway, and the train tracks. Three months later, Viv was born.

"Your papa wouldn't take me to Montreal, so he brought the Saint-Henri slums to me!" Constance repeatedly told us.

"You call it *délabré*, but this area has *potential*, Constance," our father asserted when she complained about the bums in the alleys, the halfway houses, and the parks littered with needles.

Mechanicsville was below her. Her haughty airs made it clear that she felt she was meant for something else, something grand.

People used to ask if she was a ballerina. When the neighbourhood housewives gossiped about her foreignness, so as not to appear inadequate she'd say yes, she was a retired soloist from the Bolshoi Ballet. It was a story she wore like armour.

I was born the afternoon following Vivienne's inaugural pageant, a homely, five-pound preemie who was an unwelcome diversion from my sister's victory. I came out by emergency C-section, inflicting an ugly scar on my mother's taut stomach, which distressed her so much she didn't notice I couldn't hear.

An ear infection left me deaf for my first six months. I'd never be able to carry a tune. But Vivienne was my parents' salvation. If I were them, she'd have been my favourite too. Vivienne could dance, sing, and act. Vivienne could draw and paint. Vivienne was beautiful and smart and good. Vivienne was everything I wasn't.

Like the trophy halls of high school, my sister's crowns and sashes were displayed in cases lining our living room walls. The kitchen pantry, which should have contained preserves, was stocked instead with Viv's ruffly dresses, suspended from ropes like extravagant cheerleading pompoms. Sequined shoes cast prisms along the dried goods shelves, and the broom closet held accessories and props — wands, capes, parasols, and endless bins of masks and ribbons.

Our mother collected mirrors from thrift stores and fastened them to my sister's bedroom wall from floor to ceiling. Opening Viv's door, you'd see your broken reflection scattered and distorted like faces in a funhouse. On Con's instruction, across the mirrors, our father attached a barre for Viv's warm-ups. The living room furniture was pushed permanently against the walls so my sister could rehearse her step sequences. It always seemed as if we were in the middle of relocating.

Viv participated in contests in nearby towns and then farther afield, across the provinces, where she competed at regional and national levels. Mostly the pageants were held in community centres, bingo halls, school gyms, and church basements.

I rarely went along. Constance said my appearance detracted from my sister's portfolio. She was ruthless when it came to winning. But she was no different from the other mothers feeding their girls Pixy Stix — a powdered sugar candy in a drinking straw — and Jolt cola backstage, to gain advantage over their adversaries like Olympic dopers.

I wanted to look like Viv. When she had a professional body wave done on her hair, I requested one too. Con wouldn't pay the exorbitant rate twice over, so she gave me a home perm. Instead of voluminous, syrupy curls like my sister's, my black hair came out as a tightly crimped poodle's mane. When my mother waxed the blond peach fuzz off Viv's legs, I stole my father's razor and did the same on my arms, only to have the hair grow back coarser, darker. I begged for hoops in my ears like Vivienne's, but the piercings infected my lobes, which expanded like cherries. I couldn't wear earrings for years.

The older I got, the less I envied my sister. The tanner spray and the eyebrow tweezing burned her skin. The dyeing of eyelashes, which Constance accomplished with Q-tips, made her eyes water uncontrollably as the falsies were applied with glue. Often Viv snagged an acrylic nail on her costume, tearing off the real fingernail beneath it in the process. Then there was the dental flipper, a removable partial denture that caused Viv so much pain she couldn't chew for days after a show.

My sister wasn't one for complaining, though. She even took to slapping herself in the face before heading out to competitions, to get the blood flowing. Eventually, when she came home, I asked her why she persisted with the pageanting.

"If I play along, I can do what I want. If I don't, she'll destroy me," she replied, pulling out her fake teeth and tossing the apparatus in the trash. "Whoops, I seem to have lost my flipper," she added smugly, and walked off.

Of the two of us, I was the pragmatic one. Knowing there would be consequences, I fished the flipper out, rinsed it off, and slipped it back into its protective carrying case in the medicine cabinet. It had cost our father two weeks' salary, after all.

TWO

WHAT VIV MEANT BY doing what she wanted was sketching and painting like Henry, and accompanying us on excursions during her downtime from lessons and contests.

"I am *not* bound by the sun!" she'd say, mocking our father in his fondness for trite expressions. "There's *no* such thing as bad weather, just bad clothing. We Walkers were born to walk!"

He'd tell us this when we were knee-deep in snow, goading him to finish his charcoal studies of the Gatineau Hills so we could go for hot chocolate at the chip wagon in Hull. "Constance! We've been to Hull and back!" was his standard greeting when we returned home, and sometimes she was there and sometimes she wasn't.

Our father drew mostly in winter. Bundled in multiple layers, we plodded after him in our cumbersome second-hand snowshoes, making slow progress along the escarpment while he lectured us on historical treks Up North, pausing now and then to blow his nose and to make sure we were still there.

Henry fantasized about taking us on a northern expedition. *Up North*, he'd say, as though it were a precise, cosmopolitan location like Milan. "One day we'll go Up North, you two!" His voice resonated through the evergreens. "This is practice for the Big Trip!"

Up North was the only place we'd ever see white in its purest form. He said we'd mine diamonds there for Constance. Our father was always on his way to finding a new life-altering site, an inner shrine, a revelation, although he never entirely found it.

All winter he made oil paintings consisting of overlapping slopes of white, none of which resembled his preliminary sketches. He worked in his "studio" behind the house, a poorly insulated shed with a west-facing window and a space heater plugged into an outlet that routinely emitted sparks.

He transported his zinc and titanium-white creations down into the basement to dry. Inhaling her cigarettes with half-closed eyes like a bored film star, our mother complained about the fumes. "Henri, you *keel* me with these chemicals!"

Once, Viv kicked her orange Nerf ball smack into a large canvas propped on a shelf, smearing the landscape beyond recognition. The ball left white circles on the concrete like fingerprints — marks that were still there years later when I pulled back the carpet, as I was clearing out the house.

Our father had worked on that painting for months. Viv was distraught. "You've improved it, Sport!" he said, tousling her hair and chucking the thing out onto our snowy porch, where it stayed till spring thaw.

When he wasn't painting, my father called himself the Collector of Useless Things.

He taught me to categorize paint tubes and brushes

before I could walk. He encouraged me to checklist stuffed animals and alphabetize and colour-code my books. He bought me tackle boxes to organize shells and buttons and my mother's perfume bottles, which he retrieved from the bathroom garbage — Christian Dior, Guerlain, Givenchy — ornate glass decorated with roses and doves from which I'd sniff the dregs of floral essences.

His lifelong obsession wasn't with relics themselves, which got dusty and took up space. The fixation was with the search for the exemplary paperweight or the valuable Coney Island postcard. While Constance and Viv were off at dance class or stage coaching or vocals, these quests kept him going. My father always brought me along. He said I was endowed with special artifact-finding powers, when all I did was follow him around without discovering anything extraordinary.

It was impressive the way he persevered. Saturdays were devoted to garage sale hopping, often in the rain. For hours Henry sifted through the neighbourhood's failed projects, foraging for treasures amongst soggy boxes of wool and bamboo needles, woodworking tools, lozenges of coloured glass, and fitness paraphernalia. Trappings nobody wanted to be reminded of because they were associated with a more hopeful time in their lives.

Sometimes we'd leave the city for drives on unexplored dirt roads, spending chilly mornings unscrewing antique doorknobs and hinges from tenantless farmhouses, and getting chased by dogs.

Once, we pursued a rainbow down one of those gritty stretches. I went in one direction and my father in another. When we met up again, he told me the rainbow ended on some railway tracks and that he'd walked right through it.

Then there were the estate sales, in houses like those from *The Young and the Restless*, which Viv and I watched with Constance after school. The hushed ambience, plush curtains, and locked doors thrilled me. Those sombre homes were where my father picked up his prized paperweights.

The times I watched him remove his collection from their compartmentalized boxes were enthralling. Cautiously, he would place the weights on the kitchen table with a sly smile, as if he'd crafted them himself. I remember one morning when he cooked up strawberries and bacon while I sat with my chin propped on the mint green Formica surface, gazing into these miniature universes as the sunlight moved across the room, changing what I saw.

How those swirls of colour, those flowers and animals, got inside the orbs, I couldn't figure out.

THREE

OF THE FOUR OF US, only Viv didn't have the compulsion to gather objects around her.

You'd think she'd have copied Constance, cluttering her vanity with makeup and costume jewellery, but outside the pageant world, my sister remained unadorned.

She ignored her shelves of trophies and her reams of rosette ribbons. Her room had minimal furnishings and lacked decoration other than the jagged mirrors and a dark mound of clothes at the foot of her bed. She didn't look into the mirrors and draped her sweatshirts over them when she wasn't practising at the barre. Regularly, I peered beneath the fabrics to examine myself, squeezing at the overhang of fat above my waist and striking poses to appear thinner.

Unlike Viv's spartan quarters, my room was jammed with books that Henry told me were important to my future education. I read before school and at night and whenever I could in between. I still didn't get through all the tomes, and the ones I did finish, I couldn't make sense of.

Novels, poetry, and theatre lined my closet and dresser drawers. I had the *Aeneid*, *The Divine Comedy*, the *Decameron*, *Paradise Lost*, and Shakespeare's collected works. I also had Russian novelists whose names I couldn't pronounce and dictionaries with old, marbled bindings.

I stacked volumes under my mattress and along the windowsill. Henry made me a chair from books and book steps leading up to my bed. The books were full of mould spores and I developed permanent respiratory problems that were alleviated by an inhaler.

Viv hardly read a thing. She breezed through her studies without trying, whereas the sole class I was any good at was English. When I won the school's Bookworm Contest, the teacher blew up a picture of my head and pasted it onto a worm's body that she fastened to the awards board in the hallway.

Henry picked us up from school that day. He was delighted by my accomplishment and carried my prize—an *Encyclopaedia Britannica* box set—to the parking lot. I felt weighed down by the heavy reference set as soon as I received it. I didn't want it in my room.

In the car, my father congratulated me with a thin A. A. Milne volume of *When We Were Very Young*.

"Just what you need, another book," Viv said.

"A 1924 first edition, and I found it *used*! Guess for how much!" He turned back to us, beaming.

"Ten bucks," Viv replied, her voice flat.

"A dollar, can you believe it!"

"Neat. Thanks, Dad." I turned the book over and pretended to study it diligently, not wanting to hurt his feelings.

The board cover, once a rich royal blue, had faded to drab grey. The linen was tattered and the pages folded and torn. The last bit of gilt lettering on the spine had worn off, leaving *When We Were*.

"Nice job, little one," Viv said, grabbing the book and flipping through it. When Henry pulled up to the house, she got out of the car and wandered toward the painting shed to replicate the drawings inside it.

When she wasn't pageanting, Viv drew. She inherited her artistic sensibilities from Henry, not from Constance, who didn't have a creative bone in her body unless you counted beautifying. Mostly Viv sketched birds in hollow trees and grassy beds whose shapes were barely distinguishable from the underbrush.

I went inside with my father, where he showed Con the encyclopedia set.

"About time you won something." She turned to me with her hands full of meat loaf. "Out until dinner, Édith." She was the only one to pronounce my name *ay-deet*.

I made my way to the shed. I could hear Viv rambling to herself as she drew, imitating our ill-tempered mother berating her after a contest. "It's elbow, elbow, wrist, wrist, you *didn't wave* properly. You *blew* it!" I went back to the porch and sat in the rocker, hoping to be readmitted to the house early.

Two neighbourhood boys from Viv's grade approached on their bikes. They dinged their bells non-stop and picked up speed as they pulled up in front of our place.

Paul was short and chubby with a snub nose. Andy was handsome with a face like a G.I. Joe action model. They dropped their bikes on the sidewalk, took off their knapsacks, and pelted apples at me.

"Hey, *fat worm!*"

Moving away, I muttered, "That's an oxymoron."

"What did you say?" Andy growled.

I'd recently learned the word in English. "Worms are skinny. What you said is a contradiction in terms."

Andy ran at me, pushing me hard against the side of the house, and jabbed me with a large branch. When Viv came flying around the corner, Paul was doubled over with laughter. "Lardass bug-eye fatso three-chin worm!"

Viv wrangled the branch from Andy, snapped it on her knee, and hurled the sticks at him. Then she shoved him backwards and he fell.

"Say that again," she demanded.

Paul hesitated and retreated, but Andy scoffed as he stood and wiped the dirt off his shorts. Half the school was in love with Viv. Blowing her hair out of her eyes, she shot them a fierce look until they ran off.

They were already pedalling down the block when she shook her fist in the air. "Come near her again and I'll kill you!" Pageant girls were vicious. Viv had learned how to fight back at a young age.

She came over and put her arm around me. I rubbed my shoulder where Andy had drawn blood. "You shouldn't read so much," she offered. Then she saw something up the road that caught her attention. She let go of me and walked away.

That was the thing about my sister: one minute she was protecting me with all her being and the next I could be drowning while she stood at the edge of the pool holding the life jacket, her mind elsewhere. It was as though she was in a perpetual state of leaving, following a procession led by a piper no one else could hear.

A FEW WEEKS after the confrontation, Viv knocked on the door of my room. She came in and sat with me on the bed, something she did less and less since entering her teens.

I moved some animals aside as she stared up at my walls. Along with Henry's pillars of books, I had a collection of every kind of clown imaginable, from rodeo clowns to big top performers to the mime Marcel Marceau. Figurines and clown-themed music boxes crowded my dresser, and posters of jesters and Pierrots lined my walls. Their tragic nature appealed to me — the cracked makeup and the serious mouths behind the paint.

"Man, these clowns are atrocious, Worm." Thanks to Paul and Andy, the name stuck, only Viv said it in an endearing way. "Those guys still bugging you?"

"Nah." I put Kafka down.

The boys hadn't come near me since the apple assault. The story of Viv's threat spread. Nobody hassled me at school anymore. For the most part I played alone or stuck with my one friend, the mild and timid Daphne, who enjoyed collecting rocks and bottle caps almost as much as I did.

Viv reached into her pocket and passed me a finely carved alligator. It must have been a schoolyard trade. Or maybe she was stealing.

"This is Vespers. He's made out of moonstone." She got up and shut the bedroom door, turning off the light. "Pull down your blind," she told me.

My outstretched palm took on a milky, bluish lustre. I moved the alligator around and saw that the glow came from inside the stone.

"It's Egyptian, for protection," she said.

"What's vespers?"

"It means when things get dark."

The next year, Paul and Andy went on to high school.

Within months, Viv was dating Andy. She didn't bring him home, but I'd see them together holding hands and smoking in the park, or making out on a picnic table at the Dairy Queen. It didn't last. And any time I saw Andy after Viv moved on, he'd rush past me looking crushed.

I never found out what happened between them. My sister didn't share her emotions, secrets, or aspirations with me. I wished I could get her attention more often. It saddened me that we weren't all that connected.

I set aside Proust and Rilke to read the A. A. Milne my father had given me. Children's poems were one thing I could relate to. Milne wrote about the closeness of siblings and understood a lot about feelings of uncertainty: *Where am I going? I don't quite know. / Down to the stream where the king-cups grow— / Up on the hill where the pine-trees blow— / Anywhere, anywhere, I don't know.*

FOUR

ON STAGE AND AT school, my sister had more rivals than friends. The girls in Viv's class went green-eyed over her, especially those with boyfriends. When couples walked past, Viv never failed to siren the boys' attention away as they rubbernecked to get just one look at her, like passersby at a crime scene or a crash.

Her lack of female companions worked out well for me. Sometimes I got to be Viv's art assistant by default. She had no one else and I was always there.

One afternoon while Con and Henry were out, Viv led me to the painting shed, where she'd set up buckets of supplies and warm water. She told me we'd be making a plaster positive for one of her studio assignments.

She had me lie down on the small wooden table that took up half the shed while she mixed casting goop in one of the buckets of water, squishing the clay substance with her bare hands.

"Consider this, like, your unrepressed face," she told me.

"I'm just going to slap it on you for a bit, then we're done. Easy peasy."

She put cotton balls in my ears and straws up my nose, for breathing. She told me to shut my eyes and mouth and she rubbed petroleum jelly on my skin. Then she started masking me with the same stuff dentists use to mould teeth. Since it dried rubbery, the next step was to coat my face with actual plaster, for support.

Viv was about to tackle my mouth when I chickened out at the thought of airlessness. Before she could say anything, I shot off the tabletop and wiped the goop from my face with my sleeve.

"I can't do this, Vee!" I cried. Vee was my nickname for her, stemming from when I couldn't yet pronounce *Vivienne* as a toddler.

She sighed and put a hand on her hip and tapped her foot. I'd let her down. "Fine, do me instead," she said, hopping onto the table.

I was ill at ease with the role reversal, but Viv gave me a pep talk before she stretched out. I put new straws in her nose and adjusted her headband over her ears. I bordered her clean, makeup-free face with wet paper towels and wrapped a bigger towel around her hairline, even though she'd skipped these steps with me.

I applied the petroleum jelly then covered her immaculate skin with the dental goop, including her eyes, nose, and mouth. Although she was blind now, and couldn't really hear or speak, her body language indicated she was fine. If anything, she was relaxed and floppy, like when Con brought her home from a pricey massage session.

With Viv's face gone, I got more nervous and rushed the process, sloppily pressing some cheesecloth down and caking on the premixed plaster, like she'd told me to do.

Then she was doubly lost to me beneath two layers of solidifying, thick grey icing like someone caught under a mudslide. Despite my objections—if her breathing holes got plugged up, she would die—Viv pulled the straws from her nostrils and played drums in the air until I finished.

I rinsed my hands in one of the buckets and set the timer to fifteen minutes. As the plaster warmed, I blew on Viv's face to speed things up. Then I sat on Henry's painting stool and watched her. She got so still I had to put my palm under her nose to make sure she was breathing.

When the timer sounded, I helped her up to a seated position. She sat cross-legged on the table and leaned forward with her heavy, plastered head in her hands. It was time to remove the new face.

Like in the diagram on the instruction sheet, Viv fastened her fingers around the edge of the casting material and pulled, only the mould wouldn't come off. Before she tried again, she halted me with her one free hand so I couldn't get in close. Then she pulled some more. But the solidified plaster didn't budge.

Viv started breathing hard and fast through the too-small holes. She jumped off the table and bent over and tried to yank the thing off her skin again. She stood up and flapped her hands around as if her fingers hurt. Then she wilted to the ground in a faint.

"I'm calling an ambulance, don't move!" I wailed. "I won't let you die!"

As I fumbled with the shed door and ran for the house, I heard my sister's laughter behind me. I swung around to see Viv holding her negative face in her hands.

"That was hilar."

"You're not funny, Vee!" I screamed and lunged.

"C'mere! I was only kidding, little one."

"I thought you were *dying*," I spat out, wiping the tears and drool from my chin.

"Come on, Worm, I was just messing with you. I'll buy you a slushie when we're done. I can't finish this without you."

I trudged back to the shed, still furious.

We prepared the mould to pour plaster into the negative space, and let it set. Then we had an hour to kill. I spent it out in the yard, brooding and hunting for four-leaf clovers in the uncut grass.

Eventually, Viv pried the positive face away from the mould.

"There," she said, proudly stepping out of the shed and holding her new artwork up to the sun. "My death mask!"

It had all been worth it to see her so cheerful, which was rare.

She passed the white form over to me and I cradled it. It had my sister's bone structure and really did look like her, only a more rested and peaceful version of her, without any of the distress signs Viv's face usually wore. Calm and anonymous, the opposite of Viv's pageant face.

"Isn't it a life mask since you're living?"

"Death mask sounds cooler," she said, wrapping it in a towel and putting it in her school bag. "We did it, Worm. High-five!" I got up from the grass and hopped in the air to reach her hand, overcome by a feeling of loyalty.

Maybe I idolized her so much because I'd never existed without her. There are no memories of a time when Viv wasn't there. She was in my past and my present and my future.

Yet, thinking back, even our happy moments contained a grain of anxiety. Often it was as though Viv was trying to toughen me up in preparation for some detrimental event, always inserting an upsetting incident into our good times. As a result, I constantly worried about her well-being. Like a sandfly bite you couldn't see, with all things concerning Viv, this tiny sting of panic embedded itself beneath my skin from early on.

FIVE

I ADMIRED MY SISTER'S ability to do everything to the extreme.

If Constance adjusted Viv's caloric intake before pageants, instead of shedding five pounds, she lost ten, skipping breakfasts and handing me her brown bag lunches as soon as we left the house so that I grew chubbier in my adolescence as she transformed into a sylphlike reed with large, shell-shocked eyes.

When her weight decreased too much, her fancy custom-made "glitz dresses" didn't fit, and a flustered Constance had to get down on her knees and pull crazy glue, safety pins, and duct tape from her fanny pack. More than once I observed Viv lowering her gaze at our mother with an enigmatic smile, as Constance sweated and struggled to tighten seams so Viv wouldn't be docked marks for loose attire.

Often the duct tape stuck to Viv's lily-white skin. At home, Con forced her into the painting shed, where she poured turpentine onto a rag, scrubbing Viv's back to remove the adhesive as my sister's body flared up in rashes.

Constance spent Henry's nest egg on pageantry. Dance and stage-coaching classes alone cost a thousand dollars a month. The money to fix the rickety fence and the money to renovate the bathroom went to travel and entry fees. The money for new windows and the money to build a deck went to apparel and aesthetics. So long as it made her happy, Henry didn't object.

Meanwhile, my father's zeal switched from books to coins. I was overjoyed. My collection began with a jar of pennies that he had me sort by year and country of origin—Britain, Canada, Australia, America, Ireland. Then we organized them by age and wear.

When Viv and Constance were off pageanting one Sunday, he took me to Ye Olde Coin Shoppe, a used and rare coins store that belonged to a gypsy named Serena. Tucked between the neighbourhood pawn dealer and Payday Loans, Ye Olde Coin Shoppe resembled the witch's house from Hansel and Gretel with its steep, gabled roof and brown exterior decorated with triangle pennants and the sign COINS GOLD SILVER BUY SELL. Even with its barred windows it stood out gaily, contrasting with the street's otherwise down-and-out storefronts.

We entered through a cloud of burning incense. A woman with unruly red hair and an angular, masculine face emerged from behind the counter. She was smoking a long thin cigar and she wore a glass circle over one eye, attached to her waist with a chain. Approaching us in her layers of shawls and skirts, her arms adorned with bracelets, she could have been thirty or fifty, it was impossible to tell.

She made us tart hibiscus tea that she poured into glasses rather than cups. She offered us figs from a tin with dragonflies on it, which she kept on a shelf above the till.

My father let me pick an item from Serena's grubby cabinets for myself. But as I was deciding what to choose, I was thrown off by the strange sounds coming from the upstairs living quarters, noises that neither my father nor Serena reacted to.

"What's happening up there?" I asked.

"My son," Serena said without looking up from the album she was making. "Don't hold this upside down." She slid a coin into a plastic casing and gave it to me. "A sterling obol to start you off."

My father shook Serena's hand in appreciation as I priced out my new acquisition. On one side of the coin there was a double axe and a cluster of grapes. I flipped the transparent page over. The other side had a double head stamped on it, with a bearded face looking left and a clean-shaven face looking right, sharing the same skull.

"Are these Siamese twins?"

"It's a janiform head," she explained, "named after the Roman god Janus."

"I know a Janice at school."

"Hold it around the edge. Don't put your fingers on the faces." Serena told me I was touching a 2,500-year-old coin. The lump of metal was rough and tarnished.

"What's it worth?" I asked her.

"Nothing. Twenty dollars at most."

"But it's so old."

"Some objects are like women." Serena removed her eyepiece before giving my father a beguiling smile. "They lose their value with age."

AFTER WE LEFT the Coin Shoppe, we wound through the streets of Mechanicsville to see what was up for grabs. It was late afternoon, the eve of garbage day, and a lot of people had already dragged out their junk. On these occasions Henry was like an addict. He couldn't help himself.

You can make art from anything, my father always told me. Even trash.

It was perfectly okay to rummage through strangers' belongings curbside because—contrary to what Serena had said—according to Henry, objects did *not* lose their value with wear and tear.

We found my first bike in a pile of garbage. And some totally functional bookshelves. An imitation Tiffany lamp and a gently used dollhouse.

It didn't end there. Henry never left the house without a bag in his pocket. If he saw litter in the park or on the street, he automatically picked it up, much to my and Viv's displeasure. Bending down every five minutes to retrieve trash and throw it into the nearest wastebasket was second nature to our father, as if he was on permanent custodial duty. Eternally cleaning up after the rest of us.

A few blocks from home, his eagle eye spotted a so-called gem. He pulled over, the car still idling.

"Edith, go grab it." He pointed to a grungy three-legged chair with a carved-out star in the middle of its back. As the smaller and speedier of the two of us, it was my job to pull odds and ends from mishmash as fast as I could, while Henry kept watch.

"I don't want it," I told him.

He knew this was the one habit of his that drove me up the wall. But even as I said it, I was reaching under the seat for my baseball cap and rubber gloves.

"For real, that grody thing? This has to stop, Dad."

"Just doing our bit for the environment, *mon amie*." He pinched my cheek. "I'm timing you."

The truth was, even garbage picking was fun with Henry.

If I had to plug my nose and pull my cap down low over my forehead, praying no one from school would see me, so what. I had nothing better to do. Most of the stuff we nabbed was intended for me anyhow. Even though a majority of it stayed in the garage until it got thrown away again at Con's insistence—we never got around to revitalizing most of our trove—I was touched by my father's big-hearted efforts.

In under five seconds, the rejected piece of furniture was pitched into the back of the wagon—one of the three remaining legs breaking—and I was in the passenger seat. Henry peeled off with squealing tires.

WE WORKED HARD on that little chair over the next week. We cleaned it with bleach and washed it off with the hose, and then we sanded it down. With his woodworking tools my father made two new legs and fixed the two wobbly ones. Then he took me to a paint store and let me pick out the chair's new colour. I chose Tyrian purple because Henry said it was the shade emperors wore, and that it was made from sea snails, and that the tint would get brighter with time instead of fading like other colours.

We set up shop in the backyard under the apple tree. "Viv's missing out," I told him.

"You bet." He dipped his brush.

"But not the picking garbage part."

"Your sister would never engage in such an activity," he agreed. "See? All it needed was a little sprucing up. Get it—spruce?" He elbowed me.

We stood back to assess our restoration. Displayed on a square of cardboard in the grass, it was the finest-looking chair I'd ever seen. I felt proud to have made this stellar piece of furniture with my father. Together we'd turned a hideous castoff into a work of art.

"Now my star's got somewhere to sit and think," Henry said.

"That's one *fuuugly* chair," Viv called out as she passed through the yard to the side door. She was only putting on a show. Viv had fun with the scrap collection too, even if she wouldn't admit it.

Just a year prior, when Con ordered Henry to clear out the garage, Viv had been the one to take the lead. She'd rolled a shopping cart over from the alleyway and we'd piled our father's findings high into it, balancing and interconnecting plastic, aluminum, nylon, wood, and foam items at my sister's instruction.

Viv got streamers and ribbons from the pantry and tied these to the cart's metal rungs. Then she had me climb onto her shoulders to stick a plastic wind-spinning flower on top of the pile, like a candle on a cake.

I hopped onto the end of the cart and Viv pushed me up and down the street, an old transistor radio blaring Elvis from somewhere within our mini, roving dumping ground.

"Faster, Vee!" I told her as she ran circles.

"Magical cart and all its contents for sale!" she hollered. "Splendiferous top-notch crap! I'll throw in my sister for free!" She broke into side-splitting laughter.

"That installation would sell for big bucks in a gallery, girls," Henry called to us from the front steps where he sat watching. "Tens of thousands in New York."

"Sell it to the dummies," Viv cried. "Make us rich!"

When one of the swivel wheels jammed, Viv skipped off, leaving Henry and me to drag the stubborn cart to a nearby Dumpster.

Con and Viv referred to our extracurricular activity as dump picking. That was one thing they agreed on.

As for the chair, once the paint dried, we relocated it to a corner of my room. Sometimes I'd read on it, but the wooden seat was uncomfortable. When I leaned against the chair back, I'd get an indentation of the star on my skin. I didn't tell Henry when the Tyrian purple began fading not long after.

SIX

IT'S HARD TO PINPOINT when things took a turn between Viv and Con. If I had to make a half-blind guess—like Viv dancing when one of her eyes got glued shut from lash adhesive—I'd say it was following Barbie Belles.

By this time, Viv had already started slacking in her pageants. She still won crowns, but now she came home with lesser titles. With each practice came protest, and she began making mistakes onstage.

The friction between them had been palpable all along, but until then they hadn't pulverized each other. On the day of Barbie Belles, where competitors channelled their favourite fashion doll, my mother and sister's bond ruptured into a million fragments like a pile of shattered glass at a bus shelter.

I'd helped Viv into her Supergirl gear that morning. Her exuberance seemed genuine. But returning from the contest at sundown, she catapulted into the kitchen criticizing our mother in a way I hadn't witnessed before.

"She demanded to review the score sheet, Dad! She challenged the judges in front of everyone, saying the final was rigged!" Viv dropped an electric green cape by the counter where Henry and I stood, preparing Welsh rarebits. She was like an acrobat in her long-sleeved unitard, which changed colour like the skin of a fish as she hydroplaned around the room.

"I got you a top title, *non*?" You could practically see the heat emanating off my mother's fuming body as she appeared behind Viv with her hands on her hips, an eyebrow raised. Her nails and skirt matched the wrinkled cape at our feet. She had a knack for co-ordinating her ensembles with my sister's.

"Why do you always humiliate me? You're worse than a heckler!" Viv's cheeks and neck were blotchy with resentment.

"Be thankful. My mother never stood for me. Not once."

"Stood *up* for you. Can't you understand people are laughing at your immigrant accent and your retarded outfits?"

With a year of elocution training under her belt, my sister intermittently claimed that our mother was grammatically lazy. I thought to underline that Con had taken ESL classes, but I didn't want to get involved. Was it our mother's fault that the lessons didn't help to refine her English? The accent never vexed me as it did Viv, although some expressions befuddled me. Throughout my childhood, when Con told me *all things come in trees*, I'd look up into trees for whatever it was I yearned for.

"It's you who was too lazy to hold on to your *langue natale*!" Almost imperceptibly, Con's nostrils flared. She'd long stopped declaring with pride that French was our first language. The comprehension was there, yet we hadn't retained our mother's vernacular enough to speak it.

Henry exhaled loudly, passing me the whisk. I took over stirring the mixture of grated cheddar, mustard, and eggs. "That will do, girls," he said, wedging himself between them.

"All the *sakreefees* I made." Con's voice wavered as she pushed our father out of the way. "*Mon Dieu*, you chagrin me, Vivienne."

"Yeah, yeah. Remind us." Viv kicked the cape into a corner and stepped in close to Con. "You gave up your career. You would've been a megastar if you hadn't had us. Blah, blah, blah."

In a swift, violent jerk, Constance raised her arm, her charm bracelet coming undone and flying across the room. As I dove for the bracelet, Henry bulldozed his way back between them, grabbing my mother's wrist before she could slap my sister.

"Vivienne, *go*," he urged through clenched teeth.

But Viv wasn't finished. "Reality check, Con. You're a frustrated housewife stuck in the past," she railed as she backed out of the kitchen. "You wouldn't have made it. And now you're a hag, so quit burdening me with your unlived fucking life!"

Viv picked up the cape and threw it against our mother's chest. It fell like a shroud over Con's brocade pumps.

Once my sister left the kitchen, Con's eyes went from glossy to dry. She was a pro at being on the brink of tears then swallowing them back before anyone noticed.

Still, I felt bad for her that day. She lost control and then her anger failed her. She couldn't hide the fact that she was hurt by Viv's verbal attack.

Con had grown up poor and hadn't had much as a child.

We were spoiled rotten, she told us, only in her words it came out as *you girls are a rotten spoil.*

Overcompensating by ambushing Viv with the prestige and glamour she herself hungered for, she was appalled that Viv didn't flutter toward the limelight of pageantry like a luna moth toward moonlight. Her reasoning for saddling Viv with her dreams was simple. She wanted Viv to have what she never had. To become the person she hadn't become. She was granting Viv the chance for her wings to be dipped in gold, and here Viv was, turning away from the light.

SOMETIMES WHEN CON sat by the window with a vacant stare, I wondered if she missed where she came from.

Her parents visited once. Henry paid the airfare. I was too small to remember much about it. Only that her father was a kind, funny man who looked like a bulldog and that Viv and I fought for his attention and the foil-wrapped chocolates he doled out freely.

Her mother was an iceberg—an uptight lady with thin lips and coiled hair who wore bogus Chanel suits. Constance called her Thérèse. We had no affectionate nicknames for our grandmother. She didn't bounce us on her lap or embrace us. She toted Mentos in her purse and never offered us any. She didn't send cards on birthdays.

When Pépé, her father, died, Constance locked herself in the bedroom for a week. When Thérèse died, she carried on as usual. She never spoke of either of them again.

The one story Con did recount matter-of-factly when Henry wasn't around was the one about how she'd wanted to stay a shopgirl in France rather than go back to New York and marry our father, so that she could start saving again for

Hollywood. Apparently her pregnancy was no hindrance to the game plan. You could see Viv doing the math, growing watchful then incredulous at the narration. She never outright asked Con if she would have given her up for adoption or worse—the unspeakable—but you could tell she was thinking it by the way she gawked at our mother, her violet blue eyes full of suspicion by the end of the tale. Me, I had a soft spot for Thérèse, knowing that if it weren't for her iron-handed authority I wouldn't exist.

You had to commend our mother for trying. In a sense, we'd been foisted on her. We should have given her more credit for not walking out.

It was undeniable that Con wasn't built for domesticity. Despite coming from the culinary capital of the world, she was a terrible cook. Every odourless thing she served had the same bland taste—her casseroles and her quiches and her tarts—the taste of not caring. Her neatness skills were no better. On the surface, the rooms in our house passed as tidy. Close up, you could start a dust storm by blowing on a shelf. She couldn't stand the sound of the vacuum, which gave her a migraine. If she got around to sweeping, she nudged the refuse against the walls instead of using a dustbin. Only when she was out at some rendezvous could Henry turn the Electrolux on for a thorough cleaning.

Opening any cupboard resulted in a landslide of items spilling out. Our home's chaos was hidden in drawers and closets, similar to the way my mother's arresting, statuesque face gave no indication of whatever turmoil she internalized.

She didn't teach us much or seem to care how we grew up. It wasn't deliberate neglect. Incapable of maternal nurturing, she fulfilled the minimum of motherly obligations.

In the domain of pageantry, however, she was a

perfectionist. No expenses were spared on the prodigy of our family. Until Viv revolted, Constance put all her energy into these opulent charades as if her sanity depended on it.

After the blow-up, I worried Viv would send Con packing back to France. Instead, our mother started playing Édith Piaf more than ever.

It was like mean French fairies were gnawing away at her insides, whispering frustrations in her ear, namely that she'd wasted the prime years of her life on us.

One day she put the song "Non, je ne regrette rien" on repeat. The husky, heartbreaking voice poured forth from the stereo for hours on end.

"We get it, Mom," I finally said. "You have no regrets."

"Au contraire, ma fille. Je regrette tout."

"Everything?"

"Mostly, *oui*."

I tried not to take it personally.

"Personne ne m'aime," she added as she scrupulously folded her stylishly printed pashminas.

"That's not true. We all love you."

It would have been easier if she'd pitched tantrums and got it all out of her system. But our unknowable mother conveyed her disappointments by a nearly undetectable shift in her gaze, which changed her entire countenance. Had she auditioned to sit for Leonardo's famous portrait, she'd have beaten out Mona Lisa.

SEVEN

THE MORE VIV RESISTED Con, the more my mother distanced herself from us and the more my father hoarded. Constance signed up for night classes in pottery, quilting, and weaving, and Henry's reckless spending on artifacts increased, as though shining objects and complete sets could soothe his mind.

When it came to my mother, my father was chasing a fugitive pigment, trying to turn their love into a permanent state without the innate properties required to do so. Even while their relationship waned, he continued to adore her. By his mid-forties, Henry had been reduced. Like paper going through tonal changes, he was unrecognizable as the person in the albums I had flipped through as a girl.

"That's not *you*," I'd insist. Gone was the youthful, chiselled man with wavy black hair and a challenging look in his eyes.

While Constance retained her beauty in an unearthly way, my father's handsomeness was like a flare producing a bright comet over my mother, signalling her then expiring.

ONE NIGHT AFTER Constance slipped out the door in a cocktail dress, lacing the room with her frangipani aroma as she left, Viv turned to Henry and said, "Why don't you bust her, it's obvious what she's doing."

Our father gave my sister a blank stare. He opened his mouth but retracted whatever he was about to say. Instead, he walked over to the bay window and watched our mother drive away.

I can still see his profile there in his brown sweater vest, his back and shoulders curbing prematurely, his hair thinning. Worse than this image, it's the sound of his wheezing that stays with me — the coarse rasping that came with each breath.

Viv glowered from the couch then stomped outside to the painting shed. I trailed out after her.

"No one dresses like that to go to a quilting class. See if she ever comes home with anything from those slut outings. I *hate* her!"

Viv had a point. Con never returned with any of the products of her crafting classes. She was either naive or she didn't care. Though I found it inconceivable that she wasn't enrolled in any courses and was meeting a man on the side, as Viv's accusation implied. But maybe our mother was up to no good.

"I thought you wanted her off your case."

"She can bite me." My sister chewed her nails. The skin was torn and bleeding.

That night, Henry told me, "It's time we got you a job. Get you out of your room." Summer holidays were starting. I anticipated having two months at home with Dickens.

"I like my room."

"It's not good to isolate yourself, kiddo."

"I don't want a job."

"It'll be more like an apprenticeship." He paused. "With Serena. Would you like that?"

A summer with Serena in her peculiar shop did not excite me.

"Give it a chance," he said, adding, "Her son Omar helps sometimes." As if my meeting the boy in the attic would be incentive enough.

I forced a smile. I wanted to make him just as proud as Viv did, though less so lately.

HE LET ME off in front of Ye Olde Coin Shoppe the next morning, waiting until I'd gone inside before pulling away.

Serena was hunched over like a watchmaker, with a magnifier sticking out of one eye. When she heard me come in, she placed the lens on the table, sliding it away from her like a chess piece. She stretched her arms in the air, swaying into a backward arch.

"Hello, Edith."

She pulled a cigarillo from behind her ear and lit it. The blue smoke curled in on itself at her lips. I preferred this sweet odour to that of my mother's cigarettes.

Serena picked a piece of tobacco from her tongue. She had a feline quality to her, in her wild mane and in the way she languidly moved around the jam-packed space. She sauntered over to the window, parting the curtains to inspect the street.

"Your dad bring you?"

"He's gone."

She let the curtains drop and scrutinized me. Fitting me with a heavy, rubbery apron, she led me to a wooden desk like the ones we used in class.

"So much for school being out," I joked, sliding into the seat. But Serena didn't smile.

"That's Omar's. He doesn't use it anymore."

Lifting a bucket onto the desk, she dunked her arm into the soapy water and pulled up a handful of black lumps that she plunked onto a cloth. Using a denture brush, she showed me how to scrub loose dirt off the coins. Once she was confident I'd mastered the scrubbing, she retreated upstairs and told me to call if any customers entered the store.

In the time it took her to return, calluses formed on my palms and my neck began cramping. When I heard her coming down the steps, I straightened up.

"Where's your son?" I asked as she surveyed my progress.

"Omarrrr!" Serena called. She rolled her r's like Con.

A gangly boy about my age appeared on the landing. He had inky hair and the same serious face as his mother. He wore coke-bottle glasses with a thick white band like a tennis player's around his head.

"Hi." He shuffled over and peered into my bucket. "I see my mom has you doing her dirty work."

"She's paying me," I told him.

"So she says."

He ran a finger along the glass tops of the cabinets. In among the coins and banknotes from foreign countries were other currencies — belts made from shells and beads, ivory statuettes, and shackles.

Serena was adding up a pile of receipts at the back of the room. "I'm going to take a nap," Omar said, walking over to her.

She smoothed his curls down and kissed him on the forehead. "Don't forget, we have a doctor's appointment at four o'clock."

"I won't," he said, looking virtuous.

Serena came back to my workstation with a dental pick and a coin. "See green? Scrape." When I scratched at the coin, she slapped my hand. "Gentle!"

She hoisted the bucket off my desk and dumped the murky water into the sink. Omar lingered at the counter. I continued with my scraping, not letting on as I saw him slip a coin into his pocket before he climbed the staircase. When he caught my glance, his eye twitched.

Later, I was startled by a loud, rhythmic thudding upstairs and then a howling. Serena flew up the narrow passageway and never came back down. I walked around the shop, intrigued by the sawed-off shotgun under the counter and the alarm system on the wall.

When my father picked me up, I asked, "What's wrong with Omar?"

"Hmmm?" He seemed preoccupied.

"Her kid. What's with him?"

My father lowered the volume on the radio. "Oh, Omar. He's epileptic."

EIGHT

IT WAS OUR MOTHER'S unfailing belief in the impossible that was her undoing. Toward the end of Viv's pageant career, Con was like an actor with lines memorized for the wrong play, performing in a tragicomedy of her own making.

The night before the Fairytale Faces competition, which we all attended annually, it was evident something was off with my sister.

Viv wrestled with her pointe shoes. Con had bought them from a new supplier at a lesser cost. The pointes didn't shape to her arches and were a size too small.

"Constance, these don't fit."

"Don't fret, *zouzou*. We're going to *make* them fit."

She sat Viv on the bed, squeezing her delicate feet into the hard slippers. She took a spray bottle and applied water onto the satin to stretch it out.

Viv grimaced with each step as she practised her routine. She didn't finish her final run-through. When she pulled the shoes off, her toes looked as if they'd been spattered with red paint.

"*Merde*, Vivienne. How many times do I have to tell you to tape up? You will bleed right through the shoe!"

Viv said she wasn't feeling well and she didn't touch her supper. When she retreated to her room, I followed her. "Beauty is lame," she mumbled with indifference, closing her eyes. I brushed and braided her hair until she slapped my hand away.

Viv recoiled from our family. Even though she shared an artistic talent with Henry, she remained uncommunicative with him, while her relationship with Con was a long and painful tournament of wills.

She wouldn't get close with my parents and by extension she wouldn't get close with me. Yet I didn't need her to shower me with affection to know that she loved me. Protecting me from bullies like Andy and Paul was proof of it, as were other similar and unpredictable gestures, though they were few and far between.

My theory was that my resplendent sister kept her distance so she wouldn't crack up. So I forgave her and let her be.

At four in the morning, we packed into the wagon for the five-hour drive to Toronto. Viv slept the whole way there. By the time we reached the Hilton, where the contest was being held, her complexion was washed out and she was shivering.

Con dismissed it as nerves.

In the room we'd rented for the day, she wrapped my sister in a blanket and sat her down at the mirror. Humming "Au clair de la lune," she pulled Viv's costumes from their garment bags and laid them out with care on the king-size bed.

When they started arguing, Henry and I left the room and installed ourselves in the back row of the large conference space. Soon the lights dimmed and the girls paraded out one by one: *Calista wants to be a chief executive. Her hobbies include shoe shopping and surfing. Madison dreams of being a physicist and Miss Universe. Her favourite foods are Astro Pops and KFC.*

The first segment was character costumes. Snow Whites and Rapunzels dominated. When Viv's turn came, Constance participated in the skit, as parents sometimes did. My sister had been adamant about choosing her own attire. The music was also stopped at her request. In silence, she stepped onto the platform and lay on her back for what felt like forever in pageant time. People in the audience started fidgeting. Then Con emerged all dolled up in her strapless dress and mules. With a dancer's grace, she bent over and dragged Viv out by the ankles to centre stage.

My mother attached Velcro strings to Viv's head, wrists, and knees. She took a few steps back and raised a wooden control bar high in the air, prompting Viv to sit up and turn her head from side to side.

My sister had converted one of her princess cones into a Pinocchio hat. She'd stamped circles on her cheeks with a bingo blotter, and put the cardboard cylinder from a roll of toilet paper over her nose, fastening it around her head with twine.

For three minutes, Viv entertained the audience as our mother acted as the puppeteer. There was applause and gasping when Viv snuck behind Con to fake a kick or make the strangling motion around an invisible throat with her white-gloved hands. When her time was up, Viv stiffened. She dropped her upper body down and pinned her nose against her knees, returning to an inanimate object that Constance hauled offstage.

The judges and audience roared with laughter. We all did. Only when Viv flipped Con the double bird from the curtain wing, which everyone saw except my mother, did the room go quiet.

THERE WAS A two-hour break before the final glitz-wear portion of the contest.

Back in our hotel suite, Con turned on the TV and plugged in the hair appliances. When the irons were hot, she began the lengthy activity of creating ringlets of varying sizes out of Viv's hair, over which she fastened a heavier artificial hairpiece, which stayed on with sharp-toothed metal combs that gave my sister severe headaches.

My father put his hand on Viv's forehead. Then he grabbed my mother by the upper arm and pulled her into the bathroom, closing the door. Viv turned the volume up on *Oprah*, but we could still hear them arguing about whether or not my sister was really sick. When they came out, he told me to put on my coat.

"Henri Walker, don't you *dare*."

"Hang in there, sweetheart." My father studied Viv, ignoring our mother.

My sister moved the curls away from her eyes. "I am a pageant *angel*," she said, blowing kisses weakly in our direction.

That afternoon, Henry took me to the Royal Ontario Museum. The rotunda's mosaic ceiling was the most beautiful thing I'd ever seen. It was made from a constellation of tiny squares of Venetian glass. Sea horses, falcons, dragons, and other mythical creatures sparkled in amber, turquoise, and bronze.

The main and upper floors were crammed with medieval garb and Asian sculptures. But my father led me down to the basement level, where there were hardly any visitors. There he showed me collections of Roman glass and ancient coins and, finally, paperweights. We sat on a bench facing the wall of domed tops, each one uniquely faceted, etched, and coloured.

In our quiet thinking time together, we shared a closeness that Con and Viv didn't have with each other or with us. The one thing I lacked, which Viv had in common with my father, was her talent with the paintbrush. Yet I made up for this with my wit and collecting sensibilities.

Henry and I were like bookends. We had the same appearance, personality, and interests. But our connection ran deeper than being carbon copies of one another. We were allied in our pact to create little asylums where we could—antique shops and museums being the perfect places to evade Con and Viv's feuds. And like bookends, we reinforced the pulpy novellas that made up our family library, preventing the unit from toppling over.

Plus, we couldn't get close with Viv or Con no matter how hard we tried. We had that in common too.

"Someday maybe you'll work in a place like this."

"I'd like that."

"Good, Boss. That's good to hear."

"It would be pretty to see a clown juggling these, don't you think?"

My father smiled. Then he checked his watch and said it was time to go back to the circus.

WE RETURNED TO find Viv in the lobby, enveloped in a cloud of lacquer that Constance was spraying onto her hair and her shimmering fur-lined gown. She was the personification of stardust. The costume cost two thousand dollars.

Viv was covering her eyes and coughing.

"*Enough*, Constance." Henry seized the can of hairspray from our mother. My sister smiled. She had her flipper in, so it was her phony smile. Her skin had gone from pasty to greenish.

Constance handed her some Pixy Stix. Without blinking, Viv tipped her head back and poured the contents from the straws into her mouth. Her eyes watered as she swallowed the powdered sugar. "I don't feel well," she said.

Names were already being called for glitz-wear. Constance escorted Viv down the corridor and we wished her good luck. As I followed Henry back to our seats, a girl covered in peacock feathers whispered to me as she passed, "Your mom's demented."

It was a packed house. Families came from across the country, hoping to win the lavish prizes, including electronics, canopy beds, scholarships, and cash. There were no seats left, so we stood against the wall by the stage. Behind the curtain, Viv's cramped feet were the only ones in pointe shoes.

"Number twenty-three, Vivienne!" chirped the announcer.

My sister came out smiling. Her flipper was so white, she looked like a girl in a toothpaste commercial. I waved to her as she floated back and forth across the stage, pausing every so often in a new pose until, midway through her act, she lurched forward as if the wind had been knocked out of her.

Viv threw up on her diaphanous dress and on the stage. She covered her mouth but kept vomiting. Terrified, she turned toward the curtain then back to the judges and the audience. Everyone stayed fixed in their seats. Even

Constance froze backstage. Unassisted, my father rushed over, put his arms around her, and guided her offstage to the nearest washroom.

It was the first pageant where my sister left without a crown, or even a consolation prize.

Nobody talked the whole drive home. When Viv stormed to her room and slammed the door, my father said, "You've taken it too far, Constance. She's not a trained monkey. She's had enough."

For a week, Viv stayed in bed with the flu. None of us spoke of Fairytale Faces again.

SHORTLY AFTER, ON one of those warm days when Constance forced us outside, I sat in the tree swing and watched my sister extract a pair of scissors from her pocket.

Other than Viv's pageants, our mother's only pleasure was gardening. In our postage-stamp yard there were unkempt beds and a rock garden that Con brought to life with flowers and the rich scents of herbs. She added window boxes around the house. She put a cement bird bath under the apple tree in the far corner by the painting shed, dangling feeders from the branches.

With her gleaming scissors, my sister cut the head off every bud in Constance's garden. Of all the yarrow, geraniums, and fringed bleeding hearts, the begonias and roses and daisies, she didn't miss a blossom.

Then she dragged the hose over to the wheelbarrow and filled it with water, throwing heads by the armful into the old receptacle.

"She's going to kill you, Vee," I said, and this snapped Viv out of her trance. She looked at me then back at the wheelbarrow.

Constance was in the kitchen, buttering up a pageant co-ordinator on the phone. She materialized at the window with her bulky head of curlers, sucking on a cigarette and zeroing in on us to see what we were doing.

"Over here, Con! I made you flower soup!" Viv scooped a fistful of jewel-tone petals in her hand and threw them in the air.

Constance dropped the phone and flew through the patio door, tearing down the steps. Neighbours eyeballed her chasing my sister across the street in her bathrobe, the both of them barefoot. But Viv outran her and didn't come home until nightfall.

"Vivienne, Vivieeeennnnne!" our mother shrieked. She sounded like a wounded animal.

Later, there were similar episodes. So many they melted together like a stack of Polaroids left out in the sun too long.

NINE

I ESCAPED TO THE Coin Shoppe as much as possible.

Serena had me cleaning and photographing coins. It was dull, methodical work and I enjoyed her assembly-line approach to preparing lots for sale.

She ordered most of them from England. They arrived in dented boxes covered in stamps and stickers. After their initial scrub in soapy water, they went into a sodium carbonate solution that removed dirt and organic debris.

She taught me to pick at thick clay encrustations under a microscope, using dental instruments including diamond-tipped drill bits. My desk was coated in dust and I used my inhaler frequently. When Serena swept the powder onto the floor with a hand-held broom, I'd launch into a coughing fit.

While we soaked one lot for a week, we brushed and picked the next. The coins ranged from dime size to the size of a loonie, but thicker. None were exactly round and many were split at the edges.

I took the hard dirt off with a shoe polishing brush until I saw a profile coming through.

The Roman legends were easy to read—they used our alphabet and the Latin words reminded me of English. Serena gave me a chart for the Greek coins that had short letters naming the city. Soon I recognized heads of gods, goddesses, and rulers appearing beneath the dirt. Constantine, Caesar, Nero. Diana the huntress in her miniskirt with bow and arrow, Zeus on his chariot, and Athena in her helmet, ready for war. My favourites were the coins depicting animals—lions, owls, dolphins, and octopuses. Each one's picture and text was so much more understandable than the complicated books in my room.

Once cleaned and no longer rough, I laid them like cookies on a baking tray that Serena then put into the oven at a low temperature for a half-hour to remove leftover water from the pores. Next we applied wax to the metals and buffed them, turning ugly lumps into shiny hoards.

I photographed the obverse and reverse sides and Serena put them in plastic sleeves, inserting labels with minuscule descriptions and prices before sliding them into their display cases for selling.

Omar came down often during my shifts. He was like a blue jay, visiting long enough to swipe a coin. When I caught him stealing for the third time, I aimed the camera at him and snapped as he sprang a vitrine open to pocket a medallion. Serena was upstairs on the phone, having a loud discussion in Romanian.

"How can you steal from your own mother?"

"Easy," he replied, coming over so that he was within arm's reach of the camera. He wore all black and smelled of basil.

"She'll catch you." I thought of Constance and how nothing got past her.

"No, she won't. This is a front anyway."

"For what?"

"If I told you, I'd have to kill you."

"Go for it."

"Haven't you detected a lack of customers? She offers loans on the lowdown, dum-dum. Her interest rates aren't as steep as Payday Loans next door."

I'd asked Serena why no one came in. I didn't think twice when she explained that most of her sales were made by phone or online.

"She'll think it's me stealing and fire me," I said, irritated.

"Take it easy. I'm replacing what I take with replicas." Omar handed me an obol. "Real or not real?"

"Real."

"Wrong. You can't tell it's a forgery and no one else can either." Omar took the coin back. "Give me the camera."

"How come you don't go to school?"

"I'm home-schooled. I learn in two hours what you learn in seven. The rest of my days are free." His Adam's apple bobbed up and down on his thin neck. He wasn't ugly. Behind his thick glasses, he had long eyelashes and the delicate features of a girl.

"Why?" I asked.

"I'm like this coin. My insides are a fraud, filled with lead."

I offered the camera. I didn't want him to get frazzled and have a seizure. Omar popped the memory card out and passed it back to me.

"That was half a day's work."

"That sucks." He grinned, obviously not sorry at all.

WHILE I SPENT my days at the Coin Shoppe or helping Constance purge Viv's old duds to make way for new and more expensive accoutrements, Henry signed Viv up for art camp at the local community centre. I couldn't complain. I knew I didn't have the talent for the program.

At camp, students picked themes from folded papers in a top hat. Viv's subject was amusement parks. Every day she made a different painting: a Ferris wheel, a merry-go-round, a roller coaster. Once home, she painted her darks darker. She would add herself to the scenes in pageant wear, camouflaged in among the balloons and cotton candy stands. Then she'd cover the whole canvas with a grey lacquer coating that dripped into thick lines like water going down a windowpane. The results were nocturnal carnivals where it was hard to make out the forms. After my sister finished a painting, she had no interest in it, and she let me put her assignments up among my clowns. She called my room the ragbag sideshow mausoleum.

She and Constance avoided each other around the house. At mealtime, if Henry was still at work, Viv took her food out to the painting shed or she sat under the apple tree, balancing her plate on her knees. Mostly Con brought her supper to the living room, tuning in to one of her soaps. I started eating on the floor of my bedroom, where I could spread out my coins and buttons.

At various times I'd catch one of them staring out at the pilfered garden that Constance hadn't bothered to revive.

Early mornings, before my sister was up, my mother would slide open the screen door and walk in the dewy grass, crouching here and there with her cup of coffee and her cigarette, poking her red fingernails into the soil and through sinewy leaves.

I'd watch the birds fly away from her and high up into the trees in unison.

TEN

TOWARD THE END OF summer, we went to Lake Louise, Alberta. I was thirteen and this was the unforgettable trip where we visited Lake O'Hara and I saw the unicorn. It was unforgettable for another reason also. A reason named Liam Livingstone.

It took five days to get there. As we drove in our station wagon through the unpopulated prairies, it felt as if we were the last inhabitants on earth, like passengers on a ship sailing through gold. Viv and Con were on speaking terms again, though they had little to say to each other. Theirs was a world I barely grasped. I stayed out of their snippy exchanges, reading my books on bullion and taking breaks to look out at the pastoral landscape. Part of me wanted us to stay together on that drive forever.

A BOY TOOK Con's seat on the Parks bus. Or a young man, at eighteen, I suppose. Only when I think of him now do I see him as a kid; we were all kids back then. Even Vivienne, whose thin frame and regal composure aged her beyond her sixteen years.

Viv focused her attention out the window as he gravitated to her, in the seat across from the one I occupied with Henry. Who could blame him, with her high cheekbones and long yellow braid and full lips. She was a replica of our mother, but with eyes set farther apart and of a more intense violet blue. For years I'd close my own eyes and pull on the skin at my temples, hoping I'd open them and they'd be like Viv's.

I watched the scene unfold, taking in his lanky body, his stubbly jawbone, his jeans and T-shirt and muddy sneakers.

Constance called it *coup de foudre*. I'd read about love at first sight in Dante and in *Romeo and Juliet* as some kind of heart madness. I was nauseous and giddy. I knew I would marry him.

"Hi. Is anyone sitting here?"

Viv's glance registered him as unexceptional. She pulled her paisley bag onto her lap and the boy slid in beside her.

I sensed his eagerness as he looked at my sister. I sensed his racing pulse.

"I'm glad I managed to get a spot," he said, his voice unsteady.

Viv sulked and returned her gaze to the window. The bus left the parking lot and he extracted a fossil from his knapsack, holding it out to my sister. Its surface was specked with flat white coils.

I tapped him on the shoulder. "I collect ammonites!"

He turned to me. "Get out of town."

"We *are* out of town. We're from Ontario. I'm Edith."

When he laughed, I studied him — his intelligent, roguish grey eyes, the subtle dimples in his cheeks. "Hi,

Edith, I'm Liam. And who's this?" He beheld my sister once more.

"That's Viv. Don't mind her rudeness."

Viv unglued herself from the window, swinging around to glare at me. *"Edith!* Mind your own business." This brought her body closer to Liam's. Chest to chest, inches away from each other.

"Where are you from?" I continued.

He didn't hear me.

I tapped him on the shoulder again. *"Hey.* Liam!"

"Er—oh, Ottawa."

"Us too!"

"But I go to school in Calgary."

"How come you're alone?"

"My uncle's paying me to find rocks."

"Come hike with us!"

"I don't want to impose?" He stood and leaned over me to shake Henry's hand. "Liam Livingstone," he said. Once he got near enough, I smelled his bare arm—the scent of rain on dry earth.

"The more the merrier," our father said, hardly raising his head from his trail guide.

Viv sighed and returned to her window.

"Liam *Livingstone*?" I snorted. "That's not your *real* name."

"Corny, I know. I come from a line of geologists."

My father pulled me by the ponytail. "Pipe down, Edith. Enjoy the scenery."

During the slow ascent up the fire road to Lake O'Hara, I sat on my heels, unable to stop observing them, the way I knew movie popcorn would make my stomach ache, and I kept shoving my fist into the bag, entranced by a flickering screen.

Liam asked my sister about herself until her silky face opened up. By the end of the ride they were conversing with ease.

"She has a boyfriend," I said as we arrived at our destination. At school, Viv had new boyfriends every month.

"Shut *up*, Edith!" Viv turned back and smiled at Liam.

I told him about the Coin Shoppe. Viv joked about Omar being my boyfriend. She wasn't acting like herself. "Your cheeks are red," I said to her when we disembarked.

Viv and Liam lagged behind while we tromped up the mountain. Each time laughter erupted, I slowed. *"What's so hilarious?"*

"Nothing, pipsqueak," Viv said.

"Mom wanted you to get her some of those for pressing." I pointed to a high slope carpeted with blue and pink flowers. "It's the least you could do after that stunt you pulled."

"What stunt?" Liam looked from me to Viv.

"Ignore her," my sister cut in. "She likes to invent."

When she started climbing, I approached Liam. "Why don't you come back to Ontario and study the Canadian Shield?"

"Maybe I'll have reason to someday." He winked at me then watched my sister, who was struggling to reach the flowers. "I'd better help," he said, entrusting me with his knapsack and patting me on the head before he shot up the rock slide.

I joined Henry, who was sitting on a boulder drinking coffee. That's when the unicorn appeared on the mountainside opposite the slope that Viv and Liam climbed. Once Henry confirmed the sighting, I cried out and jumped around. I watched the legendary animal awhile. Then I turned my back on it so I could find Liam again.

That day, my life became a book containing two chapters: the one prior to Liam and everything that came after, with Liam serving as the divider between my sister and me.

They returned with heaps of blooms plucked from the alpine crest. Liam made quick work of braiding the stems for Viv.

"She has a thousand crowns. Don't inconvenience yourself," I told him as he bunched what remained into a bouquet for me. Forget-me-nots.

We passed waterfalls and twisted trees and meadows of heather and mossy creeks. I wanted to push my sister off a ridge. When we attained the snow-capped surrounding of Lake Oesa, Liam turned to Viv. "I just figured out the colour of your eyes. They're lapis lazuli, the purple-blue stone."

My eyes were brown, almost black.

He was unaware that I'd snapped his picture. Or had stolen one of the rocks he'd mined from his knapsack. I rubbed the rock's coarse surface. It felt like glass slivers in my fingertips.

He exchanged personal details with Vivienne, but this didn't worry me. By the time we got home and Constance began preparations for my sister's last year of pageantry, I was sure Viv had forgotten all about him.

ELEVEN

"WHY DON'T YOU COME to school?" I asked Omar in September. It was decided I would keep going to Serena's twice a week.

"Because children can be *crew-elle*," he said, parodying his mother. "She won't let me. Treats me like a pansy. She's too scared to let me do anything."

In my fifth-grade class there had been a quiet girl named Elinore who had epilepsy. She wore lace-trimmed dresses and looked like a porcelain doll.

When Elinore had her fits, it was as if she was possessed by a demon. She'd drop to the ground before anyone could catch her. A deep moaning would rise up from her throat while she convulsed and foamed at the mouth. Once, she hit her head on the metal edge of her desk. Blood clotted in her blond hair as our teacher rolled her onto her side to prevent choking, and stuck a pencil between her teeth so she wouldn't bite down on her tongue.

At recess, boys would writhe on the ground, mimicking

Elinore. She left midway through the term. A rumour spread that she'd died.

"What are the seizures like?" I asked him.

"I check out when they come on."

"Does it hurt?"

"The headaches feel like knives behind my eyes."

"So you know when it's going to happen?"

"Flashing lights can bring them on. Otherwise it's random."

He walked around the unlit store, browsing the vitrines through his thick glasses. When he stared at me straight on, I got shy.

He deactivated the alarm panel at the back of a case, pulled a key out from under his baseball cap, and slid the door open.

I took a puff from my inhaler. "Why do you steal?"

"I'm saving for medicine in the States that'll cure me."

"Your mom won't get you that?"

"She says it could leave me brain-dead."

Expertly, Omar slid his arm in and out of the display so rapidly I couldn't tell what he'd taken. He came over with his hands in his pockets. His green sneakers made his feet seem enormous, jutting out from his scrawny legs like the shoes of the clowns I collected.

He stuck his tongue out. On the tip of it there rested the smallest coin I'd ever seen.

"Fish scales."

"Pardon?"

"They're called fish scales. For their size and their min-nowy look."

"Where do you get the fakes from?"

"My mom makes me go to group counselling. A bunch

of epileptics sit in a circle and talk feelings. There's this guy there, Grigg. He works in a casino and he's a coin collector. He deals money to make money to buy money, haha!" Omar slapped his knee, searching my face for a reaction. "Anyway, he hit on my mom, but she saw he had an agenda. He was always eyeing the coins. So one day when he was in the shop and Mom was upstairs, I told him I'd get him what he wanted. I made copies of the cabinet keys while she was in one of her sleeping pill slumbers." He gave me a sheepish look before going on. "Sometimes he'll fake seizures, it's hysterical. The rules are no more than two coins a week. He gives me replicas to replace what we take. He puts what I bring him in a safety deposit box at a bank and sells them at trade shows or to auction houses. You want in?"

"I get paid already."

"Everyone needs more money."

"What you're doing is lousy."

"You wouldn't say that if you knew my mom."

I went back to cleaning crude lumps.

Omar picked one up. "I can't make heads or tails of these," he said. Then he pulled a pack of cigarillos out of his sleeve and waved it at me. "You want to go smoke a cigar out back?"

"Buzz off," I said, and he trudged out alone.

At night in my room, I examined the pictures of Liam I'd had printed without anybody knowing.

Most were blurry. I'd snapped too fast in my fervour. What I ended up with were morsels of Liam—a leg moving forward on a rocky slope, an arm raised in the sky, his perfect ear and profile view. I smelled the photos and kissed them. I slid them under my pillow with the stolen glassy rock.

I copied his address, finding it under a pile of drawings in Viv's room. Viv would email, so I went for pen and paper. Each day after school I hurried to the mailbox. For every five times I wrote him, he'd send a short note back.

Dear Edith,
Sounds like your collection is coming along, keep it up!
How's your sister? I've been busy studying land formations
in Drumheller. This postcard shows you some hoodoos,
famous in this region.
Liam

Photographs and letters — the first secret I kept from my sister.

TWELVE

Like Houdini, Viv disappeared from the last pageant of her life.

This was nothing new. My sister wandered at a young age, and as a kid Viv was in the habit of getting lost. After panicked searches, we'd find her asleep in a cardboard box in the garage or in the attic under a pile of clothes, or farther off, in a concrete pipe in the playground blocks away.

Once, at Sears after closing time, Viv had the department store in lockdown for two hours before security found her concealed by a rack of vents in the hardware aisle. Another time, during the Santa Claus parade, she slipped from our mother's grip. We tracked her down hours later, sitting on the curb of a deserted parking lot. Her arms were loaded up with bottles, which she'd been collecting to trade in for change to call home. She wiped her sticky hands on my snowsuit and Con was livid because her ski jacket smelled like beer.

Her most impressive hideout took place in elementary school during the scratch-and-sniff sticker craze. Somehow

Viv got hold of the most bankable of all stickers, the dry martini: a tipped and grinning martini glass with big eyes, containing a single olive.

Stephanie, the most popular girl in school, offered to swap ten packs of smellies for Viv's page of dry martinis. Viv refused. She offered her allowance for a month. She offered her lunches of Pop-Tarts and pudding and pizza. When she said she'd bring Viv a real martini, my sister agreed.

The next day at lunch, some fourth-graders gathered behind the school. Stephanie extracted a jam jar of cloudy liquid from her purse. A gust of Pine-Sol hit the air as my sister pulled the dry martini sheet from her album.

Viv sat on her knapsack, unscrewed the metal lid, and took a sip, spitting most of it out in the dirt. Stephanie and her friends squealed. Plugging her nose, Viv took another gulp then transmitted the jar to the boys, who'd formed a circle around her. Daphne and I watched from further back, leaning against the schoolyard fence.

Miss Rogers, who was on outside duty that week, and who also happened to be Viv's teacher, caught on as the bell rang. She broke up the group and dragged Viv by the hood to the infirmary, where she passed out. When our mother got there, Viv woke up and vomited on Con's pink patent shoes. Both girls were suspended for a week.

That was the year Miss Rogers told my parents she thought Viv had psychological issues. Her concerns were based on the smelly sticker incident and the annual poetry contest.

Each spring, students had to write a poem for English class. A jury of teachers chose the winners, which were read out loud at assembly. My rhyming couplet about bubbles and kittens went unnoticed. Viv's poem was more troubling:

"The monster my mother / crawled out / from under the bed / and crept inside my head / through my ears."

"What's this rubbish, Vivienne?" Constance shook the scrap of paper in front of her after she'd met with Miss Rogers. "Where did you copy this from?"

When Viv went back to the elementary school after her suspension, her fourth-grade classmates teased her and called her Sauceface and Wino. She hid every lunch hour so she'd be left alone. Then came the twenty-four-hour stretch when she went missing. Police roped off the premises and scoured the neighbourhood. News crews converged near the flagpole, waiting for the principal to answer questions about pedophiles. My parents were frantic and we stayed up through the night with an inspector and his assistant. They discussed tapping our phone in case we received a kidnapper's ransom call.

The next afternoon, a maintenance worker found Viv in the school's subterranean boiler room, which was no longer in use. Nobody ventured down there. Everyone believed the underground tunnels were inhabited by the ghosts of students who died in the flu epidemic of 1918. Even the boys cowered from the space.

Viv lay unscathed on a blanket near the entrance duct, eating Twinkies, reading *Rolling Stone* magazine with a flashlight. The only thing Con said after she set eyes on my sister and before she turned and walked off was, *"Cette fille sera ma mort."* She was already looking away from Viv and the rest of us, speaking to no one in particular, to the dark air and the tomb-like walls.

THE GRAND SUPREME Prize for the Island of Dreams pageant was a trip for the winner and her family to Hawaii. Constance wanted it badly.

She took my sister to a coach who taught her a dance where her body drifted around while her head stood still. She spray-tanned Viv penny brown and ordered her a custom-designed grass skirt. She had a lei made fresh by the florist, and an anklet and crown of hard, pointed leaves, which she kept in a cooler for the drive to Peterborough. She bought face glitter and a special iron to make Viv's hair wavy. This was to be her big comeback.

Henry was working that weekend, so Con had to bring me along. She summoned and bossed me around like a personal assistant and I begrudgingly fulfilled each task relating to my sister's imminent triumph.

Minutes to showtime, when the contestants were lining up backstage, Viv accepted a hug from us before we went to sit in the audience.

"This is it, my darling," Con said, her wild eyes glued to the stage.

"Number three, Vivienne!" the former beauty queen emcee announced. And again, "Number three, *Vivienne!*"

The audience craned their necks to catch a glimpse of my sister, infamous for her roller-coaster pageant career.

The emcee moped. "Number threeee! Vivieeeeennnnnee!"

My mother's features began contorting. Her grip tightened on my hand before she released it and marched backstage in her thigh-high vinyl boots.

The emcee flipped her curls behind her shoulders. "We'll give Miss Vivienne a few secs, ladies and gents."

Mothers whispered conspiratorially to one another, anxious for their daughters to gain marks on Viv for tardiness. The judge tapped the bell on the judging table.

The emcee straightened up and stuck her chest out from beneath her sweater set. "Presenting...Vivienne!"

A ukulele and Hawaiian man's voice singing in a Polynesian dialect came on. But again my sister did not appear. The judge nodded at the emcee again. The music stopped.

"Number four, Sublime! Presenting Sublime!" A Shania Twain song bellowed through the loudspeakers. Sublime entered stage right, traipsing around in her Daisy Dukes and slinging a back handspring every so often. From the audience her mother yelled encouragement and instructed dance moves.

I went backstage. I checked the washrooms, the stairwell, and the football field. As I neared the parking lot, I heard my mother's voice. "That's it! It's over. You're officially a loser. Just what you wanted, *p'tite idiote*."

Viv leaned against the hood in her hula skirt and bikini top, her head bent low.

"I hope you're happy," Constance said. Then she lit a cigarette, shot into her seat, and started the engine. She would have driven away without me. The car was already in motion when I ran to it, my sister pushing the door open so I could jump in.

THIRTEEN

A FEW MONTHS LATER, Viv had a new friend. His dad was in the military, so he moved around a lot. His name was Nick Angel.

An aboveground tunnel connected their high school to my middle school. After class, I'd see Viv making out with him in the parking lot. She didn't walk home with me anymore. I'd pass by them and Nick would be looping her long, honey hair around his finger, pressing her up against the brick wall like in a music video.

Nick Angel was hot in a mean sort of way. He had seductive wolf eyes and a crewcut. He wore steel-toed boots and marched down the hall as though he was on a mission. I imagined him raging through the buildings with a machine gun.

"Why are you hanging out with that creep?" I asked her.

"He's misunderstood. He's a poet," she told me.

She had begun skipping classes and was coming home smelling like pot and beer. I knew the smell from Daphne's older brothers, who were stoners. Now, with her pageanting career behind her, she had a lot of spare time on her hands.

Then she shaved her head. When she strolled through the kitchen's saloon doors, my gasp prompted Con to look up from the lotto tickets she was scratching. I waited for our mother to hit the roof. But when she saw my sister, all she did was stare her down, light a cigarette, and blow the smoke in Viv's face.

Each time Viv altered her once-prized physique, Constance had the same reaction. At night, though, Con would lock herself in the bathroom and run water for a bath, only the water ran long enough to fill twenty tubs.

Their duel was wordless. Con took away her allowance. Viv somehow still had money and got along fine. Con removed her bedroom phone. Viv used the booth down the street and then she bought a cellphone. Con threatened to take her to a centre for disobedient teens. Viv barricaded herself in her room and smashed the mirrors with the base of her floor lamp. Con unhinged her door and replaced it with a transparent curtain. This went on for months.

My father wasn't disturbed by Viv's new style. Provided that she was painting—and she was, obsessively—he thought she was merely asserting herself and figuring out her identity. He said it was normal, which made me fear I'd have to go through it too.

"*Well*. This is different!" he'd say when she came home with black nail polish or an outfit adorned with holes and safety pins.

Soon Viv had piercings all the way up her ears, a diamond in her nostril, and a hoop in her eyebrow. Then she got a tattoo of a paintbrush on her shoulder blade. I wanted to take her picture and send it to Liam to horrify him. The problem was that Viv was still beautiful, just fiercer.

She traced thick sooty liner around her eyes and bought her clothes and lace-up boots from the army surplus store. Her teachers couldn't express disdain because she was still maintaining As.

Nick Angel was bad news. In the school parking lot, kids approached him and an exchange took place. He got away with it because there were no security cameras back there. His father was often travelling, so he had the house to himself and he brought Viv there after class.

"Ciao!" My sister waved to me, clutching Nick's meaty arm.

"Bye sweetheart, be good," Nick Angel called, grinning.

Constance was home less and less herself. I turned into a latchkey kid. None of us knew where she went in the afternoons and Henry's shift had changed from four until midnight.

Alone in the house, I'd go into Viv's room to inspect her graphite drawings. There were sketches all over and I was always curious to see what she was working on. To my dismay, her most recent stack were all naked pictures of Nick Angel.

I fetched a hat box from under her bed. It contained awful love notes signed *NA*. I read a few and got bored. I looked forward to telling Liam about this new relationship in my next letter.

Under the notes I found a dainty glass pipe, pale blue and shaped like a bird with a golden brown streak on its spine. It was as fine as any paperweight and I debated taking it so I could begin a new collection.

I put my lips around the pipe's stem and inhaled. The glass had a burnt, earthy taste to it. Next to it was a piece of foil, which I unwrapped. A small brown chunk fell onto the carpet. It had a strong and unpleasant smell.

Then I found two tiny zip-lock bags of white powder. The powder looked like the artificial sweetener Con used in her coffee. I put one in my pocket and returned everything else to the hat box.

I went to the pantry to marvel at Viv's costumes—I was too fat to try any on—but they were all gone. The small, vandalized space was empty and dirty. Constance must have sold off the dresses to Viv's competitors or shredded them with a knife like she'd sworn to do. The trophy cases had been cleared out too.

The following day, I told Omar about Nick Angel and showed him my finding.

"Where'd you get that?"

"My sister."

"That's nose candy. Blow."

"How would you know?"

"My mom's ex made me bag it. When she found out, she rammed her rifle into his crotch and kicked him out."

I grabbed the miniature zip-lock from Omar and shoved it into my pocket.

"Put that back where you found it," he told me.

"This is Nick's doing. He's a pig."

"You could poison him with lye." We mixed lye into our cleaning agents for the coins. "Use a dropper on the coke," Omar went on, "then return it to its place. The cops will think bad street drugs killed him."

I contemplated Omar's proposition, wondering if I could get away with it. "What if my sister snorts it?"

"I didn't say it wouldn't be risky."

He walked around the cases in deep concentration. He

paused at one of them as if something hit him, and motioned me over. I could hear Serena banging around upstairs. She'd gone up a half-hour ago to prepare us tea and biscuits. She did that a lot lately and didn't come back down because her phone rang so often.

Omar drew my attention to a tetradrachm showing a man wearing a lion's skin on his head.

"See that guy? That's Hercules."

"Your mom has taught me a few things, for your information."

"Actually, it's Alexander the Great. He was the first one cocky enough to present himself as a demi-god on his coinage."

"What's your point?"

"Know how he died?"

"I forget."

"By his *own hand*. He was the toughest hero around. He won all his feats, including killing the Hydra serpent. Then he had to cross this river with his wife Deianira. A centaur named Nessos was there and tried to rape her. Hercules shot an arrow that he'd dipped in the Hydra's blood at Nessos. As the centaur lay dying, he saturated a cloth in his wound and gave it to Deianira, telling her that if she made an elixir with it, she'd guarantee her husband's affection forever."

"Fascinating."

"Time passed. Hercules was a cheater. When he strayed, Deianira recalled the antidote for lost love. She doused her husband's shirt in the elixir and dried it. Hercules threw on the tunic and was consumed in agony." Omar was getting worked up, his eyes widening. "He built his *own* funeral pyre and jumped into the flames!"

"Weird, but whatever." I worried the thought of fire might provoke a seizure, but Omar only looked exasperated.

"My point *is*, it was his own poisoned arrow that killed him."

"So buy a bow and arrow?"

"Give Nick Angel as much drug money as you can. Eventually he'll overdose."

FOURTEEN

IN AN ATTEMPT TO bring our crumbling family together, my father bought us a membership to the National Gallery on Sussex Drive.

During the late eighties, he'd monitored the construction of the glass showpiece from his brown tower on the other side of the bridge. He disapproved of the Museum of Civilization going up simultaneously, steps away from his office and on his side of the river. A Disney of replicas, he called it.

My father was one of ten thousand civil servants working at Place du Portage in Quebec, near the confluence of the Gatineau and Ottawa rivers. Place du Portage was a complex consisting of four towers occupying a city block. My father was in Complex 1 — the first of the high-rises to go up in the seventies. Five days a week for over twenty years, he spent his days sealed away in that turret like a prince.

He always wore a suit. In the windowless locker room that smelled of fuel, where he and the other cleaning staff ate lunch, he changed into his custodial uniform. After every shift, he put his suit back on to travel home.

"I'm over at Place du Portage," he told friends, strangers, and acquaintances, without going into detail about the nature of his occupation.

It was like Fort Knox in Complex 1. Every few feet, security guards and screening machines checked staff for bombs and envelopes of white powder.

People got sick a lot in those buildings. Allegations of poor air circulation and cancer-causing bacteria were made by former employees filing lawsuits. At the elevators there were flats of water bottles and posters on the walls advising staff to hydrate.

On PD days, at a loss for what to do with us, our mother frequently took us to Complex 1 for lunch. Our father worked on floors twenty to twenty-five. Since we weren't allowed up, we'd wait for him in the lobby. "Sure these structures are abominable, but I've got a great view!" he told us, pointing to the venerable art gallery we couldn't see from ground level, while Constance scowled at the milieu.

INSIDE THE GALLERY'S glass entrance dome, Henry distributed our tickets and began his spiel on the genius of the architect. Viv cut him off to say she was going to the contemporary section and would meet us again in two hours.

A group of artsy men loitered nearby, ogling my sister in her pencil skirt, fishnet stockings, and Doc Martens. She was still shaving her head but had let one lock grow at the nape of her neck. Her shoulder blades poked out like angel wings through her sheer black blouse. She didn't ask me to join her.

Henry and Constance held hands like a couple of zombies. I walked with them through the Canadiana rooms.

Con skimmed Group of Seven landscapes without interest until she arrived at *The Tangled Garden* by J. E. H. MacDonald, in which rampant vegetation filled the canvas with a merciless kaleidoscope of colour.

"Leave me here," she said at the overgrown, uncultivated patch, as if her affinity with the artist moved her more than we could.

My father directed me to the European rooms, and to a larger-than-life painting of a pregnant woman staring out at us, naked, with wild red hair. "Ah! A Klimt opus."

From afar it was a peaceful scene. Closer, the woman seemed tense and there were skeleton faces behind her. The painting was called *Hope I*.

"Under this there's a happier picture," he went on. "She stood with her husband in a bucolic setting. Then Klimt's infant son died. So he painted over the tableau and added the faces of death."

I left my father with *Hope I* and continued on, halting at a smaller picture — *Portrait of a Young Man* by George Frederic Watts, *circa* 1870. With his pensive expression and deep-set eyes, he was the spitting image of Liam.

I stretched my arm to touch his cheek. When a security guard blew a whistle, Henry led me away, through room after room of paintings and sculptures.

He told me we wouldn't see the most glorious works of art because they were unheard of. The same went for the best poems and novels, which sat in drawers. He said these masterpieces existed someplace but it was doubtful we'd ever experience them, like those worlds inside the paperweights.

I knew he was referring to his own stuff. He'd offered up his paintings to the Gallery, on each occasion receiving a polite note of decline from the head curator. He'd also applied to be a custodian and security guard there and had been rejected.

He took me to the gift shop. I bought the postcard of the *Young Man* in his white blouse, wide open at the chest, still captivated by his uncanny resemblance to Liam.

Then we passed through courtyards hidden among the rooms of art. One of them enclosed a shallow square of rippling water. I saw my moon-faced reflection in the pool. I threw a nickel at it, wishing I looked more like my sister, but without the shaved head.

My father left me at the garden court and went to find Viv and Constance. In the plot of trees and tropical flowers, I wrote my postcard to Liam. *You have to come see this place,* I told him. *You're already here.*

I took in the stillness and the sense of relief the gallery spaces gave me. I had a premonition I'd be back. I dreamt my sister's paintings would be on the walls, and I would be their caretaker.

FIFTEEN

VIV GOT TOO SKINNY. Her complexion faded and she
coughed a lot.

One Saturday morning, she and Constance had a screaming match over a pack of cigarettes that dropped to the
floor from Viv's biker jacket. Until then Constance hadn't
noticed Viv was smoking because the smell was all around
her anyhow.

I didn't want to listen to their fighting. I went into the
painting shed, but the space heater had short-circuited. It was
late November and there was snow on the ground. I decided
to walk over to the Coin Shoppe where at least it was warm
and I'd get tea. My shift didn't start until noon, but if it meant
a few hours of free labour, Serena would let me in.

I took the alley entrance that connected to the down-
stairs kitchen, where Serena would hear my knocking. Peeking through the dusty window, I saw her drift by in a green
bathrobe, her red hair piled loosely on top of her head like
the Klimt woman from the Gallery.

She opened the kitchen cupboards in slow motion, as though she was still half asleep and dreaming. I didn't want to frighten her. I waited for her to turn my way.

Standing on the tips of her toes, she retrieved mugs from the top shelf. She went over to the coffee machine and poured herself a cup, leaning against the yellow counter before taking a sip. Then she poured another cup. An arm reached out for it and I recognized the frayed sleeve.

My father appeared with his back turned to me. He put his cup on the counter and moved in too close to Serena. He took her cup and put it down. She pressed her hands against the counter's edge and my father held her face and pulled it toward him.

My knees were buckling when Omar poked his head out of the annex window. "Don't tell me you didn't *know*. Why do you think you got the job?"

I stared up at his epileptic smirk. In that instant I despised Omar. I despised my father and my sister and my miserable mother. Most of all I despised Serena. I wanted to get away from them all.

"Of course I knew," I told him. "And I changed my mind. I want in." Constance had been making me put my earnings into an account I couldn't withdraw from. With Omar's scam, I'd have enough to leave them all behind me. Start fresh in another city, even.

"Cool." He vanished a second then poked his head out again. "Don't move."

I waited around the corner, puffing on my inhaler. The chemicals irritated my throat and made my heart race. Omar came back to the window and flicked a piece of metal at me that landed in the mud. I picked it up and wiped it off on my jacket. The coin was too light. The thin skin of yellow gold on the surface wasn't real. I rubbed its waxy sheen.

"Start with a Constantine coin. Cherrywood cabinet, back left. Code's 4321." The window thumped shut.

I stood there not moving as the wet snow turned to ice rain.

NEARING THE BOX stores a few blocks away, I thought about telling Con what I'd seen.

Earlier in the week, after a heated argument with Henry, she stormed down to the basement where I was sprawled under a quilt, immersed in *Wuthering Heights*. She told me to shove over, sinking into the couch. She'd interrupted Heathcliff on the moors, chasing after Catherine's ghost.

Sometimes I'd catch her sorting through pictures of herself down in that dark space, where boxes of her old belongings were stored. Or I'd find her hiding out there, absorbed in films—on our second, outdated TV set that Henry and I had found Dumpster picking—as entire sunny days passed her by.

The period pieces were her favourite. The ones where a heroine tumbled off a horse and a hunt took place with foxes and hounds. There were bosoms and misconceptions, the most critical conversations taking place in snippets during quadrilles.

Constance adored dance scenes. Waltzes couldn't leave concrete regret behind, she once told me. It was just the moment and then it was gone.

When I watched her watch these movies, I could almost feel her chest tightening at any sign of affection between the actors, as if the main hero was whispering *kissss me* straight to her. Filled with ennui, my mother wanted to place herself inside those screen sets. And I wondered if this was hardening her against us.

My father called to her in a gentle voice from the top of the stairs. She stood, composing herself and smoothing her hair and skirt, but before leaving, she turned to me. "Édith, there are no acts more selfish than those of a lonely person."

"You mean a person in *love*," I corrected her, not looking up from my book.

"*Non*," she replied. "It's loneliness that makes us terrible and hurtful human beings."

NOW THAT MY loveless mother had driven my father away and turned Viv into a delinquent by pushing her in those abhorrent pageants until she rebelled, I'd have to resolve Viv's mess myself. Then I could depart with a clear conscience, knowing I had done what I could to help my screwed-up sister get back on track.

Nick Angel was at the Cineplex arcade like I knew he would be. I approached him and said, "Leave my sister alone." I was dripping wet from the rain.

He sniggered and didn't stop his game of Robo Redux. "Whaaa?"

"I'll pay you to break up with Viv."

Nick studied me. His face was like Apollo's coin face and it was hard for me to be menacing.

"Don't talk to her again."

"Your mom put you up to this?"

"She has a bright future and you're destroying it." I focused on his throat.

"She did put you up to this."

"My mom doesn't care."

"So I hear." He crossed his arms. "How much?"

"Three hundred." I didn't know what Omar would get for the coin, but he'd spot me if I needed a loan.

"Deal." Nick's muscular hand shook mine.

"Meet me here Saturday morning."

"Okay," he said, returning to his game and sliding a play card into the machine.

I went back to the Coin Shoppe for my shift. Serena reeked of patchouli. I couldn't make eye contact. She offered me tea and I refused it even though I was numb from the cold.

When she went upstairs, I circulated around the cabinets until I found the Constantine coin. I switched off the alarm, coughing each time I pressed the button that made a beeping sound. Grabbing the coin, I replaced it with the one Omar had thrown down to me.

When my shift was over, I climbed the fire escape to Omar's room.

"When do I get my money?"

"Chill. Meetings are Wednesdays."

"How much?"

"Dunno. Maybe a thousand for that one. So four hundred for Grigg and three hundred each for you and me."

"I need more."

"You strike a deal with your sister's dopehead boyfriend?"

"None of your business."

"Tell you what. Have my cut this once. For a taste of the *mahhhnaaaaaayyy* . . ."

"Don't be obnoxious."

"Me? Then don't be such a snot. I'm trying to help." He barely missed my fingers as he slammed his window down.

THE NEXT SATURDAY, I met Nick Angel at the arcade. I'd tied the roll of bills Omar had given me with one of Viv's hair ribbons.

"Here," was all I said, surrendering the cash.

"Thanks," Nick replied, clumsily grabbing the money and shoving it into his army pant pocket. "Later."

That night, Viv went out. I pictured Nick breaking up with her in an unkind way, but when she got home she was unaffected. On Sunday night she came home late again. I knew she was high because of the skunk smell. She went straight to her room without so much as a hello to me.

I saw them together skipping classes that week, probably blowing all the money I'd forked out to Nick. When they came back to school, I ran through the tunnel into their building, watched and waited for them to part ways, then followed Nick to his locker and cornered him.

"What the hell?"

"Sorry," he told me. "Your sister is persuasive."

I pulled the other three hundred from my backpack and gave it to him. "Leave her alone. I mean it." He didn't look so evil anymore.

Just as Omar predicted, within a month Nick Angel overdosed. Viv came home hysterical. She made the movements to tear at her hair, but there was no hair to pull at. She sobbed so hard we couldn't understand what she was saying.

Nick had ignored her that week. She didn't know why. She went over to his house. His combative father called her a Nazi and blamed her for his son's hospitalization.

"Who is this boy?" Con asked me.

"No one. A druggie," I told her.

Later, I went into Viv's room to comfort her. "I did this to him," she professed. "I made him sell exam answers out back. He somehow got some cash fast," she said, wringing her hands. "He wanted to put it away for university. I got him to buy coke."

Nick Angel's freckly face popped into my mind when I closed my eyes. I couldn't sleep. I'd been reading *Macbeth* and I was sure his ghost would haunt me if he died.

His parents wouldn't let Viv visit him in the hospital, so I snuck into his room on her behalf. When he saw me, he went berserk, hollering that he never wanted to see me or Viv again.

As soon as he got out, his father shipped him away to a military academy. Viv was inconsolable and her grades started slipping. I didn't mention Nick's last words or how awkward it was to see him cry.

Omar said he would have gone that route regardless. That he would have found a way to OD with my money or without it. But I wasn't convinced. What scared me was what I'd been capable of. And what Omar and I were capable of together.

WHEN MY FATHER asked me why I was quitting the Coin Shoppe, I said I was tired of watching Serena bring sleazy customers up to her room. Nothing was further from the truth. He was the only man I'd seen her with, but Henry's pained expression satisfied me.

Lying in bed at night, I wondered if I'd led my father to Serena, or if he knew her already and wasn't so much intent on my learning about coins as he was on seeing her. This possibility hurt the most.

My career as a thief consisted of stealing one gold coin. Since she was sleeping with my father, I owed Serena nothing. Omar didn't ask for his money back and I didn't offer.

As far as I was concerned, he was partly responsible for what happened to Nick Angel anyway.

I still went to tell him goodbye once I announced to Serena that I was leaving. "My mom is such a witch," he said as he leaned out the window, looking down on me as I crouched on the snow-covered fire escape.

"So is mine," I told him. "I hope you get that medicine," I added.

"I hope you get away from your family."

"You too."

"Yeah."

I whistled "Somewhere over the rainbow" as a joke. Then we lapsed into silence. I got up and wiped the hard pieces of tar and ice from the back of my jeans. I put on my toque and mitts and extended an arm through the open window to shake Omar's swift, dark hand. Instead, he pulled my mitten down a bit and kissed the inside of my wrist.

"See you around, songbird."

SIXTEEN

LIAM CAME HOME FOR Christmas. When he visited us, he brought Viv a bracelet made from seashells. His gift to me was more thoughtful—a fossil of sardine-like fish on plaster. He pointed out the scales, bones, and teeth. I stored the Lake O'Hara rock in my closet, substituting it with this new treasure under my pillow.

He called Viv "Baldie" even though her hair was growing out. "Try this, Edith!" he said, patting the top of my sister's head with one hand and rubbing her stomach with the other, then reversing the motions. I approached him and placed my hand on his hard abdomen. "No, use your own stomach," he explained, pushing me away.

On Christmas Eve, while Constance and Henry were out shopping, the three of us spent the morning in the shed. From my father's stool I observed Liam and Viv fabricate a kite from kraft paper and dowelling rods. I helped paint the aircraft in bold hues and abstract forms, my throat tightening when Viv guided Liam's brush.

In the kitchen, I poured hot chocolate into a Thermos and toasted s'mores in the oven, wrapping them in foil to keep them warm. Then we loaded into Liam's parents' car and drove to the grounds of Rideau Hall.

We were like characters in a scene from a Russian novel inside that gentrified tundra. Especially Viv, in the raccoon fur and matching hat she'd liberated from Con's closet. Henry had saved up for months to buy it for our mother, yet we never saw her wear it. She claimed it wasn't soft enough.

The snow crunching underfoot, we took turns running through the white savannah and guiding the burst of colour into the air. The kite danced inside the drag and pull of the wind before it came crashing down, the wood dowels snapping and the paper tearing.

Next we went skating on the pond. Viv was as glamorous as Margaret Trudeau against the snow and ice, spinning around like a music box figurine.

We snapped photos with our father's clunky Holga. The camera took terrible pictures that seemed old because of their poor quality. Printed, we looked like a dead family from another era.

LIAM'S VISIT HAD brought Viv back to life.

She straightened out when he returned to Alberta for school. Her grades improved and she didn't come home past curfew. Constance let her have a land line in her room again and reinstalled her door. They were almost courteous to each other.

As my sister's hair grew, she began styling and curling it. Every so often she'd ask me to snap shots of her in exotic poses, which I assumed she texted to Liam. I stopped sending him my own photos and letters, ashamed of my pudgy plainness.

Through winter and spring, my body changed. I wore baggy T-shirts to school. I grew an embarrassing fine moustache above my upper lip. Hairs grew everywhere—on my arms, my thighs, between my legs. I swiped wax strips from Constance's cupboard. Each month I helped myself to Viv's tampon supply since she didn't need them—she was so rail-thin she didn't get her period anymore. I stole a fleshy-coloured training bra Viv had shoved at the back of her dresser once she'd switched to padded bras. She was three years older than me, but her chest was flatter than mine.

I listened to my sister whispering on the phone to Liam late into the night, through the thin wall separating our rooms. They weren't compatible and her interest in him was a riddle to me. I concluded that, now that Nick was gone, she had nothing else to do.

Sometimes I still went to visit Omar. I tried not to ask if he'd seen my father there. When I passed by the kitchen window, I no longer looked inside.

In Omar's room, we played cards and laughed our heads off watching porn on his computer, where slow-loading bodies moved sluggishly.

When I asked him for advice and told him about my plans for me and Liam, he suddenly developed aches and pains and made excuses not to see me. Then one day he had a seizure. Serena flew in, screaming for me to get out. "He's faking it," I told her, without knowing why I said it. The next time I knocked at his window, he didn't answer, even though I knew he was inside.

A FEW WEEKS after the school year ended, Henry took us out west again, this time to British Columbia. My mother boycotted the holiday. She'd been in a terrible mood that spring. There were phone calls from the bank manager.

I didn't want to stay home alone with Constance, but I also didn't want to go on Henry's dumb trip.

I'd grown conflicted when it came to my father. Since I'd found out about his affair with Serena, he'd gone down in my esteem, but I still adored him. And when Con or Viv were particularly cruel or dismissive, I still had the desire to protect him. In part, their behaviour made me understand why he'd done what he'd done.

Henry thought nature would be good for us. He went out and bought a canoe like Tom Thomson's. He was infatuated with the artist and wouldn't shut up about how he'd mysteriously drowned during a canoeing trip in 1917. He started repeating the story to us as soon as we hit the highway.

"We don't care, Dad," Viv told him. Nothing coming out of her mouth was nice anymore.

Our father had the hare-brained idea that we could take the canoe all the way to a place called Bella Coola since there was a big river and channels leading to the Pacific Ocean near the community. He was into Native art and wanted to buy a mask there from a celebrated Nuxalk artist. So the three of us strapped the boat onto the station wagon and drove more than four thousand kilometres to the interior of British Columbia.

Viv wrote in her journal for the entire trip and it got on my nerves. I read Thomas Hardy the whole way there and didn't speak much to either of them.

After six days in the car, on the last leg of the trip, we got to "the Hill," which led to a village so disconnected from civilization it was as if it were under quarantine. The joke about Bella Coola was that World War II came and went without anyone there hearing about it.

The Hill consisted of a series of narrow switchbacks that had been hacked through the coastal mountains by the locals. Rusted car parts were scattered over the railing-less hillsides. Even without the canoe, it would have been a tricky descent at slow speed to the valley floor. Due to the bad road, Henry decided that we'd rent a canoe on the spot instead.

Viv helped our father slide the canoe off the rack. The plan was to leave it at the top of the incline and pick it up on the way home in two weeks. But my sister jostled the vessel too close to the crags. As she walked back to the car, we heard the scraping sound of fibreglass on gravel. The canoe went flying down the cliff, straight as a javelin, before smashing into the pines.

THE BACKYARD OF the house we rented was full of raspberry bushes. Our tongues were permanently stained and our arms scratched from the bristles. Bald eagles frequently swept down, snatching up feral cats in their talons.

While Henry waited for his mask to be carved, we went sightseeing. We saw the landmark rock the explorer Alexander Mackenzie wrote on in bear fat and vermilion, when he reached the Pacific Ocean. Nearby, hot springs ran through hoses into old tubs. A garter snake with a greenish-yellow stripe on its sable body slithered around the basins, where the overflowing water formed warm pools on the ground. When Viv lunged for the reptile, foam secreted from its tail, releasing musk. My flabbergasted sister dropped the writhing creature and jumped backwards as it flattened its head and struck at her.

On the days our father was painting, Viv and I hung out at the local swimming pool. A lifeguard named Tammy invited us to a bonfire. At the party, I sipped on the same lukewarm bottle of Budweiser all night while Viv pounded them back. Then she put the moves on Tammy's boyfriend and got into a scrap with some Native kids. One of the older girls called Viv a skank, pulled a knife, and nicked her on the cheek.

Blood gushed down her jawline and neck, making the cut seem worse than it was. I gave Viv my favourite blue sweater to press against her skin as we rushed through the pitch-black town to the house. She threw my sweater into the garbage as soon as we got there.

It was the middle of the night and Henry was enraged because we'd snuck out the window. We sped to the region's small hospital to get Viv's face stitched. As we sat in the waiting room, a man was wheeled in on a stretcher, lying on his stomach. He'd been mauled in the rear by a grizzly at a logging camp. My still-drunk sister found it priceless.

The next day was our last. At the general store, Henry bought me rabbit fur moccasins and made me choose porcupine quill earrings for Constance. Viv didn't want anything and waited outside, her hands shoved deep into her jean pockets, her swollen cheek covered with a white bandage. Henry got her a T-shirt printed with *I survived the Bella Coola highway! You can too!* And then we began the long journey back.

We had two spare tires in the trunk and we used them both to get up the steep slope out of there. When we got home and unpacked the mask from its crate, there was a split straight through the middle. It had cracked in transport, presumably on our way back up the Hill.

Our mother had a conniption when she saw Viv's cut face. She called Viv a nitwit and a disgrace, even as she reached for a French skin balm in the kitchen drawer to rub on my sister's cheek.

As for the mask, Con was relieved. The second she laid eyes on it, she said it spooked her. Viv suggested to Henry — who sat at the table with his broken sculpture, appearing defeated — that we drive back to Bella Coola for a refund. She'd had fun with those kids, she told him.

I made an album commemorating the long voyage. The best shot was one of Viv standing in a bear trap with a dangling elk carcass. She'd completely disregarded the Do Not Enter Or Touch sign. In my doodly writing, I captioned it *Sis Entrapped*.

Viv was determined to see a grizzly that summer, even after we returned home. Eventually our father took us to the municipal dump to catch black bears on digicam. The bears moved like shadows through the mound of metal and glass. Viv was seventeen, I was fourteen. That was our last big road trip together.

SEVENTEEN

IN THE FALL, VIV dropped out of her final year of high school. She said she was bored.

"How well do we ever know our children?" Henry slammed his fist on the table, knocking over the salt and pepper shakers. I heard them roll and smash on the floor.

"How well do we ever know our *parents*?" my sister retorted. I was listening to it all from my bedroom.

"Don't be such a scaredy-cat, Vivienne," Con said.

"I'm not. I don't agree with the system."

"I hardly got a job with my diploma, you can't be an artist without graduating. You'll regret this," Henry seethed. Then came the sound of my parents stomping outside after Viv.

"Keep going to school to do what? Clean people's trash like *you*?" My sister's voice carried loud enough for the whole neighbourhood to hear.

I reached the porch in time to see Constance shrugging her shoulders at Henry. "She'll be back," my mother said, easing herself into the rocking chair. Viv's figure was already diminishing down the street as she marched away in her paint-encrusted boots and plaid blouse, her army duffle on her back.

"Where are you going, Vee?" I had asked while she shoved clothes into her bag.

"Yukon. Whitehorse for starters."

"Why?"

"To see the northern lights and paint gold."

"You mean pan."

"I'll paint it."

"You tell Dad?"

She didn't answer, testing a Zippo.

"Can I come?"

"No, Worm."

"You'll hurt his feelings. He wanted to take us there."

"But he didn't, did he." She turned to me, raising an earringed eyebrow.

DESPITE HER ROMANTIC vision, Viv wound up five minutes from home. She moved into a cheap industrial loft in Chinatown, above a pho restaurant. She would stay until she saved enough to buy a used car and go north, she told us.

She'd sold enough paintings on the side at school — mostly of superheroes and vampires — to cover her first month's rent. She took a job at a greasy spoon that offered all-day breakfast and at night she painted on cardboard from boxes left out on the curb. Often her pictures carried fishy odours and she sold small ones at craft fairs.

Once a week, my parents and I dropped off bags of food. Initially, Con refused to go. "If she wants to live by herself, she can feed herself," she insisted, examining her nails.

But my father had softened after Viv's departure. "You left home at seventeen too. Wouldn't you have appreciated some help from your parents?"

"I got nothing from my parents. *Rien*."

Henry threw tubes of paint and brushes in among the loaves of bread and tins of tuna. We rarely stayed longer than an hour. It was humiliating to watch him go on praising Viv's work in strained conversations when you could see she didn't want us there.

Our voices echoed in the steel loft. A futon was set up in one corner and a metal utility table in another, with two hard grey chairs pushed against it. On the table was the deluxe iMac with designing software Henry bought Viv on credit, despite Con's fury at the expenditure. At the back of the room, a mustard yellow General Electric fridge emitted a steady, low hum. There was a counter next to the fridge but no kitchen sink, so Viv washed her dishes in the shower down the hall.

Otherwise the space contained only my sister's paintings, carelessly scattered across the floor like the flyers that littered the parking lot behind her building.

She reinvented common objects: a lone egg on a shelf, a battered shoe in the gutter, an umbrella wet and drooping like a wilted flower. The way she portrayed these plain things, it felt as though we were being shown their soul.

When Constance walked around the bare quarters, glancing here and there at the piles of cardboard, her lips thinned and her eyes went glossy, but she didn't say a word.

LIAM TRANSFERRED UNIVERSITIES and drove out in early January, at the coldest time of the year. He arrived full of stories about black ice and ditch rescues along the Trans-Canada Highway. His parents had since moved to BC and

Viv said he could stay with her.

He phoned once he got close to the city. Viv was working and gave me the keys, asking me to meet him to let him in. When he pulled up along the busy street, I was afraid he wouldn't remember me. He'd spent the summer excavating in South America. It had been more than a year since we'd seen each other.

He got out of an suv that looked like it had come from an auto wrecking yard, and stood for a few seconds in his puffy down coat and Sorels. He seemed younger and less intimidating to me now. I was catching up to him.

I made the concession to wear a scarf, but I was frozen in my thin coat and flimsy blouse. By the time he came over and picked me up to spin me around, I couldn't feel my arms or feet.

"You've grown, lima bean! Where'd you get those legs?"

"You're like the Michelin Man in that thing," I told him, peering with difficulty through my hair. Con had recently cut my bangs to cover the pimples on my forehead.

Liam slung a bag over each shoulder. I led him through the restaurant's noisy kitchen, past chickens lined up on a cutting board and steaming vats of slimy green soup, to the back door leading up to Viv's.

"You came all the way out here for her?" I asked above the noise.

"And you, of course!" And me. Of course.

He followed me through the narrow entranceway. When we got inside, he took off his coat and looked for a place to hang it before dropping it on the floor. Then he rolled up his sleeves and went over to Viv's paintings, getting down on his knees to flip through them. He turned to me, astonished. "Your sister's talented."

"She's good at everything. Drives me crazy." I wanted to touch him. He was more attractive than ever. A tingling sensation rushed through my body.

Liam sniffed the air. "What's that smell?"

I VISITED THEM often on Somerset Street, where the odour of oysters and fried noodles lingered on the gauzy curtains that billowed into their illegal living quarters.

Even through winter they kept the factory-sized windows open to cool down the space that overheated from the exposed pipes running the length of the ceiling. Snow blew in around our feet like the ghost of a lake.

I got into the habit of stopping by after class. Liam bought beanbag chairs for my visits. He was always welcoming. Ceremoniously, he'd pour me green tea then lie down on the mattress with his books, the both of us studying while Viv painted, sipping teacups of rye.

Liam had brought his turntable and records. Mostly Viv played Jacques Brel.

Their phone was always ringing, they always had plans. Once in a while I snuck out my window to join them for parties in underground clubs. On those occasions, my ravishing sister secured her lengthening hair into a twist with chopsticks and painted her lips a deep burgundy. Liam and I ritualistically observed her getting ready, awestruck.

Now and then she and Liam swallowed smiley-faced tablets before going out, but they never offered one to me. I wasn't interested anyway. I liked being in control of my senses at all times. Viv also kept a thin silver flask in her beaded purse that she drank from throughout the night. She used it as a mirror to fix her makeup. When she pulled it from her clutch, it gleamed like a blade against her face.

Everybody at the parties seemed to be her friend. Liam and I always headed home long before she did. Sometimes when she went out, she'd be gone until the next day and I'd get shaky calls from Liam, telling me he'd had enough. "My sister's such a jerk," was all I could think to say.

Keep your enemies close, Omar taught me. Not that Viv was my enemy, but I knew her well enough to know she'd tire of Liam. So I continued practising self-restraint. It was becoming hard for me to veil my growing feelings, but I wanted Liam to turn to me of his own accord. I figured all I had to do was wait.

But Liam had other plans. He pushed Viv to take her last year of school through correspondence, and she did it with ease. Then he convinced her to apply to art academies. He bought a costly digital camera and helped her put together a portfolio.

When Viv was offered a bursary to the Emily Carr Institute, Liam moved to Vancouver with her. "Your sister needs to slow down," he said as he hugged me before climbing into his dented-up suv, packed with their few possessions. "This move will do her good."

"Buh-bye! *Arrivederci! Au revoir!*" Viv called from the window, with an undertone of *good fucking riddance*.

I stood with my parents and watched them drive away. I bit down hard on the inside of my cheeks, waving and trying not to cry.

Years after they vacated their place in Chinatown, it burned down along with the entire city block. The fire left a gaping void where nothing was rebuilt.

EIGHTEEN

With Viv gone, Constance's wrath petered out. Her face softened, as did the crow's feet at the outer corners of her eyes. The sharpness in her voice gave way to foreign melodies.

But sometimes, getting up to pee in the early hours, I'd see that my parents' bedroom door was open. Con had bouts of insomnia and started taking walks in the middle of the night. From the bay window I watched my mother passing beneath the street lamps in her cotton nightgown, a plume of smoke extending from her fingers like a magician's last trick.

When she decided to fix her attention on me, I knew it wasn't because of a growing affection. My mother was a woman who couldn't be alone and I was the only one left.

It seemed as though we were the sole inhabitants of the house now. I barely saw my father anymore. He left for his shift right before I returned from school, and sometimes he worked on weekends. When I did see him, he was absent-minded and tired, just going through the motions. After Viv left, it was as if his spirit had been extinguished. I noticed with a pang that he walked by garbage and didn't pick it up anymore. "Aren't you going to get that, Dad?" I'd say.

"Oh, sure, Chief. Got a bag?"

I missed the old Henry, and our artifact-finding escapades, which we hadn't gone on since forever. Not that I would admit this to him. Instead, I held on to my pride and said nothing.

EVERY AFTERNOON WHEN I got home from school, Con wanted my verdict on the villains in her soaps. She consulted me on her wardrobe and hairstyles and nail colours. She had me ironing her clothes and enlisted my help on her errands for obscure drugstore products and random groceries. While I shopped, she rested in the car in her head scarf and cat eye sunglasses, tilting the seat back and listening to opera.

Following supper, she'd leave the house sometimes. Eventually I tailed her and was perplexed to find her entering a church. There were no services going on, which meant she was either praying or seeking spiritual counselling. This made no sense since Con was the least religious person I knew.

When she was gone, I'd phone Viv and Liam. I didn't mention the church, but I told them about the diets Con put me on, and the magnet she'd added to the fridge: *Warning—I May Be Habit Forming.* I entertained them with re-enactments.

"Tell her to go fuck herself," Viv said.

"Edith, you're Rubenesque, don't change," Liam told me.

I really wanted to lose weight and wasn't just humouring Constance, complying with her regimens. One week it was a paprika, lemon, and water fast. The next it was an all-beef diet and next, cauliflower soup. She even had me jogging around the block while she drove the car at my heels, honking the horn if I slowed down. She made me scramble up the metal playground slide until blisters formed on my palms. She had me suck on licorice root for its dietary properties, even though the wooden sticks made my tongue itchy.

"How queer. With all we do, you stay *toutoune*."

"What's *toutoune*?"

"It means fatso."

One night in the drugstore, rounding a corner with some Aspirin, a carton of cigarettes, and two bottles of Dr. Pepper in my arms, I slammed into Serena. Constance was waiting in the car reading *Vogue*.

Landing against her cushiony body repulsed me. She smelled of celery. I jumped back and found I couldn't swallow.

Serena had aged. I was glad to see her roughened in her bohemian attire.

"How are you?" she stammered. "How is your father?"

"You tell me."

She picked up the carton and the Aspirin from the floor and handed them to me with a remorseful look. "You smoke now?"

"They're for my mom. Have you two met? I'll introduce you. She's outside in the car."

"Another time," she said, moving toward the exit.

I wanted to ask after Omar. But she was gone, her red hair blazing behind her like a scarlet letter.

At night in my room, I cried into my pillow. Without

knocking, Constance came in and sat on the edge of the bed. She patted my ankles and rubbed my back before crossing her spidery arms in and around herself.

"*T'inquiète pas, chérie*. Someday what's between them shall mean nothing. They will sabotage it themselves in time."

I didn't know if she was talking about Viv and Liam or my father and Serena. Her words increased the tightening sensation in my chest. The same way it felt when Viv used to pin me down to sit on me, not hurting me because she was so light, but causing enough discomfort to give me trouble breathing after she got up and walked away.

LIAM FINISHED HIS geology degree and took a job with an oil company. He was sullen when he told me. We both knew it wasn't what he'd dreamt of doing.

He admitted to paying for my sister's classes and completing most of her course-based work. "All she does is paint. I've created a monster," he said kiddingly during our calls. Long after the other students relinquished their easels for the bars, Viv popped caffeine pills and stayed in the studio till dawn, garnering acclaim for her abstracts.

For Easter, Henry bought me a ticket to fly out to see them. I accepted ungraciously. In the kitchen, he'd erected willow branches in a bucket from which he hung hollowed-out eggs with thread. Each time Constance came through the door, the eggs swayed like pendulums, tapping into one another.

"Hoppy Easter, Edith." He slid an envelope across the table. "Now hop on over to Vancouver and tell us how your big sister's doing."

I pulled out the ticket and folded it, sliding it into my back pocket as if it meant nothing to me. "Thanks. I hid you a gift too, in the shed," I lied. It tore me up that he was hardly around anymore. It didn't occur to me that maybe he had to work overtime because of Con's overspending.

Liam met me at the airport with a hand-painted sign: *Welcome to Vancouver beanstalk!* His hair was longer and had lightened to the colour of sand. His face was unshaven and he had dark circles under his eyes.

We stood facing each other. I kissed him on the cheek then hugged him. "You still smell like rain," I told him.

He reddened. "Sheesh. You're almost as tall as me."

"Where's my sister?" I was glad to have him to myself.

"Working. Sorry."

"Picasso couldn't take a break?"

He didn't respond and looked mildly tormented when he took my bag and put his other arm around me, leading me to the parkade.

We drove into the midday sun. Liam put the visors down and reached across to pull some aviator glasses from the glove compartment, offering them to me.

I examined myself in the rear-view mirror. "Can I have these?"

He glanced at me then turned back to the road. "Very becoming. They're all yours."

We drove by a strip of old hotels and bars interspersed with junk shops and pizza and tattoo parlours. I thought of the Coin Shoppe.

At a red light, a shirtless man rapped his knuckles on my window, motioning for me to roll it down. Liam told me to ignore him.

He pulled up on a dilapidated street, indicating a camera on a nearby building when he noticed my confusion. "This whole neighbourhood's under surveillance, it's actually safe. Cops everywhere."

Someone in a hoodie walked by, kicked a beer can, and punched the air. "This is the shadiest campus I've ever seen," I said, half joking.

Unbuckling his seat belt, Liam managed a smile. "It's not so bad. You'll get used to it."

We all thought they were living in student housing. But since Viv's bursary included residency for just one boarder, she and Liam had decided to rent their own place. Their warehouse dwelling resembled the one they'd left in Chinatown, but this time it was in the Downtown Eastside. Because of its proximity to skid row, or the Great White Way as Viv called it, rent was cheap.

My sister greeted me at the door with a glass of red wine in one hand and a paintbrush in the other. A jazzy black woman's voice carried through the empty room.

"Worm!" She hugged me, spilling her drink down the back of my blouse. Her collarbone jutted out from beneath her smock. I felt her spine and ribs when I held her. Her teeth were stained and her eyes shone.

"Geez, check you out." She put her glass and brush down on a wood crate, grabbed me by the shoulders, and turned me around. We were almost the same height. "So the Con is totally starving you, that bitch."

Viv pulled two more glasses from under the crate, pouring wine for Liam and me. She took a gulp from her goblet before refilling it to the rim. Pointing to an air mattress at the back of the room, she yelled, "Your bed! Hope you like it, we got it specially for you!"

Liam turned down the music.

"It's perfect, Vee," I told her.

Though damp and cold, the apartment had exceptional southern exposure. Half the space was taken up by Viv's minuscule canvases, no larger than a regular-sized sheet of paper. Each one had its own hypnotic pull. The forms still came from life matter, but she didn't title the oils anymore, she only numbered them.

The botched shapes mystified me. "I don't get it. Can't you say if this is a spoon or a vase?"

"Formulate your own interpretation."

"That's silly," I told her, fuelled by the alcohol. "Can I have the one over there?" I pointed to a blue semicircle above a withered orange crown. I was jealous that she could turn common things over in her mind like that. I could never be so imaginative.

"Take what you want," Viv said, cartwheeling across the loft with a cigarette dangling from her lips.

WE RENTED BIKES in Stanley Park. We drove to the north shore and took the Skyride up Grouse Mountain. We went on the ferry to Victoria and walked for hours on the beach.

We didn't stick around their neighbourhood until the end of my stay, when Viv took us to a blues club and then to a squalid after-hours bar disguised as a diner. It felt unsafe in there. Deviants circulated to make deals, while at other tables people talked to themselves or walked around with soiled pants, eyeing handbags.

Liam and I ordered pancakes and coffee. Viv got a Coke bottle of dark rum with a pink straw. She seemed at home, sketching the roller skating waitresses in lines and swerves and talking to individuals Constance would have flagged as degenerates.

When we pushed the loft's metal door open, dawn was

coming in through the filthy windows. Liam went into the bedroom, partitioned off from the rest of the space by surrealist triptych panels Viv had made. I keeled over on the air mattress while my sister rifled through the cupboards and the fridge.

"Where's the gin?" she sang out.

Liam emerged, toothbrush in his mouth. "You drank it last week."

My sister frowned. She returned to the cupboard and stared at the shelves. Then she reached for a small bottle, which she uncapped and tipped back in quick sips, gasping after each swallow as if her throat burned.

I closed my eyes. The room was spinning. I overheard arguing in the bathroom. "I know you're fucking him. That's how you're passing, wasted. Do you model for him too, is that how you got the A in studio?"

"I don't have time for this, Liam. Back off."

"Don't lie to me, Vivienne." Liam's low, pleading voice drifted from me.

In the late afternoon, I awoke to a dead calm. I dragged myself to the kitchen and poured a mug of orange juice, then another. I ate some cereal over the sink and placed my empty bowl next to the empty bottle of vanilla.

Liam drove me to the airport that evening as the sun went down on the mountains and the sea, distilling them with whisky light. We didn't talk on the drive. He pulled up at Departures without coming in with me, saying he had to get back to Viv.

He held my hand a moment. "We'll miss your funny face."

"I love you," I told him. Then the traffic patrol was beside us, honking for Liam to move his vehicle.

"We love you too, bean. Take care of yourself." He

retreated inside the suv and vanished into the sunset's tawny flash.

I didn't visit them again. They broke up a few months later.

I'll miss you Edith, Liam wrote after he'd moved out. *But life with your sister is like skipping rope on ice. I'm not cut out for it.*

NINETEEN

SOMEWHERE AROUND MY SEVENTEENTH birthday, Henry acquired a sallow look. A supervisor from Complex 1 phoned to say he'd gone to the hospital with shoulder pain. By the time we got there, doctors had run tests and told him about a spot on his X-rays.

There was a CT scan and a biopsy. An operation took place that same week. The surgeon removed the tumour and a small part of his lung. Over the next four months he received a biweekly blast of chemotherapy that turned him into an emaciated version of himself.

Constance tried to quit smoking. My father sought answers, insisting he'd grown up in a house insulated with asbestos and that he'd been exposed to it his whole childhood, working with his father on the farm. He blamed painting with oils and smoking a pipe during his New York years. He blamed the polluted city and poor air in the Place du Portage buildings. He blamed everything but my mother.

Six months after his chemo and radiation, the chest pains came back. The coughing up blood. The wheezing. The cancer had metastasized from one lung to the other, blocking his airflow and slowly asphyxiating him while spreading into his bones, liver, and brain.

"I think the doctors gave me cancer hormones by mistake," he reported after his last trip to the oncologist. "Crummy hoodwinkers."

Every time I called Viv and asked her to come home, she stalled. It was almost Christmas.

"We could use your help."

"I'd stress Con out."

"Home care's understaffed and she's exhausted."

"She doesn't sleep anyway. What's the difference?"

"He keeps asking to see you, Vee."

"I have to wrap up my projects. Besides, flights are oversold until the New Year."

"I'll find you one."

"Fucking hell, Edith. I'll be there as soon as I can."

I wrote to Liam, hoping it would prompt a call. He sent a card addressed to the three of us. It was embossed with white lilies and contained a formal message, as if my father was already dead.

BEFORE HENRY STOPPED eating solids, he had a candy bar craving.

He had a penchant for generic candy bars. The ones in bright yellow wrappers. We discovered them all over the place—in the glove compartment, in the basement, in his shed. He liked them with a pear and club soda.

We were going stir-crazy by then. There was nothing to eat in the house and it was the nurse's day off. Constance cut a bar into squares and put them in the oven. Within minutes, the pieces melted into thin biscuits that she peeled off the cookie sheet. The kitchen smelled like smoky toffee and peanuts. We put the wafers on a plate and brought them to the bedroom with sparkling water and a straw.

He was dozing, a Sotheby's catalogue open on his legs. I moved it, knowing that anything touching his skin hurt him. Although we'd been turning him every two hours, he had painful bedsores and looked ninety years old.

His eyes grew large when she placed the tray in front of him. He managed a few bites. My mother and I had one too.

"Strange you never liked Oh Henry! bars," Con said.

"Better than truffles," my father replied. Minutes later he threw up.

We stayed in the room while he slept. The sound of the oxygen tank rhythmically giving off puffs of air lulled me.

"Forgive him, Édith. I encouraged it—I knew about Serena."

I wanted to cover his ears, even if he was in one of his morphine-induced sleeps and wouldn't wake for hours. When I stood to leave, she followed me out of the room.

"What are you talking about?"

"We needed money. She provided loans. I put us in debt with those pageants. Great debt. I tried the casino and racetracks. We lost more. I tried praying."

So she'd been gambling and betting, those nights she got dressed up and Viv thought she was cheating on our father, attending pretend night classes. Still, I couldn't listen to this.

"You turned a blind eye to Dad having an affair, just to get a loan? You knew the whole time?"

"I necessitated your father to borrow from her. What happened after that, I do not condone. But I am telling you that I am partially to blame."

"Why are you protecting him?"

"Do not hate your father, Édith. *Sois pas comme moi avec ma mère. Elle me hante.*"

"You're right. You should have forgiven your own mother before she died for whatever she did, which I can't imagine was any worse than what you've done to us. But I'm not like you. I always felt sorry for Dad for having to put up with your undignified schemes. You should have divorced him ages ago and left us all alone."

I didn't forgive Henry for cheating on our family, but Con had driven him to it. If that red-headed temptress lured him in after she loaned my parents some money, it was because Con never showed him any love. She'd single-handedly wrecked our family with those deranged pageants. Her tolerance of Henry's infidelity also sickened me. They had both equally betrayed me.

"We had no choice." She was tearful, but I knew she wouldn't cry. She never did.

"Here's a choice. How about getting off your ass and getting a job like the rest of us? Then none of this would have happened."

I left her on the couch with *Days of Our Lives* blaring. I put on my boots and coat. Outside, I kicked the painting shed again and again until my feet were like two blocks of ice, feeling nothing.

THE NEXT DAY when I entered my father's room, the nurse was sitting in the old rocking chair we'd dragged inside from the porch, knitting and reading a Harlequin. She rose when I approached her. "Have a seat, sugar. Won't be long," she said, dutifully closing the door behind her.

I leaned forward and picked up my father's claw-like hand. His nails were long. A massive blue vein swelled where the IV drip was inserted.

Dipping a cotton swab in water and dabbing his lips, I thought of how little my parents had in common, and how my father would have done anything for my mother while in return she only ever seemed lukewarm with him. "She's a remarkable woman," he'd said about Constance a week earlier. "She didn't choose me. I chose her. Don't be too hard on her, Edith."

When he opened his eyes, they were opaque. I waited for deathbed confessions. None came.

"Where is Vivienne?" he kept asking.

"She's on her way, Dad." I took puffs off my inhaler.

"I won't die, will I?" was the last thing he said to me, looking over my shoulder to the wall.

HE DIED ON a bitterly cold day in January, a day when trees of frost appeared all around us like glass sculptures.

Viv flew home and stayed for three days. She wore jeans and a sweater ten times too big for her to the funeral. Whenever she moved her legs during the service, bottles clinked in the purse resting between her feet. She and Constance mirrored each other, my sister an untidy version of our impeccable mother staring straight ahead, unflinching.

After the service, someone touched my waist. Omar was taller than me now. He'd combed his hair and parted it to the side. He wore a suit that was too small for him, his arms and legs extending from the cheap navy fabric like plant stems.

Behind him, I could see Serena at the back of the room, in a tent of black. "Sorry. She demanded to be here," he said.

"It's good to see you," I told him.

"You're thinking it should have been my mom. Especially with those cigars."

"Mine smokes more." I watched my mother eyeing Serena. She maintained her poise and raised her chin a fraction.

Omar blinked at the floor before asking, "So what's next for you?"

"School, I guess. You?"

"Omaha."

"Why?"

"My aunt lives there."

"What about the coins?"

"She's selling the shop to Grigg. If you ever need a favour, he's your man." Omar pulled a token from his suit pocket and pressed it into my hand. "For luck."

"Is it true your mom gave my parents money?"

"Yeah." He flushed. "It was all business between them at first. But then, well, your mom's plan backfired."

I stared at Omar's feet, mortified by my family. "At least you can get on those trial meds now."

"Nah. Mom busted me."

We said goodbye. When I hugged him, my head was level to his chest. Through the blue suit, his heart beat like a bird in his breast pocket.

After Omar walked away, I inspected the coin. It was blank on both sides. A medallion he'd probably shaped himself. A gold, flat disc as round as the sun.

AFTER MY FATHER died, it was like having a magnificent work torn from the walls. Suddenly, a rectangle of bright nothingness that had been hidden for decades came into view. Surrounding the rectangle was the rest of my life, unimaginably grey since its removal—something I hadn't noticed until then.

In the months after his death, I dropped thirty pounds. Nobody recognized me. Constance bought me a new wardrobe and harassed me into applying to university.

Viv phoned once in a while, her voice distant. I told her I'd got into school in Calgary, but she didn't seem to care. "Say hi to him for me," was all she said.

I didn't tell her that I'd decided to stay home with Con. Like the medallion I wore around my neck now, the knowledge was dear to me that Viv wasn't even aware that Liam had left the country.

He had written to me from the Andes, where he was researching lapis lazuli. He hadn't stayed in touch with her the way he had with me.

TWO

TWENTY

I MEMORIZED THE MESSAGE on the postcard, which I routinely pulled from my backpack to study. At first the archaic-looking script was hard to decipher, like hieroglyphics I had to decode. *Lapis chunks of an impossible ultramarine here, the size of pickup trucks. Painters grind it down for pigments. Cleopatra used its powder on her eyes. Thinking of you. L.*

The photograph was a forlorn scene of a dirt road winding through grey hills under a reddish-blue sky. It was the only piece of mail I'd received from Liam since his arrival in Ovalle, Chile, four months prior. He was thinking of me thousands of miles away. Or he'd thought about me momentarily — the date stamped across the postage sticker was five weeks old already.

I enrolled in museum studies at the local community college. Classifying objects was the one thing I knew how to do, as if a genetic predisposition landed me in a field populated by compulsive types lacking social skills.

I kept to myself at school until I met Raven. She was

my partner for a conservation course in a white laboratory where rows of microscopes were arranged like soldiers. There, we learned methods for designing mounts and storage containers for tenuous objects such as paper and minerals.

Our teacher, Galina, who resembled Dr. Ruth, was in the middle of discussing the mechanics of stress and strain when Raven came flying in through the double doors, removing her cap and saluting Galina with a curtsy.

"Apologies, madame!"

"Nice of you to join us, *Ravine*. Take place and be quiet." Galina checked her name off the list before continuing with strategies on how to counteract gravity.

Raven disappeared behind some lab coats and reappeared at my workstation. I sensed her assessing me as Galina scribbled diagrams on the board.

She took a square of paper from our stack of supplies, folded it again and again—sticking her tongue out in concentration—and produced a small origami flower that she slid over to me.

At break, she shoved the epoxy putty and mat board aside, pulled herself up onto the steel table, and retied the laces of her yellow high-tops.

"Hi, I'm Raven. Has anyone ever told you that you look like Nevertitty?"

"I think it's Nefertiti."

"Ya, whatserface." Her smile revealed eye teeth that stuck out like fangs.

She was from Winnipeg and had that prairie frankness about her. She had spiky ebony hair and a sapphire nose stud that accentuated her brown skin and blueberry-black eyes. "Are those real?" I asked of her eyelashes.

"Injun lashes, real deal."

Raven's dream was to go to massage school. She disliked museums and all the dead things they contained. She told me she was in the program to please her mom and because it was subsidized by Northern Affairs.

"After this, I'm doing massage therapy. Then I'll open my own place. I'm calling it Body Poets."

"Thanks for the flower," I said.

"You married?" she asked.

"No."

"Boyfriend?"

"Sort of. It's complicated."

"What's complicated's name?"

I paused, unsure how much to disclose. It was the first time I spoke to anyone about Liam.

"Liam Livingstone." Liam. Liam Livingstone. Edith Livingstone. Liam and Edith Livingstone. Mrs. Livingstone.

Raven crinkled her nose. "Sounds like a stripper."

"Are you?"

"Am I what? A stripper?"

"Married?"

"Going on four years." She pointed to a crescent moon tattoo on her neck above where her spine began, telling me about Zachary. "We met at a yoga retreat in Halfmoon Bay. We got matching tattoos and eloped to Niagara Falls. He's from Ottawa, that's why I'm stuck here."

"You're young to be married for that long."

"I'm twenty-two with an old soul." She twisted her back to the right then to the left, cracking it. She was Viv's age, then.

"My sister has a tattoo," I offered.

She cocked her head. "Why are you here? Who made you do it?"

"I want to be here."

"Is this, like, your calling?"

"I guess so."

"Yikes. Not a passionate one, are you." She put on a pair of tortoiseshell glasses, sizing me up. "Bet you end up at the National Gallery." She took off the glasses and handed them over. "Use these to get in. They're a prop."

AFTER CLASS, I'D take the river path home, passing a small island covered in black-backed gulls whose high-pitched cries bounced off the rocks, through the wind and waves.

The terrain was similar to Vancouver's stone seawall that I'd walked along with Liam and Viv. Only Place du Portage loomed on the other side of my bank, obscured by smokestacks sticking out here and there like my mother's cigarettes in the sand bucket on the porch. She was smoking furiously again.

Fishermen on the shoreline occasionally nodded at me, but mostly they continued staring into their watery silence.

I thought about my sister, coveting her life. She barely called me. She was too busy playing the rising talent, the hot young west coast artist mingling in elite circles.

Based on her recent success in the art scene, I figured she'd cleaned up her life and wasn't partying hard or popping pills anymore. I pictured her at galas and soirées where handsome, wealthy men fell at her feet. During her current stint of fame, she told us her organic forms were selling so much to galleries and collectors that she hadn't finished her degree and couldn't take time off for a visit home.

Yet when I phoned her, the odd time she picked up, what she said didn't quite make sense. She spoke in broken phrases, all jumbled together, which created nonsensical conversations that reminded me of the griffins with mismatched body parts that I used to clean on coins.

I felt like I was talking to Alice in Wonderland. She'd left me behind and gone off into a brilliant world I couldn't infiltrate.

TWENTY-ONE

I WAS A NATURAL at collections care. Fast-tracking my diploma, I finished in eight months and then I applied for jobs across the city. No one returned my calls with the exception of one employer. I took a cab to the interview, crossing the interprovincial bridge into the barren concrete landscape along with thousands of civil servants, returning to the federal government towers where my father had spent his life.

Inside the Chaudière complex, the Heritage receptionist accompanied me through a maze of grey cubicles. The odour of instant coffee attached itself to my skin and hair. She led me to a windowless room for a two-hour exam.

She closed the door, but I opened it when I sensed my usual anxiety coming on. I took two puffs off my inhaler. A janitor came by with a bucket on wheels, setting his mop aside to empty out the garbage cans by the window with a vista of the river and the Gallery. Just like Henry would have done, day in and day out.

I couldn't write a word. When the receptionist returned

to bring me to the interview panel, I told her I was late for a meeting and I left.

I sent the taxi away and walked to the river's edge. I crossed the long steel truss bridge that my father had driven on twice a day for all those years. The wood boardwalk creaked and vibrated while cyclists and cars flew past. The bridge railings were littered with love locks—padlocks fixed there by couples, who threw the key into the water below to express their undying love. Thousands of these toy keys corroded at the bottom of the river. I hoped the relationships had lasted.

When I reached the art gallery's glass dome, I remained fixed there in the grass, looking up at the structure. Eventually some incorporeal presence propelled me around to the staff entrance. A security guard unlocked the sliding window.

"I'd like to speak with someone in Human Resources."

"Do you have an appointment?"

"No."

"You need to be on the roster."

"My father died. He wanted me to work here."

"That's nice." The guard stood up and adjusted his pants. The radio hooked to his belt emitted voices through the static.

I pulled my resumé from my knapsack and raised it to his window. "I just want to drop this off"—my voice got croaky—"please."

My poly-blend dress clung to my back. I hadn't taken the time to cool off after crossing the bridge in the scorching sun.

He exhaled until his shoulders slumped forward. "You can't walk in unannounced," he told me. "But I'll give it to them for you." He took the papers from my hand and slid his window closed again, turning back to his surveillance screens.

A MONTH LATER, I was called in for an interview.

When I arrived, the same security guard was there. This time he treated me like a proper visitor, asking me to sign in before taking a seat in the waiting area.

A woman whose hair was blacker than mine and who wore a denim jumpsuit and fur sandals appeared at the doorway.

"Miss Walker, pleasure. I'm Jeanette." The hand I shook was decorated with an enormous topaz ring. I followed her through the doors as she went on, "Lucky for you, we happen to be desperate. Three of our juniors defected to the War Museum, where the pay's better. I'm thinking of going there myself. Come in."

Once we were seated in her office, Jeanette scanned my file. "You've worked with coins?"

"A little."

"How's your eyesight?"

I removed Raven's glasses. "These are an accessory."

"You'd be taking measurements and recording numbers. Essentially, it's a data entry job."

"I can do that."

"Do you collect?"

"Not anymore."

"Why not?"

"I have few things to which I'm sentimentally attached."

"Excellent." She rearranged her pencil holder and stationery on her spotless desk. "Hoarders tend to have messy offices, and that doesn't reflect well on the institution when funders tour around. Where did you get that necklace?" She pointed with her pencil to the medallion.

"A friend. He was a collector. We lost touch."

I must have seemed nostalgic because Jeanette opened up then. "It happens," she said, her almond eyes glazing over. She looked a little heartbroken. "Some people. Nothing we can do about it."

I STARTED THAT same week. When I told Raven about the job, she asked me to find her something there too — anything, she said. She was working at a hosiery store called Fancy Sox and she detested it.

On my first day, Jeanette brought me up to the fourth floor and introduced me to Alejandro, a middle-aged, slender man with a dark goatee who wore a pinstriped suit. Alejandro would train me on Avalon, the database I was to work with as a cataloguer.

Two desks took up the snug room. Once Jeanette left, Alejandro moved a stack of magazines over and motioned. "You can sit there, but the chair's broken." Then he angled his monitor toward me to demonstrate how to complete tasks in Avalon. "It's a temperamental system that's going to crash and thousands of hours of entries, all the history, will be gone," he told me. "This is technically not my problem. I've voiced my concerns and no one listens."

Alejandro went on. "Avalon estimates that we show 4 percent of our collections to the public. Most mornings you'll be in the vaults for at least an hour or two with a laptop, pencil, notepad, and tape measure, cataloguing the other 96 percent. It's riveting work."

Vault doors stayed closed at all times. He confided that he doubled his lab coats while in storage to keep warm in the strictly climate-controlled environment. He pontificated about handwashing and the ban on lotions and jewellery, and how dust was the enemy, its particles tiny daggers causing irreparable damage to surfaces.

Alejandro also explained the coding for the works on paper, stored in archival black boxes one on top of the other like rectangular coffins on steel shelving units.

"Light and humidity levels are verified daily. It's freezing in there and coffee's not allowed. I slip chocolates and power bars into my pockets, but if you do it, be careful. You don't want to be on your knees collecting crumbs when a curator walks in. There are infestations to think about, insects and mice."

In the afternoon, Alejandro gave me a tour of the viewing room, which we would alternate supervising, bringing works on paper to researchers arriving with permission letters.

"Make sure they don't have pens or chewing gum, and that they don't spit onto the art while talking. In my opinion, the buggers should wear masks," Alejandro said. "And ask that they leave their bags at the door. Give them gloves from the desk drawer and check in on them once per shift. Otherwise you're free to do whatever."

The viewing room had the most windows and light in the entire complex. It was on the top floor. The ceiling was a skylight and the front wall was all glass.

My new refuge steadied me and lifted my spirit.

I stood at the window, gazing down at the river and the iron bridge. The gulls and clouds swept down so low, it was as if they were inside with me.

I HARDLY NOTICED the seasons passing. I sent letters to Liam via a general delivery address, but I was uncertain if he had received them. I ploughed through Avalon, correcting typos and inaccuracies, knowing that in the future someone would go in and alter the information I'd entered until every digit was swept away like a sand mandala.

The watercolours, prints, and drawings I catalogued were deteriorating at varying rates and were as translucent as petals. Each one had its own digitized consultation chart like a patient in rehabilitation. I was almost paralyzed by the thought that one false move, one slip or catch of the sleeve, could destroy a work forever.

It was an unglamorous job, but it suited me. If I was in the storage cage a day too many, the skin of my fingers cracked and chapped, sometimes I speculated about what course my life could have taken had I any real talents like Viv.

The female Gallery workers were as striking as my sister. Especially the managers in their silk skirt suits and impressive heels. A flock of forward-thinking, handsome curators had landed on-site like stately monarchs, replacing academics who'd died off and been buried all at once like terracotta warriors, Alejandro told me.

He said affairs went on behind the scenes after hours, when these important individuals laboured into the night, preparing for blockbuster exhibitions—*Bernini and the Birth of Baroque Portrait Sculpture*, or *Egyptomania*, or *The Great Parade*, showcasing artists as clowns, which caused children to run screaming from the galleries. I regretted having missed that one.

I caught glimpses of these luminous beings flashing past the door to our small office, or wandering through the vaults where I was stationed. They heaved lugubrious sighs and my imagination teleported them into trendy bistros and romantic symphonies, recruiting them into one large-scale orgiastic canvas titled *The Lucky Ones*.

Little by little, I let go of the life I'd planned.

Liam had not written back. I felt like a woman seated at a loom unravelling a tapestry or standing on a cliff, skirts and hair blowing wildly — *Woman on Precipice*.

I found Raven a job in the membership sales department. It was temporary, while she and Zach settled in and he moved up the ranks in Foreign Affairs. Then she'd open her massage place.

"I went to school to make cold calls and you're no better off with your data entry," she repeated on our outings.

We had lunch together weekly. Since buying a house, Raven was consumed with decorating. One day it was an ecru bed in a bag, the next it was a chenille pillow. Heading for the department store, we often stopped in the ByWard Market's stone courtyard, where windowsills were covered in nails glinting in the sun to ward off pigeons.

We ate our sandwiches on a bench then strolled down Sussex Drive past exclusive boutiques — the children's clothing shop with its chaotic display boasting *designer swaddles! beanie pods!* and the haute couture bridal shop where daughters of government leaders and the city's prominent businessmen shopped.

Dresses of twill and silk floated in the window front on headless mannequins. I pressed my face against the glass, thinking of my future with Liam. A chandelier hung above a few gowns dangling from a rack like exquisite skinned animals. Two ethereal women with pearls and kinky tresses turned away.

FINALLY A POSTCARD arrived.

It was a picture of a blue stone mask. Liam's note said that he was coming home for a university job in Earth Sciences. He was going to arrive in a month and wanted me to help him find a place to live.

I'd been thinking of moving as well. Constance was selling the house and buying a condo where, she'd not so subtly told me, there wasn't much room.

I wrote back saying that he could stay with me and then I rushed to find a downtown rental. I secured an apartment on the main floor of a turn-of-the-century house with crown moulding and hardwood floors so uneven I had to prop slats under the furniture. It wasn't unusual to hear the plumbing in the units above and beneath me, and the steaming radiators clanked as though someone was taking a hammer to them. But there was a garden, big windows, and stained glass. My father would have liked the original light fixtures.

It was mine and I was finally on my own. I stood at the window holding the postcard and waited for Liam.

TWENTY-TWO

WHEN I HELPED CONSTANCE pack up the house, I found Henry's white scenes rolled in the attic like obsolete maps, covered in dust and cobwebs.

She was selling our home for next to nothing and could easily have doubled the price. Our once-sketchy neighbourhood had been gentrified, its main street lined with pet groomers and gourmet food shops—but she didn't care. Con wanted to move on.

"Forget the past. Swim forward like a shark. That's how to survive, *ma fille.*"

Beside the neglected rolls, there were more paintings on an old flat-top trunk. Ones that were stretched and tacked onto wooden frames, stacked neatly beneath a clear tarp. I tore off the sheet of plastic. From each of my sister's small works there dangled, like an earring, an exorbitant price tag from one Vancouver gallery or another.

"He wanted to encourage her. Not my idea." My mother sat on the floor in her kelly green jogging suit, a matching kerchief tied around her head. Mirabelle, the teacup Yorkie she bought after my father's death, was asleep in her lap. Letters surrounded her, and as Con leaned against the couch, she glanced at the piles of envelopes, setting a few aside and throwing others into the garbage bag beside her.

"*Dad* bought them? Viv said she had clients!"

"Your father used different names. She didn't ask her agent who purchased. She wasn't interested."

"But who's been buying lately?"

"He left them a sum to continue. *Mais* . . . I'm sure that's gone."

"How could he afford it?"

"Second mortgage."

"What about the debts —"

"I told you" — she cut me off — "who helped us pay those off. I don't want to discuss it again." She picked a yellow mailer from the floor with my father's handwriting on it, pulled the papers out, leafed through them, and tossed them in the garbage bag.

"Then why is she so broke she can't fly home for a visit?"

"We helped her get a name, a reputation," my mother replied, avoiding my question.

"Who wrote those newspaper reviews?"

"One teacher in particular was very fond of her. He had journalist friends."

I remembered the fight between Viv and Liam on my last night there. "She wouldn't forgive you, if she knew," I told her.

My mother stood up without removing Mira from her lap. The dog dropped to the floor like a duster. She went over to the mantel that held my father's ashes, picked up the brown urn, and examined it thoughtfully before pressing it against my abdomen.

"I don't know where to spread them." She sat down on the floor again, lit a cigarette, and opened another letter. Mira crossed under the path of smoke and hopped back onto her legs.

"What did you do with Dad's collections, his memorabilia?"

"I gave all that to the junk collectors. The diabetes foundation didn't want anything."

"What about my purple chair? My clowns and Viv's carnival scenes?"

"I saved you the glass balls. *Prends la Buick.*" Her red '96 Buick Century was over ten years old. She'd recently bought herself a Lincoln Town Car.

I felt my hostility rising. "I want the paintings."

"I'm retailing them online." She gave a small cough, tapping her cigarette into the ashtray at her feet. "You can have one of each."

"You're wasting your time. Her work won't sell anymore." My mother couldn't fathom that the art world was fickle and that Viv was likely already a has-been.

She ignored my remark and passed me an audio cassette. "That's a funny one," she said. "Listen when you can."

"Where's the tape player?" I asked, looking around the room.

"I threw it away."

I slid the cassette tape into my bag and went back up to the attic. I dragged a lamp with me into the crawl space, ducking to avoid the rafters. I sat on a ragged bath mat and began unrolling my father's canvases, going slowly to prevent cracking.

While my sister's compositions were disguises underpainted with hidden realities, my father's combinations of seashell, ivory, cornsilk, and lace were images of a cold loneliness. Ashen government towers tainting the sky. Snowbanks trailing utility corridors in winter fields. A train passing through interminable spaces of white impasto. My father painted human solitude.

I chose one titled *Estuary* that depicted a large mass of still, open water. A canoeist paddled the shoreline. In the background was a row of storefronts and a hotel—a ghost town without dimensions, like a movie set. Above the scene my father included a soaring eagle, painted crudely, as if an afterthought.

I couldn't tell who was in the boat. Probably Viv. In Bella Coola, Henry had rented a birchbark canoe that he and Viv took out a lot while I stayed at the public pool. Or maybe the canoe portrayed in my father's painting was the one not used on any lake. Maybe it was the one we lost before reaching the valley floor.

I didn't recognize any of the works in my sister's stack. They were made after I'd been to Vancouver, and I was surprised to see she'd titled them. One painting stood out from the textured, geometric shapes. *Myrtle and Leo* was by far the smallest work, maybe six by eight inches. In it was a deep maroon oval with spindly bullets all around it, indicating motion. A vibrant coral orb floated above the oval.

I knew the story behind the painting. I was stunned that it had marked my sister enough for her to re-create it years later.

Myrtle was the neighbourhood mutt. A solidly built mastiff with a coat the colour of apricots, who didn't belong to anyone and whom every house on the block took turns feeding.

Leo was a tabby kitten. The runt from a litter we found

under our porch one spring. To appease us, Henry let us keep Leo when he took the rest of the brood to the Humane Society.

One day Viv and I brought Leo out to the park across the street. My sister moved back and forth on a swing, holding the kitten while I dangled a ribbon, which Leo kept pawing at and missing as the swing receded.

Our laughter increased when Myrtle appeared and Leo hissed. Myrtle lay down in the dirt a few feet away with his usual baleful expression, barely acknowledging us as Leo kept clawing at the ribbon. Then Leo fell from Viv's upturned palm, landing on all fours in the dirt.

Myrtle bore his teeth and lunged at the kitten. The dog's muscular neck swung from left to right with the kitten in his jaw before he released the animal like a rag doll. Leo tried dragging himself away, but his hind legs were crushed. Viv took a step toward the kitten and Myrtle growled at her. He tossed Leo in the air and knocked him around some more. Each time he clamped his jaws down on the kitten, we heard tiny bones being crushed like the sound of biting into a sandwich of crisp lettuce.

When Myrtle was finished with Leo, he came over and released the dead kitten from his muzzle. The body dropped at Viv's feet. The dog wagged his tail and looked at us expectantly.

After Myrtle trotted away, my sister insisted we bury Leo. There was a pine tree near the swing set and we dug a hole. When we got home, Constance scolded us because our fingernails were so caked with dirt they wouldn't come clean.

A week later, Viv told me we had to exhume Leo and bring him closer to home. She wanted to make a proper grave for him under the steps where he was born, so he'd be comforted by the scent of his mother and siblings.

We went to the pine tree and uncovered the small mound, repositioning soil until a foul odour hit us. Viv swiftly kicked the dirt back over the maggot-covered carcass. We decided to leave Leo where he was.

We disowned Myrtle after that. Whenever the dog approached, Viv would make as if to kick him or throw stones at him, even though her hands were empty.

BACK AT MY place, I sat among cardboard boxes I hadn't unpacked with Viv's and Henry's paintings and paperweights. I played *Chill with Satie* and made poutine. I stood by the sink and ate in the dark, so I could spy into the neighbouring windows.

I watched the family in the brick house across the alley. It was as if all the light of the city were contained inside their home. The small boy practised piano in the living room beneath a warm, hive-like lantern. In the kitchen, the mother lit candles and stirred dinner in a large pot on the stove. The father was in the den, reclining in an easy chair, the room blue and flickering. I wondered if their minds were quiet. I wondered if they were happy.

I phoned Viv to say I'd moved and to give her my new number, but got no answer. A few weeks later she returned my call, reporting that she'd been in the hospital. "Pancreatitis. Don't tell the Con," she added. I hung up irritated and concerned. I didn't tell her Liam was coming home. Yet I felt she was jinxing my plans, purposely dampening my excitement about his return with her bad news.

On my way to work, I wove through downtown toward the Château Laurier, which appeared before me like a hardened sand sculpture. Each morning I passed beneath a canopy of oaks in a park overlooking the river, and at the bottom of the incline was my glass edifice — its multifaceted dome and Great Hall and *Maman*, the thirty-foot-tall bronze spider balancing on the plaza like a black firework.

Maman guarded the Gallery like a humongous paranormal being. Tourists all wanted their picture taken with her, posing under her abdomen, leaning on a graceful leg. The sculptor, Louise Bourgeois, made *Maman* when she was really old. It moved me to think of this tiny, flinty lady with her blowtorch and goggles, welding the biggest homage she could achieve to her dead mother, who was a tapestry restorer.

Suspended from *Maman*'s underside was a wire-meshed sac of marble eggs. A hidden camera and loudspeaker above the Gallery's entranceway was aimed at her. When kids got up to their pranks, climbing and groping *Maman*'s legs, or when visitors chained their bikes or dogs to her, a booming voice commanded them to step away from the spider.

Nearing the building, I sometimes got apocalyptic visions of the glassworks exploding and the city going up in flames. In the aftermath there would be no world left, but the monumental spider would still be standing. Other days I envisioned a great hand piercing through the clouds and flicking her like a mosquito off the earth's skin.

More often, though, as the Gallery window washers dangled against the panes like newly hatched arachnids, and the Gatineau Hills shifted inside their pinks and purples, *Maman* towered over me and I was overwhelmed with a devotion I couldn't rationalize. Then I descended through the parkade's granite façade, cut square like a crypt, and made my way beneath sixty-five thousand works of art, following signage to the Curatorial Wing.

That day, over lunch, I told Raven about Viv.

"Pancreatitis at her age? Not good." She looked down at her polka dot socks, shaking her head.

Raven's dad was a drunk. She divulged this when we were students. She didn't bring it up again, but that night at the bar Raven told me about the jugs of homebrew and how happy her dad was when he drank, and how good he was to her and her sister, at first.

When he wasn't drinking, he got achy teeth. In abstinence his teeth bothered him so much he'd bite into glass rims until the glass broke in his mouth. My pop's the glass chewer, Raven said.

Then she told me how her mom stayed with him even when he was most unlovable. He drank anything—Listerine and Pepsi, rubbing alcohol and Kool-Aid, hand sanitizers. Over the holidays, Raven's mom put ornamental bottles with potpourri floating in them throughout the house. He drank the decorative liquid until it debilitated him.

Once, he tried to cut down a tree while trashed and dropped the electric saw on his bare toes, losing half his foot. He drooled and became belligerent. He saw people outside their windows when there were none. He called Raven and her sister whores. He smacked them and locked them in their rooms. Then he went AWOL for three years.

After he was found dead in a ditch, Raven's mom became a fanatic about keeping a clean house. She covered the furniture with sheets. She vacuumed twice a day and went through a gallon of bleach every week. Raven and her sister had to sleep with plastic on top of their mattresses. They couldn't put toys down on the floor. They ate in the bathtub, and every time they got sick, their mom sent them away to her aunt's.

"Viv had a lot of pressure on her as a kid," I told Raven once she'd finished her sandwich. Her hair had grown out since university. She divided it into three parts and evaluated me as she plaited it.

"Spare me. From what you've told me, you were the neglected one."

"I don't get why she can't quit."

"Try to catch a river in your hands." She pulled a compact from her purse and checked her eye makeup.

Across from us in the courtyard, a boy coloured on the cobblestones, working at a frenzied pace, gripping his chalks so hard they kept breaking. "What about wings?" his mother coaxed from the bench.

The jittery child added a flurry of plumage to the bodies. I thought of Viv's bird sketches and how, later, she spread paint around dead birds that she then withdrew from the canvas, leaving negative imprints of life in their place.

TWENTY-THREE

THE GALLERY BORROWED A unicorn called *The Child's Dream*. It was on loan from the artist. The fabled animal was set in a formaldehyde vitrine, framed in gold-plated steel. It also had a gold horn and golden hoofs.

To support the tank's weight, a team pulled up the exhibition room's hardwood planks and laid down a steel floor, then set the wood back in place. If the case leaked, the poisonous fumes could be fatal. An emergency shower was set up by the fire exit — a showerhead on a tile wall with a safety lock on the pull cord and a small drain in the floor — which visitors kept mistaking for a Duchamp.

Damien Hirst made *The Child's Dream*. He was one of the richest artists alive, notorious for mixing taxonomy, myth, and spectacle and selling his creations for millions of dollars. Some offended critics purported that Hirst's encased, rotting cow heads covered in flies crossed the line. Once, a cleaner thought his art was garbage and threw the whole thing out.

Before opening hours, I went to see the unicorn. I walked

down a narrow corridor, listening to the echo of my steps as I approached the dream.

I had the room to myself. The preserving fluid magnified the unicorn's features and the hair covering its slight body. Its coat was rumpled as though a hand had just passed through it and its mane seemed fixed in a breeze, each hair moving upward as if it had been given a jolt of electricity. Its lashes extended downward as if a butterfly had landed on the glass bottom of the tank, attracting the unicorn's mournful gaze.

The snow-white foal was alive with an unsettling stillness and I waited for it to move. My memory of the unicorn on the Lake O'Hara mountainside came back to me.

Then the track lighting came on and the TVs and audio recordings from installations in adjacent rooms dispatched jarring, noisy voices, disrupting my reverie.

When Liam arrived, I was bandaging a paper cut.

I looked up and there he was, leaning against the office door with a tree under one arm and a huge backpack at his feet.

He came in, sat down, and placed the potted tree with exposed roots between us. Then he reached across my desk and took my wrist and, raising my arm in front of him, examined my finger.

"What would happen if you got blood on the art?" His thumb was on my pulse.

I hesitated then said, "It would never happen." From the moment the paper caused a stinging sensation to the moment the drop of blood surfaced, there was ample time to pull my hand away. It was an automatic reaction, like being burned.

I explained, half joking, that paper-cut emergencies were part of my training. He released my wrist and slid the bonsai toward me. "A gift from the smallest park in the world," he said.

"How did you get in?" I asked, taking in his tan and laid-back composure. There was a distance to his demeanour that was unfamiliar.

"Your friend swiped me through. The woman with plaid leggings."

Raven would have been on the lookout for him. I'd told her he was coming.

I extracted the spare set of keys I'd had made the day before from my purse and tried to remain nonchalant. "Welcome back."

"Thanks. It's a drag my parents stayed in BC." He pressed my hand into his, asked for directions to my apartment, and then left.

AFTER WORK, RAVEN drove me home. I asked her to go easy over bumps and not to break suddenly. "God, it's a plant, Edith, not a child." She adjusted her rear-view mirror. "So cruel, the way those are grown. Same principle as binding Japanese women's feet. You sure he's over your sister?" She stopped in front of my place, guzzling down the last of her coffee from her I Hate Cats travel mug.

"He's staying with me, isn't he?"

"Personally, I'd steer clear. Now scram." She slapped my knee, gesturing for me to get out.

When I walked into the apartment, Liam was standing barefoot in the kitchen, stirring spaghetti sauce. "Hi. Hope you're hungry." He turned to me smiling, but he still seemed changed somehow. "I'll be out of your hair soon. I already have leads on a condo."

I'd set up the pullout and bought new sheets and towels. "It's no hurry," I said casually. "Stay as long as you want."

I put the bonsai on top of the bookcase in my bedroom, near a window framed by vines. It was a flowering mock orange tree with thick, glossy leaves and creamy flowers and rough, cracked bark. I almost expected insect-sized birds to fly out of the foliage.

It would live fifty years if soaked and pruned with miniature utensils, producing leathery fruit called capsules, smaller than my pinky nail. The blossoms gave off a subtle fragrance. When I switched on my reading lamp, the tree cast itself onto my wall like a shadow puppet.

That night, Liam collapsed onto the fold-out early, while I was still washing dishes. I thought we'd be up talking for hours, but I let him sleep. I covered him with a blanket and knelt down next to him.

The muscles at his temples twitched. His eyes moved around rapidly beneath their lids, as if he was struggling to exit some unpleasant trance. I gently blew on his eyelashes and the movements ceased. I resisted putting my head on his chest as I watched him, absorbed by his abdomen moving up and down under his T-shirt. Then I accidentally fell asleep on the rug beside him, curled up like a dog. I awoke before he did and retreated to my room.

Those first few weeks, I slept with my bedroom door closed to give him some privacy, although I often sat on the other side with my ear to the wall, listening to his breathing.

After his arrival, my tasks, my days, my life no longer seemed mundane.

I felt happy. People looked at me differently. Even Raven noticed.

"What the hell's wrong with you?"

"I'm in love."

"Infatuation ain't love, my pet. Once you've tolerated the bullshit and the smells and annoying habits you can't stand, get back to me."

Liam and I started having lunch together. He'd bike over from campus and we'd sit in the open-air amphitheatre behind the Gallery, on the windy promontory above the river and the bridge between provinces. After eating, he'd tilt his head back and close his eyes. Or he'd scope out the sculpture on the point, called *One Hundred Foot Line* — a ten-storey tapered spire that came out of the hill like a giant thorn and disappeared into the air.

One muggy afternoon, the metallic hum of cicadas caught his attention. The sun was too strong, so we sat on the grass, shaded by the *Line*. "Music from the bug that spends most of its life underground," he said, biting into his apple.

I was aware that when cicadas emerged from the soil, they removed themselves from their shells. Every summer, Viv had collected them from trees and planted them around the house to scare Constance.

Other than the rare flashback, when I was with Liam entire days passed where I didn't think about my sister. He didn't bring up Viv either.

Alone at night, though, a succession of images associated with her involuntarily flashed through my mind while I slept. But these were dreams I tended to forget on waking.

TWENTY-FOUR

ON THE MORNING OF Liam's birthday, I gave him a rock and a globe and wrote him a note that said, *You Rock My World*. He hugged me and told me I was sweet before clipping his bike helmet on and rushing out the door.

I avoided Raven at lunch that day and went to a lingerie shop, where I spent a hundred bucks on a black lace bra and bikini briefs.

Hurrying home from work, I showered and applied makeup. I curled my hair and put on the black dress I'd kept, meant for my father's funeral but purchased several sizes too small by Constance. It didn't fit me then, but it fit now.

I cued up some Nina Simone and poured bubbly in Dollarama flutes with wedding bells on them.

Liam whistled as he came through the door. "What's all this?"

I offered him his drink and tipped my glass against his. "Happy Birthday." I went on tiptoe to remove his bike helmet. Then I took his hand and led him to the bedroom.

He was confused. "Wait a sec..."

"Don't worry," I told him, trying to undo my dress. The zipper was caught in the lace.

"Edith, I don't think..." He stepped back.

"It's fine," I cajoled.

"Seriously. We can't do this." He kissed me then pulled away. "It's too weird."

But I was already undressing. Suddenly, his expression changed. He got a strange look in his eyes as he watched me remove my clothes. Then he stepped toward me and kissed me on my neck and chest.

"When did you get so hot?" he said, then, "Tell me what you want."

I figured it was obvious what I wanted. "You," I told him, returning his kisses.

He pushed me onto the bed. Within a few minutes, it was over.

He passed me a towel and asked if I wanted to use the bathroom. I said no, so he got up, a bit too quickly, I thought. While he showered, I changed the sheets so he wouldn't see the blood.

It wasn't what I'd anticipated, but that didn't matter. After years of waiting, I'd finally walked the tightrope from fantasy to reality.

FROM THAT DAY on, he slept in my bed. Usually he dozed off long before me with a book still in his hands. Occasionally, in the middle of the night, he'd reach for me in the dark. We didn't talk about what was happening between us. I based how he felt about me on those carnal nights.

We fell into a routine like a married couple. Each day I'd prepare his coffee, toast, and egg, sitting calm beside him as he ate and reviewed his teaching notes. He gave me a peck on the nose goodbye, then it was my turn to get ready for work. We met for lunch less and less, but we still came home around the same time.

Liam was the one to make dinner each night and I was the one to clean up. Afterwards, he'd study his rocks, spreading them out on the table and examining them with his magnifying glass, or he'd grade papers and I'd lie on the couch pretending to read, observing him and daydreaming about the trips we'd take and what our children would look like.

We drank tea and went for evening walks in the autumn. I stitched his socks and shirts and learned basic cooking skills.

After a few months, Liam stopped mentioning the place he was going to buy. Like a gambler on a winning streak with my rabbit foot charm, I couldn't believe my luck. I was on top of the world.

If there was a nagging feeling that some emotional element was missing, I brushed it off my shoulder like a feather. If I was tempted by rashness in our quiet domestic bliss, thinking how I wanted to suck on his fingers, pull his hair, or slap him, I restrained myself for fear of scaring him off.

But I began serving wine with meals and keeping beer in the fridge, noticing that after a drink or two he relaxed. With a couple of beers he'd let me run him a bath and wash his body after a tiring day. He'd welcome a massage in bed and was more affectionate with me. These were the moments I lived for.

TWENTY-FIVE

ONE NIGHT, LIAM CALLED to say he had to work late. I thought it would be romantic if I brought him a picnic. I packed deli sandwiches, candles, strawberries, and Chardonnay. I put on a white dress I knew he liked, and dabbed the Chanel No. 5 I'd just bought behind my ears.

I was freezing cold as I walked to the campus. My dress was for summer, which was long since over. Then it started raining. Within minutes, the blue dye from the jean jacket I held over my head was dripping onto my dress as I tried to hail a cab.

The Earth Sciences building was deserted. Inside, I passed vacant auditoriums and lecture halls before entering the faculty corridor. I found a washroom and tried reshaping my ratty hair and removing the streaks of makeup running down my cheeks. Wringing my jacket out, I put it back on over my ruined dress.

I'd never actually been to Liam's office. One door was open at the end of the hall, with brightness ricocheting from it. I took a few squeaking steps then removed my shoes to approach more quietly.

As I got closer, I heard the flirtatious voices of girls. "We need to find you a wife, Professor Livingstone!" one said coyly. "It's no wonder your shirts and ties clash," the other giggled. A young male interjected then with, "Leave him alone, Brianna."

Liam hadn't mentioned any study group. I peered into the doorway to see him leaning back comfortably in his chair, giving them that intoxicating smile he'd used on me so often. "I'll be single forever. Too much important work to do," he told them. Then everyone was looking at me, standing there like a madwoman in my tie-dyed dress, clutching my wet shoes and sopping basket.

"Here's your supper, Professor Livingstone," I said, dropping the wicker hamper on the floor and turning back down the hall.

"Edith, hang on!" he called out.

As I rounded the corner, I slipped on the polished floor. If Liam heard me fall, he didn't acknowledge it or come after me. I limped to the taxi stand, my hip throbbing.

The library tower glowed in the distance like a light sabre. The rain had subsided and I stood for a minute in the cold darkness, watching students in their carrels that lined the windows. I envied them in their partitioned wooden desks, thinking and memorizing, their laptops like crystal balls illuminating their faces. I had the fleeting thought that maybe I'd made a mistake, missing out on university life.

WHEN LIAM CAME home later, he immediately entered the bedroom and sat beside me on the bed.

I moved away from him and crossed my arms. "If you don't want to be with me, say so."

"Let's not get melodramatic, Edith."

"Do you regret this?"

"Of course not."

"Why don't you mention me to anyone?"

"I don't discuss my private life."

"You could have introduced me."

"Let me make it right."

He'd brought the basket on his bike even though the rain was coming down hard again. His clothes were wet and the more I tried to kick him off the bed, the more he tried to embrace me. I finally relented and we had sex and ate the strawberries. I decided to forgive him.

My hip ached for weeks. I hated having to sleep facing the wall, but lying on my side facing Liam hurt too much.

After the picnic debacle, he was always busy.

I started waiting for him to come home, adjusting my habits around that waiting. He missed dinners, alluding to mid-terms. I kept cooking my simple online recipes — flavourless casseroles and stir-fries that never looked like the pictures. I'd leave his plate out for a time then chuck the whole dish into the garbage when I didn't hear from him.

I went to bed nervous, angry, and alone each evening. I debated following him then talked myself out of it. When he'd kiss my temple while I slept, or when he brought me a rock, shaking me awake to describe its qualities to me, or if he suggested we take a midnight walk so he could tell me about his day and use me as a sounding board, all was forgotten.

I was like a circus performer, constantly working on tricks to impress him. Swanky feasts and erotic outfits galore. Clever books I left out for him to see, although I never actually read them. It worked for a while, but Liam's attention span with me was finite. I could only hold him so long, like a unicyclist throwing torches in the air, hoping they'd land back in my hands right-side up and with the flames still burning.

WHEN OUR TIME together ebbed into what seemed like interludes between parts of a larger production I didn't have a role in, it was because Liam had valuable work to do. I should expect less and accept his eccentricities, his absences. This is what I told myself the afternoon I opened the door to find him in suit bottoms, ironing a shirt.

As he explained about the awards banquet, his mother called to say they were ready to be picked up from the hotel.

I finished his ironing as he spoke to her. The dove-grey shirt was new. It felt expensive. I pressed it to my body then gave it to him.

"Are you the one getting the award?" I asked.

"Fellowship." He wiped the steam from the bathroom mirror to straighten the knot of his tie. "It's no big deal."

"You look good," I said, my voice quavering. "Your parents must be proud, coming all this way."

"They insisted."

"No dates allowed or what?" I pursued, smiling too hard.

"You'd be bored," he said, dropping his keys and phone into his suit pocket. He pinched my cheek as he headed for the door. "Hey, let's do something fun this weekend. Just us."

"Okay," I answered, reassured.

After he left, I flipped channels until I came across a French film called *Noce Blanche*, about a young woman named Mathilde who becomes enamoured of her teacher,

François. The two begin a torrid affair. François loses his marriage and his career. When he comes to his senses, he moves away, into a self-imposed exile to Dunkirk—a township in northern France, on the sea. Mathilde follows without him knowing, taking an apartment with a view of the school where François teaches. She pines after him in his classroom through a prison-like window, living as a recluse and letting herself die. But not before scrawling, *L'océan, François, il y a l'océan* on the wall of her cramped quarters.

I thought Mathilde was pathetic. Then I reconsidered. If this was revenge, she was a mastermind. François would be haunted by her for the rest of his life.

I fell asleep on the couch. When Liam got in, I sat up and watched him get a glass of water, the phosphorescence from the fridge hitting his chest in a celestial way. When he turned and saw me, he jumped.

"Jesus! You scared me," he said, then laughed and drank.

"Where's the prize?"

He took an envelope from his breast pocket and set it on the table.

"Did you make a speech?"

"A short one."

He took off his jacket and loosened his tie. Unbuttoned the dove-grey shirt. He was about to say good night.

"Are you that ashamed of me?" I asked before he could retreat.

He turned to the fridge again, put both hands on the appliance, and stood there spread-eagled.

"You know how to devastate a girl," I told him.

He smacked his forehead on the fridge. Once, twice, three times, slow and hard. "I'm not fighting with you, Edith."

I went over to him and placed my hand in his. "Congratulations," I said, and drew his face to mine.

He made love to me in a frantic, aggressive way. Despite himself, probably. There was an inner tension in him. A complex conflict he wouldn't talk about, like an Escher drawing, light against dark.

After, we lay there not speaking. I had Piaf's "Hymne à l'amour" in my head and I hummed it.

"Please stop," Liam told me. "You can't sing."

"What do you think about unicorns?" I asked, kissing his shoulder.

"I used to think anything was possible." He turned to the window, adding, "I think they're made up."

"Do you want to take a walk?"

"I should do some work," he said aloofly. "I have papers to grade."

He slid his boxers on. He stood and stretched, taking a swig of water from the bedside table. He went over to the window, opening it to let in the cool night air. Then a black form shot into the room.

The bat flew erratically, lower and lower, flitting overhead, skimming the surface of the bed and furniture. I crouched down to move out of its way.

"Wait for it to land!" Liam bent down beside me.

I could hear the wingbeats and sensed its panic. Liam grabbed a towel from the floor and tried throwing it over the bat, missing several times before trapping it. The creature made clicking noises beneath the fabric.

"It's trying to bite through," Liam said, carrying it outside rather than tossing it out the window in case it flew in again.

I pulled the glass pane down and sat on the sill. Liam walked over to a tree, shirtless, and placed the towel with the bat in it on a branch. When he took a few steps back the small body swooped down then flew off.

He stared up at the blackness for ages.

He was melting away from me and there was nothing I could do. I was like a wax artist working in a sweltering climate.

"I hope that's not bat luck," I joked when he finally came inside.

A few weeks later, Viv called.

"I'm home, Worm," she told me. "Sorry I haven't been in touch."

TWENTY-SIX

I HADN'T SEEN VIV since the funeral almost three years earlier.

I left work to meet her in a grimy downtown coffee shop. My goal was to keep her visit from Liam.

It took me a while to locate her. She waved from a corner table. A trucker's cap covered her matted blond hair and there were broken blood vessels under her eyes. She had a large purse at her feet with various articles of clothing overflowing from it onto the dirty floor.

Her hygiene shocked me. Sitting across from Viv, the only recognizable part of her was her voice, though it was weakened and hoarse. She was antsy in her seat. I caught whiffs of a sharp, rank smell. My unclean sister stank.

Along with a rising sense of worry, I felt a brisk thrill. Liam would never be attracted to her the way she looked now.

"That city was toxic. I'm starting fresh," she said.

"Are you all right?"

"Great! Listen, I'm a bit short on cash."

I gave her what I had in my wallet, amazed that she'd let herself go to this point. "Are you still painting?"

"Definitely. No word of this to the Con, okay?"

"Don't call her that," I said. Regretting my tone, I asked her where she was staying.

"With friends," she said ambiguously.

We'd become strangers, distancing ourselves with mutual relief. I still hadn't quite forgiven my sister for not flying home before our father died. Now she was back in my life and I didn't know what to do with her.

I tried not to stare at her bitten-down nails and at the squiggling scar on her cheekbone, which had stayed with her since Bella Coola like a chalk drawing of the hot springs snake.

Watching the shaky hand that held the coffee cup, I pitied her. "Don't be stupid, Vee. Come home with me."

She didn't argue, telling me she'd wait in the Market until my shift ended. I left her near some vegetable stalls. I turned back to wave, but she was already entering the Lafayette bar.

When I got to my desk, I phoned Constance. She'd just returned from a trip to Florida with her boyfriend Pierre. She was rarely home more than a few weeks at a time these days. It was an unspoken rule that we didn't discuss Pierre even though he'd been around for almost a year. When my mother spoke of him, it was in passing. It was the same when we talked about Viv. Although we didn't talk about her much anymore.

"Come visit. We went outlet shopping. I found you the most billowy dress, I hope you haven't put on weight."

"How long are you home?"

"Not long. I have some news—*Non, pas là! Pas là, Mirabelle!*" she snapped.

"Viv's back."

"*Quoi?* I've heard nothing."

"She's staying with me."

"Give me her email, Édith."

"I doubt she uses it."

"*Give* it to me." The pitch of my mother's voice rose. "Let's have her over for brunch!" When the dog started yipping, she hung up.

I TOOK THE elevator to the viewing room. The afternoon shifts were the best part of my job. When the sun came through the panes, it enlightened every object and person like gold-leaf manuscript illustrations. When it rained hard, it was like being in the undercut behind a waterfall.

I hoped there wouldn't be any researchers there. I was cataloguing seventy-nine variations of a foot by Hans Schlippenberger and I wanted to finish my notes so I could move on to a more interesting series. But when I came in to relieve Alejandro, there was a figure stooped over a table at the back of the room.

"He has the Gauguin file, so no breaks." Alejandro swept up his magazines and walked out before the glass doors swung shut. By the time he reached the elevator, he had a cigarette in his mouth and was squeezing a hand into his leather pant pocket in search of a lighter.

I settled in and scanned the register. Dr. Theo de Buuter. Nobody I knew, probably a volunteer. Gallery volunteers were a territorial subculture of wealthy retirees not to be interfered with. The staff avoided them and they ran the place in their own parallel universe, leading tours, holding silent auctions, going on art-themed trips through Europe. Once, I took water from the cooler by their lounge and they sent me a reprimanding note.

I walked over to the old man's table. A couple of prints were laid out in front of him. We owned twenty-two Gauguins of moderate artistic merit—one sculpture, two oils, some woodcuts, and a few zincographs. With the exception of the sculpture and the oils, these stayed in storage for the most part. Sometimes smaller institutions borrowed them, headlining *Gauguin Masterworks!*

He was bent over, scribbling away with one of those tiny pencils we supplied—the ones barely long enough to rest on the soft expanse of skin between the thumb and index finger. I cleared my throat until he removed his glasses and closed his notebook.

He tried pushing his chair back, but it kept catching on the carpet. Once he stood up, he towered over me, though part of his height may have been due to his outrageous hair.

His pencil rolled off the table, landing soundlessly. He bent over to pick it up, grunting. He wore a blue bow tie, the only splash of colour on an otherwise dreary palette. A professor, I re-evaluated.

"Hi. If you need anything, let me know." His nod implied, *is that all?* Gulls cackled through the thick panes above us. "We close at four," I added, then went back to my desk.

I catalogued five more feet. Logging off Avalon, I looked up to find old De Buuter staring. Not at me but through me, as though I were a hologram. There had been talk of holograms around the Gallery. Senior management wanted to put all the collections into storage and have virtual holograms on display instead, so nothing got damaged.

At a quarter to four, the closing announcement came through the intercom. Dr. de Buuter shuffled over, initialled the register, and left. As he went by, a trace of lavender lingered in the air, smelling like clothing that had been stored away for a long time in a drawer with sachets.

I rolled my trolley to his table to prepare the Gauguins for re-shelving. Curious, I opened the top file to see which print he'd examined.

The woodcut was of a long-haired woman squatting on the ground beside a large bird. Next to the bird there was a dog biting into the bird's back. There was a set of eyes in the background, and two other female faces—one cloaked as if in prayer and one tilting her head back as if in elation. The text *Le Sourire* was written above the dog. Evidently our curators didn't care much for the print. According to the file, it hadn't been viewed in more than ten years.

I packed my purse and locked up, detouring down the glass ramp to get outdoors. I passed under *Maman* and ran my hand along one of her legs. Her bronze was warm from the afternoon sun. "Hey, spinner," I said as I leaned on her limb before moving on.

Hey spinster, she replied.

I FOUND VIV outside the Laff, talking to a guy in a toque whose jeans were so low-riding I wanted to pull them up for him. I called to her from across the street. She pecked him on the cheek and ran over. She was so thin her purse looked like it weighed more than she did.

"Garbage head," she said breathlessly.

"Huh?"

"That guy. He's a garbage head."

"What's that?"

"A junkie."

"You don't do drugs, then?" I stopped walking and stood in front of her.

"Hell no."

"I found a pipe in your room once."

"That's a lifetime ago." She turned to keep walking.

I grabbed her wrist. "Promise?"

"*Yes*. Let *go*." She wrenched her arm away, pulling sunglasses from her purse and checking a cellphone.

"How can you afford a cell?" When she didn't respond, I studied her protruding cheekbones. "Why are you so gaunt?"

"I have a fast metabolism. You know that."

I didn't warn her that Liam was staying with me. I needed him to see her as she was now. So he'd be over her once and for all.

When we got home, Viv asked if she could use the shower. I offered to put her clothes in the laundry and I made up the pullout. Then I ran to the pizza place on the corner. By the time I returned, Liam was storming out of the house.

"What the *fuck*!"

"You're early. I was going to tell you —"

"What's she doing in the *bedroom* half *naked*? What the *fuck*!?" He paced back and forth on the sidewalk.

"She has nowhere to go."

"Do you ever *think* before doing anything, Edith?"

Viv materialized at the door in one of my sweaters. I reached for Liam's hand, self-conscious now that my sister was watching us.

"It's for a few days. I couldn't let her stay on the street."

Liam turned to Viv, who was drying her hair. "Christ, Edith. She's manipulating you."

Viv smiled and waved then went back inside. Liam threw his bag through the door, got onto his bike, and rode off.

When I re-entered the apartment, I found Viv staring at her painting and our father's beside it on the wall. I put the pizza on the kitchen counter. She turned to me as she combed through the knots in her hair.

"Nice of you to let me know," she mumbled.

"I wasn't sure how to bring it up."

She pulled a slice of pizza from the box and picked all the toppings off.

"Where's the nearest liquor store?"

"Two blocks that way." I pointed. "Shouldn't you rest?"

She fished through her purse and slid on some flip-flops.

"You'll catch a cold wearing those," I said as the door clattered behind her.

I sat down, displaced. Twenty minutes later Viv came back with two magnums of white wine. The first she put in the freezer. The second she opened. There was a glug-glug-glug before she brought us each a glass, carrying the bottle under one arm. She put it on the floor and took her cigarettes from her purse.

"I guess I don't need to ask what's new with *you*." Her upper lip curled into a snarl.

"You can't smoke in here."

She dropped the remote in my lap, picked up her glass, and went out onto the porch.

I turned on the TV and flipped channels, stopping on a show called *Birding Adventures*. The episode was about red-footed boobies in Belize. I thought of that old man in the Gallery and questioned what he was doing there studying Gauguin's crummy prints. He wasn't fit enough to be a birder. What was his story? I wondered, watching the seabirds plummet into the ocean for fish and squid, until I heard muffled voices on the other side of the door.

Liam had returned. Their discussion got louder and became argumentative. I let them have it out.

Then things got too quiet. With stealth, I approached the window. They were sitting on the front steps side by side, their skin almost touching. Viv put her hand on Liam's arm. When he looked at her, I realized my mistake.

A half-hour later, Liam came inside, then Viv. I told him that we should let my sister rest. We said good night to her and closed the bedroom door. In bed, he didn't touch me. Instead, he got up to go to the washroom a lot. Each time he left the room, I heard him talking with Viv.

It rained in the early morning. When the sun appeared, I went out onto the deck. Along the railing there was a web strung with quartz-like water pellets. My senses were heightened from lack of sleep.

I examined the spider and its fine weaving that had survived the downpour and the wind.

It was a miraculous insect that unendingly rebuilt what got torn down. Being near this industrious spider, which had an inner strength I didn't seem to have, bolstered me. I felt the same way when I stood by *Maman*. Then I thought of Constance, our resilient and defensive matriarch. Our protector and our predator. Catching my sister in her threads, spinning her dreams and fears and desires around her to entrap her.

Viv was gone. The empty bottles were by the back door.

"Did you tell her to go?" I asked Liam when he came out, trying to hide my relief.

"I didn't have to. That's Vivienne for you," he said. "She'll be back when she needs something."

The wind rose and shook the leaves from the trees. The leaves snapped off branches and rattled around our feet. The rusts and golds were fading like my sister's loveliness. I stared at them intently, knowing that, within weeks, only a hint of colour would remain.

TWENTY-SEVEN

AFTER VIV'S CAMEO, LIAM was even more standoffish and moody. When I tried getting near him physically, he invented excuses and shut me out.

"What did you two talk about?" I asked one night. He'd been working at the kitchen table for hours and hadn't said a word to me.

"Hmmm?"

"You and Viv. On the porch."

"Can't remember."

I sat down beside him. "I have a right."

Liam, morose, closed his laptop obligingly. "It doesn't concern you, Edith."

"Tell me," I persisted. Our relationship had become like a towel washed too often, its softness gone.

"Fine," he said, turning to face me. "I asked if there'd been someone else while I was with her. I always had this feeling she was keeping something from me."

"Why are you still thinking about that?"

Liam didn't answer. He looked apprehensive. "Let's get some air," he proposed.

We walked along the canal under boughs of crabapple trees, the branches weighed down by ruby fruit. Apples were ripening in the grass and turning to mush on the walkway, giving off a sour, woody odour.

"I've accepted more fieldwork," he told me.

What I was hearing was illogical. I reinterpreted his words.

"Can you still bike? Is it nearby?"

He stopped walking and squeezed my shoulder with one hand, swatting away wasps with the other.

"What about our camping trip?" I asked, staring off at the path where white wild roses clung to their low shrubs like crumpled Kleenex. It was late October and they should have been dead already.

Then Liam said he had work to do at the university. He left me to walk back alone and told me not to wait up. He would crash on his office couch.

Once home, I sat on the bed and took off my socks, rubbing my heels. I should have paid more attention to Liam's feet. I should have drawn them. As I'd learned through Schlippenberger, one of the most difficult parts of the body to sketch was the foot. Maybe if I could have brought him to his basic geometrical form and detailed on paper what, in essence, the entirety of Liam rested on, balanced on, moved on, I would have better understood him: his contours, shapes, and shading. His angles.

That night, I hoarded all my Liam memories. The more details of him I accumulated in my mind, the more I could afford to lose, like preparing for strip poker by wearing too many layers.

My bonsai pot was a permanent fixture on the bookshelf, although the tree was no longer alive. Within weeks of Liam giving it to me, the tiny flowers had shrivelled up. I'd watered it like I was supposed to. I'd misted it and kept an eye on light exposure and still the leaves continued falling on their bed of pebbles, revealing intricate branches like lacework.

I'd wanted so much to see it produce its orange fruit. Liam hadn't masked his aggravation when he noticed it was dying.

"What did you do, poison it?" He took a butter knife from the kitchen and scraped a bit of bark off the trunk. Beneath the bark, the wood was greyish where it should have been green. Liam tsked and said, "I won't be trusting you with *my* life!"

The dead wood sculpture still possessed an eerie beauty. This weathered tree bleached from the sun, after all else had fallen away. All that remained was a stark, bone-white hunger.

He didn't say when he'd be taking off and I didn't ask. One day I came home early and it was as though he'd never been there. His toothbrush was gone, and all his clothes from the dresser. His books and his papers and his rocks. Only his bike leaned against the wall near the door, the seat and handlebars wrapped in plastic.

I poured myself a glass of wine. I removed an earring and dropped it into the saddlebag. In due course it would snag on his fingers like a fish hook and he'd think of me.

I made his favourite macaroni casserole. I set the table and put on the skimpy velvet dress that drove him mad. I poured another glass of wine then smeared on some crimson lipstick. I sat on the couch and kept drinking.

An hour went by before he pulled up in a U-Haul. "Oh, hey," he said, coming in. He didn't expect me to be there. In all likelihood he'd prepared a note.

"It's your going-away party," I told him, opening a second bottle.

"This is too much," he murmured. He was unfocused, glancing around, looking everywhere but at me.

"Can't have you slinking out of here without a goodbye." I gestured for him to sit down. I turned on the radio and lit the candles even though it was still bright out. While he checked his phone, I slopped half the dish onto his plate then daubed ketchup from the squeeze bottle all over it.

"More wine?" I asked. He covered his glass as I refilled mine.

"No thanks."

"I gather you're ready to take off." I gave a lighthearted giggle. The upper layer of shells was burnt. He was having a hard time swallowing. "Tell me about it," I said too forcefully.

"Let's not do this." His cutlery clanked on his plate.

"What is it?" I asked, getting up and going over to him. I crouched and blew in his ear. Licked his cheek. "You want to go at it one last time?"

I increased the volume on the radio. Some down-in-the-dumps jazz was playing. Moving to the slow piano, horns, and snare brush, I closed my eyes and swayed to the music as exotically as I could, stumbling once or twice. I put his hands on my waist, ran them up my body. When I peeled the top half of my dress to my hips, he stood abruptly.

He grabbed my wrist, but I kept dancing, half naked now, pressing against him until he got hold of my other arm and shook me. "Stop it, Edith. This doesn't become you."

His grip burned my skin. When he let go and walked away, I stomped after him. He wouldn't turn toward me, so I removed a slipper and threw it at him. There was a small whipping sound as it slapped him in the back.

"I thought you *liked* your girls like this." He stood at the window with his hands in his pockets. "Look at me, Liam. *Look* at me!" His composure made me want to explode.

I smashed my plate on the floor. Macaroni and pieces of ceramic went sliding across the hardwood. I took his plate and hurled it against the wall. The noodles stuck to the surface like a grotesque abstract.

That caught his attention. His eyes were on me again, so I picked up where I left off with the dancing until a sharp pain shot through my heel, causing me to yelp. Liam kept watching, not offering help as I hobbled over to the chair.

My nails were too short to pull the shard from my heel. The more I dug around, the bloodier my foot became. Soon I gave up. I felt so tired. I leaned on the table and rested my head on my crossed arms.

"Why can't you let her go?" I said, enunciating each word carefully.

"Because *you won't let* me, Edith!" Liam screamed.

I rubbed my eyes and surveyed him. He was visibly baffled. "She's the way she is now because of *you*," I told him, trying not to slur. "You destroyed her life and mine!"

He detached his keys from the ring and placed them on the table. "I was going to stay the night, but I'll go."

"You're dead inside like your rocks. You can't feel anything."

I didn't resist when he reached out to slide my arms through the straps, pulling the dress back up over my shoulders. "Get some sleep," he told me. He rolled his bike to the door, closing it tactfully behind him.

I rose early with a migraine. I staggered to the bathroom for Aspirin and removed the shard from my heel with tweezers. Then I lay in the dark for an hour before getting up for juice. Nothing quenched my dehydration. I wondered how Viv could drink so much, but then Raven had said real drinkers didn't ever get hangovers. Instead, they woke up wanting more.

I wrote a long letter to Liam that I deleted. The email I eventually sent simply said, *I'm sorry. I love you.* Part of me believed that was all it would take.

I never heard back. I thought he'd return, but he didn't.

TWENTY-EIGHT

ON THE SEVENTEENTH FLOOR of Sunset Towers, the door flew open and my mother drew me into her cloud of rose-water perfume while Mira yipped at my ankles. I pushed the dog away with my foot.

"Where is your sister?" She glanced down the hall.

"No idea."

This was a lie. I'd seen Viv hanging out at the Lafayette since she'd left my place. The drinking tavern was a few blocks from the Gallery on a seedy corner in the Market. From the sidewalk the scent of warm hops emanated over vendors' stalls of strawberries and tomatoes. Getting produce there on my lunch break, I'd gone by the Laff and spotted my sister inside at least a half-dozen times, sitting on the vinyl bench against the wall. I never went in. Instead, I rushed by, hoping Viv wouldn't see me.

"Ah." Con's face dropped. She recovered with a radiant smile. "Next time!"

I eased myself onto the peach couch in the living room

and slipped off my shoes, running my toes along the shag rug. Mira hopped into my lap, turning circles before settling. A children's barrette secured the dog's hair in a spurt between her ears.

My mother was tanned and thin. Her new hairstyle, an upsweep of blond and grey tints in a loose chignon, suited her, showing off her dancer's neck.

"And how is Liam?" she called out.

"Gone."

"*Non! Le maudit.*"

She came over to the couch and sat down beside me. When I stifled a sob, she took my hands in hers.

"*En amour*, it is better to be with someone who loves you more than you love them," she said with conviction.

Suitcases were stacked beneath the pearly mantelpiece cluttered with framed pictures. My eyes fell on the black-and-white shot of a voluptuous Constance on Henry's lap in a smoky Greenwich Village café. She kept these old ones up like artifacts among those of her and Pierre on beaches and in yacht clubs. Maybe at a certain age widowers incited each other to display their past selves. This was me in my other life. Look what I did. Look what I had.

There was a picture of me and Viv up there too, from when we were maybe four and seven. Lodged into the rocking chair on the porch, wearing cowboy hats our father found at a yard sale. We wore those hats until the straw dried up and crumbled.

There was also a shot of my teenaged sister on the mantel, in the backyard assembling an easel. In it, Viv was deep in concentration, kneeling in the grass with her chin on her knee and pieces of wood all around her. Our father's shadow projected along the pavement. There was a strong breeze that day. You could see it in the way the uncut grass bent, and the striped curtains from my bedroom blew like signalling flags. I lay on the bed reading. Through my open window I heard our father say, "You have a gift, Vivienne, use it." They didn't see me peek out, as Constance put her arm around my sister. From then on I waited for my parents to tell me what my gift was, but that day never came.

"Did you have a nice birthday?" my mother asked, tearing open a suitcase and flinging a seafoam dress at me. The garment hovered in the air before landing on Mira.

I set it aside and followed her into the kitchen. She popped frozen waffles into the toaster, opened a can of mandarins, and pulled Cool Whip from the fridge.

We brought our plates into the solarium with a view to the river and the copper Parliament rooftops. The Gallery dispersed white light, clear and colourless like a diamond on the horizon. We sat in her universal plastic chairs, eating without talking while Mira nibbled on the potted herbs.

"We have a sculpture made out of these," I said about the chairs. "It's called *Shapeshifter*."

"Bizarre."

"It's the skeleton of a whale suspended from a ceiling."

"*Pourquoi?*"

"A statement on consumerism. How we contaminate nature."

"*Ah bon.*" She sipped her coffee and lit a cigarette, drawing heavily on it before letting it burn away in the ashtray.

When Mira hopped on my mother's foot, she lifted her onto her knee, unsnapped the barrette, and ran her fingers through the tangled fringe impeding the dog's vision. Mira sneezed. Her matted coat, once silky, was coming out in Con's hands as she combed her.

"What's wrong with her?"

"Alopecia." My mother kissed Mira on the nose.

"Why are her eyes so gunky?"

"Oh, leave her, Édith! She has allergies." She pulled a tissue from her pocket, licked the tip, and wiped the inner corners of Mira's eyes. "*Alors.* Tell me how you celebrated your birthday."

Liam left days prior to my twenty-first birthday. Neither he nor Viv called.

I lied to my mother about a dinner party. In reality, my day passed without incident, most of it spent in storage. At lunch, Raven brought down a cake and gave me a gift card for a facial, and some green and black checkered tights. She also brought me a book called *The Unabridged History of Unicorns.* She'd noticed I'd been spending my lunch hours in the *Child's Dream* gallery.

"I had a party," I told Constance.

"Wonderful!" She dropped Mira onto the green turf. "*En passant*, we're moving."

"I don't blame you."

"We found a home in Naples."

"Italy? Great."

"Naples, Florida. Near Sawgrass Mills."

"Where?"

"It's one of the largest malls in America! A short drive through the Everglades and you're there."

"Wow."

"Houses are so sheep *là-bas*. Pierre is finalizing. We'll keep his place here for our *pied-à-terre. Tu vas adorer ça, chérie.*"

But I knew I wouldn't be taking many trips to Florida just as I knew she wouldn't come back once she left for that sunny, harmless state.

I looked out to the War Museum, immovable in its open field like a cement casket. If I visited Constance once a year and she lived until eighty, I would see her thirty more times. If I visited twice a year, sixty. That was two months. Even if she lived until ninety, we'd have a maximum of eighty visits, and chances were I would visit on average 1.5 times per year, which brought us back down to sixty. Two months remaining with my mother.

I LEFT HER brewing another pot of coffee and went to the aesthetician's for my facial. Jacinda, a perky girl with pigtails and sparkling eyeshadow, lathered creams and pastes on me in a dimly lit room. She rubbed my temples, snapping her gum and chatting above the New Age music. Unfortunately, I couldn't enjoy the experience. Lying there with all that sludge on my face brought to mind the time Viv wanted to make my plaster positive but, because of my cowardice, we'd ended up creating my sister's death mask instead.

Afterwards, Jacinda handed me a binder and suggested I flip through it. She endorsed Vajazzling: the act of applying jewels to a woman's nether regions for aesthetic purposes. "It's all the rage," she told me as I turned the pages, scanning images of intertwined hearts, flowers, and butterflies.

The butterflies got me thinking about the sarcophagus we had at work—*Pavane for a Dead Princess*—a limestone vessel with a glass lid, lined with silk on which an assortment of butterflies were pinned. The specimens were meant to investigate mortality and transformation and the notion of the soul. It was unnerving, seeing those classified wings in their final resting place.

Then each butterfly had to be removed and fumigated because, as it turned out, the silk lining was infested with moth cocoons. When the moths hatched and started eating the butterflies, the conservators dismantled the display.

I began reminiscing about Liam, and the time he took me to a butterfly exhibit at the campus greenhouse. He told me to wear red that day. Inside, hundreds of exotic butterflies fluttered around us, drawn to my maraschino top. It was humid and I fanned myself with a pamphlet as he led me off the walking path, away from the visitors, to a wall covered in flowers covered in butterflies. I stared in amazement.

Liam told me then that butterflies have taste buds on their feet. When starving, they feed on incredibly low concentrations of sugar diluted in water. He said that their sensitivity to sweetness was more developed than that of our own tongues, and that some species after drinking fermented dew can't fly away for days.

Before I left the spa, Jacinda asked if I wanted to book a Vajazzle consult. When I gave her the seafoam dress my mother had bought for me, she hugged me.

TWENTY-NINE

IT WAS WEEKS BEFORE I noticed the missing paperweights.
I'd been saving up to have a cabinet custom-made. When
I went to retrieve them from the linen closet, I found the
empty box.

There were twenty-seven weights. Viv must have stowed
them away in her coat and in her enormous handbag, accus-
tomed to toting large quantities of glass.

Did she pawn them or did she launch them over a bridge?
Did she sell them to buy more, full bottles, or did she find a
body of water and wade into it, pulled down by the frozen
landscapes? I preferred to think she traded them in to an
antiques dealer and used the few thousand dollars to move
to Mexico, maybe to one of those inland artist communities
where living was still cheap.

All I had left was the *millefiori*—"a thousand flowers" in
Italian—that I kept on my office desk. Within its crystal-
line dome there were cross-sections of moulded glass rods,
stretched and sliced like hard candy to form a multicoloured

carpet. The rod faces had flowers on them. There was a silhouette of a dancing devil inside the largest, middle rod, which had fascinated me as a child.

Henry was convinced the paperweight came from the St. Louis factory in France. If there had been an identifier on the bottom and if the glass had no yellow cast or air bubbles, it would have been valuable. Instead, it was deeply flawed and worthless.

THE NEXT DAY at lunch, I dropped the millefiori into my cardigan pocket, grabbed my purse, and roamed through the Canadiana galleries. I thought about how Henry likely came here on his lunch breaks too, before his years on night shift. He probably stood in the exact same spot I was standing in now, in front of *The Jack Pine* by Tom Thomson.

Pictured was a dark green, solitary tree on a rocky shore, its threadbare branches deformed against the yellows, cobalts, and carnelians of water and hills and sunset. It was my father's favourite work. We sold laser reproductions, mugs, serviettes, T-shirts, and magnets of it in the gift shop. I bought Liam the *Jack Pine* hotpot holder after we'd planned to go camping in Algonquin Park, but I never saw him use it.

In the same room was *The Tangled Garden*. This painting, which soothed my mother all those years ago, had the opposite effect on me. The closer I got to it, the more I felt as though I was suffocating. It wasn't a lithe garden. It was the tumultuous garden of all summer endings. Where cyclopean sunflower heads drooped and other flowers lost their petals in the shadows, surrounding the viewer in vibrant mayhem. There was no sky, no air. I passed it as quickly as possible, puffing on my inhaler and detouring through the Hirst room on my way back to the office.

Nobody was in there. I approached the vitrine, searching for air bubbles in the formaldehyde—those signs of imperfection my father had trained me to seek out when examining hand-blown glass. But there were no bubbles in the blue liquid.

I sat on the visitors' bench and pulled the *millefiori* orb from my pocket. I put the paperweight to my eye like a monocle, transforming the unicorn into a blurred, indistinct form.

I was slowly making my way through the book Raven had given me for my birthday, reading about how the unicorn popped up in historical accounts from different parts of the world that couldn't have communicated with each other.

The Greek unicorn was a wild ass with a white body, a red head, blue eyes, and a multicoloured horn that resided in insurmountable mountains. Persia's unicorn was a three-legged donkey with six eyes and protective powers. The medieval unicorn was a chaste, fierce white horse with a goat's beard. Knights hunted it, using maidens as bait to slaughter the animal.

But there was no physical evidence for unicorns and no one could procure a horn, so the Church Council forbade using it as an allegory. When the Vikings caught on, they harpooned narwhals from the North Sea for their tusks, throwing in triumphant stories about entrapping the unicorn. Tales spread about the horn's cure-all properties—it could rid people of ulcers and blindness, it could cure melancholia and it could remedy gout. The powder was the most expensive apothecary ingredient. Kings and popes carried horn bits around in pouches to ward off the plague. Royalty wouldn't eat without it, using it to detect poisons in food and drink.

People didn't care about the animal's existence; all they wanted was the horn. Demand was so high that any shrewd salesman could make a fortune selling unicorn cups and amulets carved from elephant ivory.

Then a beached narwhal was found along the coast of Norfolk. When a zoologist proved the tusk was one and the same as a unicorn horn — also called an *alicorn* — realists banished the animal to the realm of legends.

Peng Lau, my neighbourhood herbalist, claimed to sell alicorn powder to "heal grievous wounds." Along his walls were hundreds of neatly arranged jars and drawers lined up like counters on an abacus.

When I purchased ginger capsules for my colds or prescriptions consisting of twigs, seaweed, and roots to correct what Peng called my yin-yang imbalance, I'd point at random and ask, "What's inside there, Peng?" It was a game between us. "Wondrous remedy for what ail, lady," he would answer, handing me a paper bag so light it could have been empty.

Peng said unicorns were like angels. They brought you back from the dead.

THIRTY

THE WINTER MONTHS BLENDED together like an unremarkable pastel drawing. I used my inhaler more and more.

Only at the Gallery did I experience moments of contentment. Alone with my documents damaged by sunlight, moisture, and insects, I was almost tranquil.

Yet while locating, organizing, and cataloguing, I increasingly perceived disfiguring brown blemishes manifesting on artifacts. The papers I touched were discoloured and brittle and on the verge of crumbling. There was nothing I could do when I found an archival work eating away at itself, acidity overtaking its pores like an unkillable beast.

Constance checked in periodically from Florida, asking after Viv.

"Is it church people she's with?"

"You mean the mission. It's possible, I guess."

I listened to my mother tapping her acrylic nails on the countertop. I pictured her in her paradise surrounded by palms, standing in a bright kitchen in her gossamer blue dress. Soon she'd be picking up a rag to wipe spotless the surfaces around her, scrubbing harder and harder as her shoulders inched upward.

Not once did she ask me to go find Viv and not once did I volunteer to do it. Exchanging trivialities, we always said goodbye jovially, as if neither of us had a care in the world.

At the end of winter, crocuses stuck out of the ground like candied flames.

I still hadn't heard from Liam.

In May, when the phone rang at two o'clock in the morning, enough time had passed that I knew it wasn't him. Still, my pulse was heavy in my throat when I reached for the receiver.

"I'm in North Bay. Can you pick me up?"

"I'm sleeping."

"Please, Edith. I need to get out of here."

"Take a bus."

"I'm at the station. I don't have enough for a ticket."

I hung up wishing I hadn't answered. I tried to go back to sleep but couldn't, so I made tea and stood at the window—the one from where I'd watched Viv and Liam together on the steps. That day felt like a century ago now.

As the light changed outside, the earth and trees appeared lifeless. Then there came a blood-red sunrise and I got this prescient feeling, so I packed my bag and drove the four hours to get her, calling in sick to work when I was halfway there.

When I pulled up at the bus station, Viv was on the curb with the same duffle bag she'd left home with seven years earlier. I opened the trunk and she came around to throw in her bag, awkwardly wrapping her arms around me.

"Hey, Worm."

"Hey."

I forced myself to look at her. There was no trace of the puffy face and yellow eyes that struck me when I'd seen her half a year ago. She'd gained weight, and as she walked over to the passenger's side, I noticed her old lady's gait had lessened. Her hair was shampooed and her jeans and T-shirt were clean. She was nearly pretty again.

Before picking her up, I'd debated what to do with her. She told me she would regain tenancy of her apartment on Monday. I didn't want her staying with me or at Constance's even though she was in Florida. I decided to go to Algonquin Park with her, which was roughly on the route home anyway. At the city limits I'd stopped off at a twenty-four-hour Walmart for a stove, fleece jackets, a cooler, and a flashlight. I still had sleeping bags and a tent in the back of the car from when Liam and I had planned a camping trip the previous fall. Like his empty coffee cup by the kitchen sink, I hadn't had the heart to remove these from the trunk yet.

Viv slept for most of the drive. From time to time I'd glance over at her. She was a replica of our mother, not just physically—the long neck, the fair skin—but in how she moved unconsciously and in the flinching and sighs, as if she was bored by her dreams but couldn't be bothered to wake up. And like our mother, when she was awake, she stared out the window, chain-smoking.

"You're asking for a heart attack."

"Me and the Con have good genes."

We picked up some groceries then drove to Canoe Lake, where Tom Thomson drowned. We'd visited the area often with Henry when we were growing up.

The lake was still. At the edge of the dock, Viv gazed out to where anglers cast their fishing lines. "Flashback central," she said, stepping on her cigarette. I put the butt in my jean pocket.

We drove on to one of the open campgrounds—most of them were still closed this early in the season—choosing a spot with a narrow entry onto another lake. Before unpacking the gear, we went down to the water, pushing branches aside on the overgrown, muddy path. Minerals gave the lake a teal hue and through the pines there were gleams of hills—yellows, blues, and pinks, which I hoped might inspire my sister. But Viv remained uninterested and we climbed back to our site after only a few minutes.

We struggled with the tent. I laid a plastic tablecloth out on the picnic table, then bowls and spoons and condiments. I walked to the pump and filled a jar with water, picked some flowering weeds, and placed the bouquet on the table. I heated soup and tea on the stove while Viv went looking for more wood.

It got dark fast. Viv kindled the logs with fuel and newspaper, and rolled some tree stumps over for seats. We ate smokies and stared into the flames. If I looked from the fire to my sister quickly, her eyes looked like two gold coins.

"How are things at the art gallery?" she finally asked.

"Someday they'll want your work, Vee."

"Fat chance."

"Where did you store your paintings?"

"Garbage."

She poked at the embers, opened a bag of marshmallows, and stuck three onto her branch.

"Ever hear about that marshmallow-eating contest?"

"A kid choked to death."

"Mhmm." Her marshmallows blackened and caught fire.

"Have you been in touch with him?" I asked.

"Nah."

"Is he why you moved back?"

"Nope." She tossed her stick into the pit and rubbed her legs, massaging them with force.

"You don't care, then."

"About what?"

"Liam. That I love him."

"I figured as much."

"We're taking a break. But I think he feels the same way." It was a relief to get my feelings out into the open.

"Good for you."

"And we might make a life together. Like, something everlasting."

"Do what you want, Edith." My sister looked back into the flames without a word.

I knew she'd never cared for Liam the way I did and I didn't expect my confession would upset her. I wasn't seeking my sister's approval, yet I wanted her to be happy for me. Her indifference hurt.

WE ROSE EARLY, easing ourselves onto the dew-covered stumps, drinking coffee as the sun spread its light across the ground like spilled sangria. Viv gulped her coffee; she gulped everything.

At the docks, we rented a canoe. "Remember Bella Coola?" I ventured.

"Of course. Did that thing ever fly down the mountain." She laughed for the first time.

We paddled in silence, our skin damp and shining. We found a flat rock and anchored there. We made cushions from our towels and I opened the mini cooler containing vegetables, sandwiches, and juice.

Viv rolled up her jeans and shirt sleeves. There were what looked like burn marks on her shoulders and behind her knees. Small circles like fish scale coins, red and blistering.

"Jesus, Vivienne. Are those needle marks?"

"No, little one." She tried to placate me. "These are old. I've got it under control."

We ate staring out at the lake and across the water, to an area where trees had been razed to make way for an RV park.

"Dad would have hated that," I said.

My sister only nodded.

"You know, Mom's not the one who cheated," I went on.

"I don't want to know."

"What went down is different from what you think."

"Quit meddling, Worm. Why the fuck you carry such meaningless baggage around is beyond me," she said, almost with spite.

"You'd hate her less if you'd let me explain."

"Yeah, right. Are those yurts?" She pointed to some circular tents. Then she got up and skipped a rock across the water's surface. When she turned back to face me, I snapped a picture with the old Holga, which I'd salvaged before Constance could throw it away.

From the forest, there came the sound of a sorrowful voice on a crackling record. There was opera music coming from speakers on the other side of the lake.

Viv lay down and closed her eyes. "Tino Rossi. 'Je crois entendre encore.'"

"Pardon?"

"From *The Pearl Fishers* opera. Bizet."

"How do you know?"

"Con had the CD."

ON OUR SECOND night, a group of twenty-somethings put up their tents beside our site. Their campfire blazed three times the size of ours and they invited us over. The sound of beer cans opening echoed through the trees and Viv kept stealing glimpses, eating marshmallow after marshmallow as the group got louder.

"Why did you take the paperweights?"

"Because I couldn't find your wallet," she said. Then her expression darkened. "I was broke. I'll get them back."

"What were you doing in North Bay?"

"Treatment."

"Guess you changed your mind."

"That's not what happened."

She told me she'd been in a local facility for the last month while on a waiting list for the one in North Bay. The centre called because someone dropped out. She had to be there within two days or the next person on the list would get her spot.

"The bus ride was eight hours. It stopped in every town. It was past nine by the time I arrived. I took a cab from the station to the building and they buzzed me in. I smelled food. I was starving. They even told me I'd have my own room." My sister added logs to the flames. "After I filled out the paperwork, the nurse excused herself and came back with her superior, who took me into his office. 'When did you last use?' he asked. I told him four weeks, which was fine, you had to be clean for two weeks—they didn't do monitored detox. His hair was like Johnny Cash's and he had these thick black eyebrows. He fixed his beady eyes on my throat and said, 'You're lying.' I didn't know what he was talking about and I told him so. 'What about the joint four days ago?' he asked. 'My doctor suggested it if I sensed the

DTs coming on. I don't even like pot,' I said. 'We can't admit you with marijuana in your system,' he said. 'But it's not in my system.' 'Yes, it is.' 'My problem is with alcohol.' 'Those are the rules. If we made an exception with you, we'd have to make one with everybody.' He told me I could reapply and that the girl at the front desk would call me a taxi."

Viv zipped up her fleece, glancing over at the drinkers through the trees before pulling in closer to the fire.

"If only I'd lied on the form," she said, her voice monotone. She tied her hair into a ponytail. "I grabbed his arm and begged him to let me stay. 'Miss Walker, I encourage you to reapply,' he kept saying. I lost my temper. 'What is this, fucking Juilliard? I'm asking for help, isn't that what you people are supposed to do?' He motioned to the security guard. I told him to get his hands off me. I grabbed my bag and tried leaving, but the doors were locked. I couldn't get out. The admissions girl, who looked like a junkie herself, rushed over to open them.

"I felt like a thousand eyes were watching me from inside that godforsaken place. The cab took forever. When the driver let me off at the station, it was eleven. There was no one else there and the bus wasn't due till six. I sat down in one of the rows of hard bucket seats. Couldn't even spread out or lie down. And then I saw it, across the road from the terminal. A sign was flashing *Bar* on and off like some sick joke.

"All I had was a twenty. The centre was going to bus us back to the city when the program ended and we weren't allowed to bring in any money. I walked over to the vending machines, but none of them took bills. And the change machine was out of order.

"I could get change in the bar. Or I could order four pints.

I could hit on whatever guy was in there and have him buy me rounds for two hours solid. Or I could go around back to off-sales. Last call would be 2 a.m. and the bar would stay open till three. I stared at the flashing sign, my body screaming. Then I called you. It was the longest night of my life."

The group was jumping in the lake. We could hear them in the distance, the laughter, the splashing.

When we drove home the next day, Viv asked that I drop her at the apartment. She'd made a call and arranged for the key to be left under the mat since she was arriving a day early.

She was renting a unit in a basement on a residential street known for its gangs and crime, not far from where she'd lived with Liam in Chinatown.

"Are you sure you shouldn't go to that transitional place?"

She shook her head. "There's bedbugs. Thieves."

We stopped off at Home Depot and bought an air mattress, a folding card table, and chairs.

"What about blankets and pillows?"

"Have some."

"Let me get you a few things."

"It's okay."

"How long will you sleep on that?"

"Till first pay." She had a telemarketing job with a phone company.

"What about food?"

"I have what I need. Go home."

I helped her carry her belongings down. We set up the table and unfolded the vinyl chairs. Viv put batteries in the mattress and turned the motor on until it inflated.

I looked around the grim space, no more than five hundred

square feet. "Maybe you could start painting again, Vee."

She raised her arms then, like a surgeon in pre-op. They shook. "Wake up. I can't paint."

"Your hands will get better."

"That ship has sailed, little sister."

"You're still young."

"Edith, I'm tired. Please go."

I decided to get her blankets anyway. I knew she wouldn't have money for weeks. I went to the nearby Giant Tiger and chose cheerful yellow sheets, a duvet, some pillows, and a shade plant she could hook from the ceiling. Then I returned to her place.

Before knocking, I peered into the basement window, a habit I'd picked up since being traumatized by my father's affair. Through the pane I caught sight of my sister in deep concentration standing at the sink, pouring a purple jellied paste from a can into a white sock then squeezing the sock she held above a glass. The Sterno cooking fuel from the box of camping supplies in the trunk of the Buick.

She shot a glance around the room until her eyes landed on the small, dirty window. When she saw me, her expression changed into that of an ensnared animal. I shot up from where I stooped, hitting my head against the wood beam from the deck above.

I rushed back to the car and sat with the keys in the ignition, waiting for the pounding to subside. I touched my skull and my fingers came back red. I worried about splinters in my scalp and the possibility of infection.

The car wouldn't start. I'd flooded the engine and had to wait outside her building on the dismal street for another half-hour.

THIRTY-ONE

I ROLLED UP MY sleeve and Dr. Shaw cuffed my arm with his black band, closing the valve on the rubber bulb and pumping it rapidly. He was our physician growing up. Even then he seemed old, with his caterpillar brows and wiry hair sprouting from his ears. He'd seen us through chicken pox and mumps, through stitches and injured limbs. He'd filled out the death certificate at my father's bedside.

"What's the problem, young lady?" He opened the valve, allowing the pressure to fall.

Other than having him check the cut on my head, I didn't know how to express what was wrong. Liam had been gone seven months. I wasn't pregnant. Yet everything set me off lately. I couldn't take a walk in the park without getting choked up at passersby. When I saw families and babies, that upset me too.

"My heart's been racing. I'm not sleeping."

He ran his cold stethoscope down my back. I looked up at the shelf displaying a three-dimensional model of clean, pink lungs while he shone the head of a light instrument in my ears.

Feeling for the glands beneath my jawbone, he inquired, "How has your energy level been?"

"I'm not depressed."

"Broken heart?" He hit my knee with his little red hammer. "If that's the case, I assure you you'll be fine." He reached into a jar of wood depressors. "Tongue. How's work?"

"We have a unicorn."

He laughed and scratched his head. "I think a holiday, maybe."

"Or sleeping pills."

"Are you still using an inhaler?"

"Once in a blue moon."

"You grew out of that. Technically, you're not asthmatic anymore. Do you recall our discussion about crutches?" He'd stopped prescribing Ventolins to me years ago. I got them from walk-in clinics.

"We're done here." He pulled the curtain, dividing me from his desk heaped with manila files. He was one of the few doctors who hadn't made the switch to computers yet. "No concussion, no stitches. You won't die."

"This office was so big to me when we were kids," I told him, pulling the curtain back and lacing my runners. Dr. Shaw gestured for me to take the chair across from him.

"The universe has a way of shrinking as we grow older, doesn't it." He blinked up at the lungs. "How is your sister?"

"She's an addict. We lose track of her sometimes. I'm sure my mom told you."

"I wasn't aware." His expression didn't change as he wrote in my chart. "Well, my dear. Do yoga and cut back on caffeine. Stimulants cause palpitations." He paused before adding, "And take some time off."

"From what?"

"From whatever gave you the goose egg." He was out of insights to offer. He retrieved a sucker from the jar on his desk and handed it to me the way he used to do when we were small. "So that adventurous mother of yours is back from Florida, is she?"

"She is." I pulled the candy from its wrapper. "But not for long."

WHEN I ARRIVED to replace Alejandro in the viewing room, the old man with the unkempt grey hair was there again, along with a few regulars. "Have fun," Alejandro said, grabbing his jacket off the back of the chair and his *Hello!* magazine from the desk.

I decided to get my rounds over with so I could work through the afternoon uninterrupted.

"Hi, Maud, need help?" Maud was the daughter of a renowned Canadian cartoonist who hadn't left his family anything; it had all gone to the mistress, who donated it to the Gallery in her will. A retired schoolteacher with a dejected air, every week Maud came in to audit her father's drawings with a magnifying glass.

"I'm fine," she said, rubbing her eyes.

Arnold was at the next table over and he only came to the viewing room because of Maud. They'd met at a volunteers' luncheon. The sun came through the skylight onto his reddening, bald head. "Arnold, do you want to move? You'd be cooler over in the corner."

"No, no, Edith, I'm content here."

"What are you reviewing today?"

"Oh, whosits and whatsits," he replied, opening a portfolio onto a flat sketch of rotting fruit beside a pocket watch.

Dorothy was farther back, grumbling to herself as she took notes on Dürer. She was my least favourite client—a curator forced to retire, who came in nearly every day.

"All good, Dorothy?"

"I need more place markers." She held up the empty box without greeting me, shaking it. "And these pencils are unacceptable." Elaborate layers of clashing fabrics swathed her obese body. I took the box and moved on to the table at the very back, where the old man sat.

"Hi. Dr. de Buuter, right?" It had been a few months since his last visit, but I remembered him. He glanced up and nodded before returning to his notebook. His worn leather shoes reminded me of a Van Gogh painting and his watery eyes bordered on black, like mine.

"What did you say was your name?"

I detected an accent. "I'm Edith."

He stood, lifting his chair and moving it aside easily this time. "A pleasure to meet you." He gave me a solid handshake. I'd expected a frailer grip.

I took a step back to give him space. There was this great stockiness about him. His hands, feet, and shoulders were all too big, and his features were off kilter—the wide jaw and the aquiline nose, his sunken eyes and arched brows set on a low, deeply lined forehead.

I found it hard to make eye contact with him for more than a few seconds. I moved my gaze to the table. He was studying the same Gauguin woodcut.

"His better work is in the Post-Impressionist room," I ventured. "I can show you if you'd like."

"Thank you, but I have seen all of Gauguin's œuvre."

"All of it?"

"Unless some are in hiding." He took a handkerchief from his pocket and wiped his eyes.

I wondered if something was wrong with his tear ducts. I'd heard about such a condition that came with ageing.

"I'll leave you to it, then," I told him, rolling my trolley away.

I catalogued some shoddy still lifes. For the last half-hour of the day I read my book on unicorns. I'd set it aside and had only recently returned to it. Growing up, when Constance told me that in times of duress the first thing that went was the ability to read, I thought it was a pretext for her not to peruse anything longer than the two-page features in her fashion magazines. Yet ever since Liam left, I hadn't been able to concentrate on anything for more than five minutes.

Maud exited and Arnold followed shortly after. At five to four, Dorothy waddled out. In my peripheral vision I could see De Buuter slowly packing up. When he arrived at my desk, I noticed he was using a cane. He tucked his notepad under his arm to sign the ledger. I put down my book and he paused when he saw the cover.

"'The unicorn lived in a lilac wood.'"

"Pardon?"

"'The unicorn lived in a lilac wood, and she lived all alone.'" His coarse lips stretched into a smile. "*The Last Unicorn*. Have you not read it?"

I shook my head. "A lot of cultures still believe in it," I remarked, thinking of Peng.

"Yes." He gave me a contemplative look. "There have been sightings, as recently as a few years back." He leaned his cane against my desk to adjust his glasses. "There is usually an explanation, though. A lot are rhinoceroses.

Or gazelles, seen far away from the side." He pointed to the book cover, adding, "Often there is no comprehensible boundary between memory and imagination."

I'D STOPPED COOKING after Liam left, reverting to my old habits.

When I got home that night, I made a grilled cheese sandwich and heated a can of soup. Then I read about the highly regarded German naturalist of the seventeenth century, Gottfried Leibniz, whose belief in unicorns was based on a skeleton excavated in a mountain quarry in Germany. Leibniz sketched the skeleton in his book on fossils so his brute could take its place in the natural classification system.

I took a bath and before going to sleep I examined the ludicrous drawing. It had no hind legs, so it stood on two feet with its tailbone resting on the ground. The skeleton was later proven to be a fake made out of rhinoceros and mammoth bones. Leibniz the great scientist was ridiculed.

Turning off my bedside lamp, I thought about this animal that had gone from the highbrow discipline of science to the bedrooms of girls across North America, in the form of mass-produced toys accompanied by fairies. Viv had a crown with an enamel unicorn on it, which Con embellished with rhinestones. Whenever she wore it, the unicorn jutted from her forehead like the adornment of a prophetess predicting a dazzling future.

THIRTY-TWO

I STARTED HAVING THIS recurring dream.

Liam is at my door. When I open it, he says, "I've fallen back in love with you."

I tell him, "I know this is a dream because no one ever says they've fallen back in love. It doesn't happen."

"I was testing you," he replies from his shaft of light.

When he steps toward me, his hands and feet are made of hard blue stone. He tantalizes me with kisses and says, in a whisper that gets progressively louder, "Your sister is dying your sister is dying YOUR SISTER IS DYING YOUR SISTER —"

One night, after waking from this scene, I was unable to sleep. I started reading about the unicorn's demise. In Biblical stories, unicorns were thrown from the Ark, into the deluge. Or they were expelled from the boat by Noah himself because they were too high maintenance. Other historians insisted unicorns swam ashore and still existed in their lonesome hinterland. Then there were those who said that civilization would never see a unicorn again because they weren't granted passage on the Ark, but no one knew why. Or they stubbornly avoided boarding. Like in that Irish Rovers tune played at Finnegan's pub, where Liam and Viv used to sneak me in.

They had barrels of peanuts at Finnegan's that you scooped up with straw baskets, the saltiness making patrons thirstier. The floor of that place was slippery, littered with shells. People kept falling.

In the song, the unicorns missed the boat because they were frolicking in the rain. As the Ark sailed, the singing slowed to an ominous narrative. The unicorns were stuck on rocks in the rising flood. The unicorns were drowning.

ONE WARM JUNE day, I came home to three messages asking me to come to the hospital. I was my sister's emergency contact.

I called Constance, who happened to be in the city that week. When we arrived, Viv was complaining that she couldn't feel her arms or legs.

"That's the least of your problems," the doctor said, consulting her chart. He blandly explained that the painful tingling and numbness was caused by a vitamin B deficiency. Viv's body could no longer absorb and store thiamine, which was affecting her nervous system and her heart.

My sister shot me a nasty look when she saw our mother. She shared her space with a comatose man whose forehead was bandaged. He had no visitors.

When she fell asleep, the doctor—his name was Dr. Black—led us into a claustrophobic room that smelled of menthol, to inform us that Viv had cirrhosis.

"Blood work indicates a possibility of coexistent auto-immune hepatitis, a disease that usually affects young females and progresses to cirrhosis if not detected early and treated. In Vivienne's case, excessive alcohol use has exacerbated her condition and accelerated progression to the end stage."

From our disbelief he could see we thought this was a medical blunder, a mix-up of charts. Only lifelong drinkers and lurid old men died from liver failure. Viv had just turned twenty-five.

"Definite proof of AIH would come from a liver biopsy, but that carries a certain amount of risk," he explained. "And the results wouldn't modify the actual treatment, which is transplant, since the disease has already advanced too much."

He told us the condition was irreversible.

In a stupor, I watched the lips on his weary face reiterating the same speech he probably delivered day in day out to other families. "The transplant wait is two years and, frankly, people like Vivienne aren't at the top of the list. You're better off going to the States or India. I'd avoid Mexico and Jordan."

The gasp I let out sounded like laughter. Con looked at me with disgust before returning her attention to Dr. Black. The skin beneath his eyes was puffy and the rims of his eyelids were red. He looked unhealthy. Haggard and out of shape, like a veteran drinker.

"Keep in mind, some centres exclude patients with an addiction history," he went on. "She'll need to take her own donor if you go out of country. A family member with the same blood type, under fifty-five years of age, preferably." He looked back and forth at us before he outright studied me. "They'll give her a portion of your liver, which will grow back if all goes well. And provided you're compatible. You need an evaluation first. Blood and tissue tests, et cetera —"

"*Wait,*" I interjected. "Let me get this straight. You're asking me to pass my internal organ off to my out-of-control sister like it's a football?"

"Not at all," he replied coolly. "This is up to you, not us. Many families in this situation decide to let nature take its course."

"This can't be happening," I stuttered, and looked to Constance to come to my defence, but she just reapplied her lipstick and smiled, accepting the doctor's card. Then she asked about Viv's strange complexion. Dr. Black said it was because her liver wouldn't filter bile.

I couldn't process what I was hearing.

We returned to Viv's room. Con moved like an automaton as she drew the divider curtain and installed herself in the chair by Viv's bedside. "You've done it, *chérie!*" she said uneasily, moving Viv's hair out of the way to kiss her, leaving a red stain on her forehead.

Viv stared at the wall. Her messy braids added to her innocent appearance in her oversized hospital gown. There was no mistaking that her skin had a greenish aspect. Her eyes had a yellow tinge to them again. And her stomach was distended like that of a malnourished child.

A baby blue hospital bracelet encircled her stick-thin wrist as though she was a bird banded for studying. None of us talked for a while. When Con went outside to smoke, my sister turned to me, perturbed.

"I know what Doctor Death was explaining to you and the Con. I'm not taking anyone's liver. So no need to freak," she said.

But she looked petrified and, despite my misgivings, the contempt I felt for her fell away.

"You have to eat more, Vee." I held her bony hand and tried to be witty. "You're like that waif from *Les Mis*. And FYI, your skin's green."

"That's envy," she said. Her mouth was dry and she ran her tongue over her teeth. "You're lucky she left you alone." Then she made a face and said, "Screw off, Worm. I'll gorge myself tonight. Get lost."

DRIVING AWAY FROM the hospital, I suggested to Con that we start organizing our medical evaluations straight away.

"There is nothing more we can do, Édith. Maybe one day she will grow up."

I slammed on the brakes and my mother flew forward in her seat. Pulling over, I told her, "This is *your* fault. You have to pay for it!"

"Your sister wasn't strong like you." She clipped on her seat belt and checked her hair in the side mirror.

"You pushed her too hard."

Beneath her cashmere stole, my mother stiffened. "I did that to boost her self-confidence. *En plus, j'n'ai pas d'sous.*"

"Is that why you're with Pierre, because you have no money?"

"*Oui,* Édith. That's why."

I screeched away from the curb to get her back to Pierre's. "*Great* job, Mom. Those pageants sure paid off for Viv and Dad. I hope it was worth it," I said, almost sneering. "And another thing. Any decent parent would die for their child without thinking twice, and you won't do a simple surgery? You're still under fifty-five and you *owe it* to her after what you put her through. If there was a prize for worst mother in the universe, you'd win it, hands down. Bravo."

In her listless silence and washed-out expression, I knew

I'd gone too far. She exerted herself getting out of the car, holding on to the handgrip.

Then she turned back to me and said, "With mine she will do the same thing. It will not help her. *Think*, Édith. I'm not the same blood group, *puis*—"

"And your smoker's health sucks, I know. How convenient."

"Or she could have it. I have little enough to live for."

"Right. Con the martyr. Enough said."

She wobbled to the door like she'd twisted her ankle or her sensory functions were out of whack. Or maybe there had been an accumulation of changes in her body I hadn't noticed, since I had been preoccupied with my own issues.

BEFORE GOING HOME, I went to see Peng. He was sitting behind the counter with his eyes closed when I walked in. At the sound of the door chimes, he opened one eye a fraction, registered me, and closed it again. Ancient-sounding music of silk-stringed instruments and bamboo flutes droned from the radio.

"Hi, lady. Long time no see."

"Am I interrupting?"

"Meditating."

"I can't sleep, Peng."

He sighed and opened his eyes. Flipping his ponytail over his shoulder, he put on his wire-rimmed glasses, assessing me. Then he climbed the ladder up his wall of dried potions, taking down three jars and scooping from each of them into a paper cone.

"Also, I'll take some of that unicorn horn powder. Remember, you said you had some?"

"All gone."

"You don't have any? Not even a bit?"

"Gone."

"When's the next stock coming in?"

"No more. Never. You meditate?"

"No."

"Guilty conscience. That why no sleep. Too many predicament." He gave me the bag and tapped a few numbers on his old till. The wooden drawer popped out.

"What do I do with this?"

"Four dollar. Make tea then bed."

"I'll be up all night."

Peng wasn't interested. He'd already walked away through the beaded curtain, into the storeroom.

ONCE HOME, I went online and read up on LDLTS—living donor liver transplants. It seemed relatively straightforward. Viv's diseased liver would be extracted and replaced by a portion of my healthy liver and both our livers would grow back and magically regenerate to their full sizes within a few weeks.

Our chance of dying was low. The success rate for recipients was 90 percent, while for the living donor the risk of death was one in three hundred.

Everyone had given up on my sister. I knew that I had no choice—no one else would rescue Viv anymore.

I messaged private clinics. Transplants across the border averaged anywhere between three and six hundred thousand dollars, or sixty thousand in India, where there was virtually no waiting time.

We'd have to stay in India for three months, and I had hardly any savings.

As I calculated the finances in my head, my fantasy of

travelling the world with Liam evaporated. Up until this point, I still carried the hope that he'd send a postcard, after realizing, like in the dream, how much he missed me.

The absurdity of the situation was too much to take in. I felt as though I was in some bad made-for-TV movie. There was a dull ache in my chest and it was worsening by the hour.

I logged off the computer and went over to the window. Outside, the full moon's imprint hung low and heavy like a ghostly paperweight. Tomorrow was recycling day. Here and there I could see the shades of downtown's homeless rifling through the blue bins lining the sidewalk, ransacking the streets for bottles and cans.

I boiled some water for Peng's tea. But the infusion tasted putrid and after a few sips I poured it down the drain.

Eventually the unicorn book helped me fall asleep. I read how in Florida in the 1560s there was believed to be a river inland that had healing properties, because unicorns drank from that water and dipped their horns in it. Explorers wrote about the locals wearing pieces of alicorn, found in that area, around their necks.

I nodded in and out of consciousness, thinking how, if I could get one of those therapeutic hunks of horn for my sister, our dilemma would be resolved.

THIRY-THREE

A BANNER OF A nude went up against the glass ramp to promote a nineteenth-century French photographs exhibition. Before a gaudy backdrop, a young woman stared into the camera, kneeling on drapery in a provocative pose.

As I neared the parkade leading to the curatorial wing, there was old Theo de Buuter, his eyes on the picture. When I approached, he looked over, gave a wave of recognition, and closed his notepad. I sat beside him on the bench.

"Hello. I was just considering my lost youth." He removed his fedora and placed it between us.

I glanced up at the plump girl, her creamy skin and breasts and auburn hair brushed in sepia tones.

"Would you like a date bar?" He secured his coffee cup between his knees and produced a tinfoil square from the pocket of his corduroy blazer. His hands trembled as he unwrapped the packet and extended it to me.

"Thanks," I said, glancing over at the black felt hat, the lengthwise creases deep and worn. My father had owned a similar hat. Once, I left it on my parents' bed and he went mental.

"What is it with hats on beds?" I asked Theo.

"They foretell death. Like a hooting owl or a bird flying into your house."

"Do you believe that?"

"I believe the worst happens without omens." He removed his glasses to dab his eyes with his handkerchief.

"What brings you here?" I looked to the church across the street. He didn't respond, instead following my gaze. I took a bite of the square, the oatmeal topping crumbling onto my skirt. "What are you researching?" I raised my voice a bit.

"Oh. A bird." He opened his notepad, turning to a page where he'd made a rough sketch of *Le Sourire*. "In one of your woodcuts." He put the tip of his pen down on the bird in the dog's mouth, circling it. "Gauguin's mystery bird."

"So you're an ornithologist."

"I study birds and other animals. I am a cryptozoologist, actually."

"I see." Only I didn't. I'd have to Google it. "Your accent. Are you —"

"Dutch."

"I always liked salt licorice."

"*Dropjes.*"

"You can find it at Sugar Mountain in the Market."

"I did not know this."

"And you can buy those windmill cookies at the German delicatessen."

He continued watching the church. As the bells rang the hour, a priest in robes emerged from the carved doors like a figurine from a cuckoo clock.

"Who's your favourite Dutch painter?" I asked.

"Vermeer."

"Me too. We don't have any here."

"No," he concurred. The wind picked up and he replaced his hat on his head and adjusted his bow tie, pale green like beach glass.

"He puts his women near windows a lot."

"This is true." Theo smoothed out his piece of foil and folded it.

"His paintings are calming. The warm light and quiet scenes. I like his purples."

"He attained those shades by underpainting his reds with lapis lazuli pigments." Lapis. Of course. "With Vermeer paintings, objects acquire luminosity by soaking up the colours that are near them." Like some people, I thought to myself.

I gave him directions to the candy shop. I suggested he walk over since he still had an hour until the Gallery opened to the public.

Theo made his way across the plaza, through *Maman*'s legs. He idled in the middle of the sculpture, tilting his neck back at the underbelly of the spider. When he saw me watching him, he tipped his hat in my direction then carried on.

I SPENT THE morning in storage, measuring a donation of wave drawings. They were skilfully rendered and I took my time with them, examining each watery movement, the flow lines, the slow churns and swirls.

But thoughts of Liam distracted me, and triggered a keening in my chest like the ocean inside a shell. To boot, my asthma had flared up and I was having a tough time breathing.

I was almost finished with the drawings. As I'd done so often, I opened the last hinged frame, pulling off the sheet of tissue covering a work titled *Rogue Wave*. The thick white lip of rushing water—the curls, spray, foam, and base—had a mesmerizing effect. Then my nose dripped.

The drop of mucus landed on the crest of the wave and instantly expanded on the rice paper, smudging the fine black lines for the radius of a quarter—a substantial amount for a drawing no larger than a playing card.

I thought about hiding it in one of the reference books, which most staff had abandoned for online fact checking. No one would find it there for decades, if at all. Or I could tear it to pieces, or slide it under my sweater and take it home. What I needed to do was fill out a damage report and transport the drawing to the conservation lab. Bungling curators punctured and creased art through rough handling all the time. Yet I couldn't bring myself to report this mistake brought on by my own absent-mindedness.

When Raven banged at the metal door, I drew the paper back over the drawing and closed the frame on it, sliding the rogue wave under the other waves, hoping the tidal surge would erupt under all that pressure, erasing itself.

RAVEN PULLED HER shamrock socks up to her knees and got down to business. She needed sandpaper and sample paint pots. "Let's take King Edward, keep it real," she said, veering me away from the boutiques leading to the hardware store in favour of a detour cutting through the most downtrodden blocks in the city.

She'd given me her honest opinion when I'd called her after seeing Viv in the hospital. "Let's not sugar-coat it, your sister's probably a lost cause," she told me.

Today, as we walked, I admitted, "I've decided to do the transplant thing for Viv."

"Nice try." She whammed her bag into my arm.

"*Ow*, are you carrying bricks in there?"

"Don't be a moron, then."

"It's safe. I've done the research. Plus, I've always wanted to see India."

She snapped her fingers an inch away from my face. "*Earth* to Edith. Which planet are you on?"

"I don't exactly have a choice, Raven."

"I'd like to slap you." She slammed her palm to her forehead, her lips tightening as she fumed at some wild swans in the park.

When she turned to face me again, her fists were clenched and the veins around her temples pulsated. "Your mom's the only smart one, giving your sister tough love. All you do is enable her."

"That's not fair."

"It's like those imaginary unihorses you think are real," she went on. "I shouldn't have encouraged you with that dumbass book, which was a joke, by the way. They're not real, Edith. In *this* reality, only your sister can save herself, and she's not doing that. Open your eyes and stop being so naive. Has she shown any desire to get the transplant? Is she asking to get on waiting lists here, to find other donors, like, dead ones? Has she talked about staying clean? Course not."

"You're wrong," I snivelled, wiping my nose on my sleeve. I blinked hard and shook my head until she put an arm around me.

"I know this sounds harsh. But I don't want to see my best friend wreck her life for nothing. You can't fix this."

We passed the Shepherds of Good Hope, where I was

sure Viv had stayed. *Three hots and a cot*. Instinctively I scanned the faces of the men and women crouched against the buildings, asking us for change. When the traffic light turned red, half a dozen teenagers jumped up with cups, pulled off their hoods, and wove between cars, moving fast.

Raven insisted on taking this route every few months to distribute the granola bars and cookies that she amassed in her office from the lunches Zach prepared for her. As she sprinted into alleyways here and there, I waited on the street, hugging my purse.

When she was back at my side, I tried picking up our pace, but she was in a punchy humour and didn't catch on. She was in one of her moods because Zach was pushing the baby question. Before getting married, she told Zach she didn't want kids. Zach had changed his mind since they bought the house.

"Sinister that there's no Indians here. In Winnipeg that's all there is."

"That's good, right?"

Some men formed a semicircle on the sidewalk. One of them wore a suit and a skullcap and had a ring on every digit. With each step he took, there was a metallic click on the pavement. He moved in front of us, blocking our way. I stared down at his beige tap shoes.

"Ladies. Can I interest you in some meth or cock?" He had bloodshot eyes and the tattoo of a knife running down his neck. Raven grabbed my arm and went around him, finally walking faster.

He spat and swore. "Fucking cunts!"

I felt the saliva on my neck, through my blouse.

"And that's another thing." She was on a rant now. "You dress your homeless up too well here. Half the time they're so tidy that I don't know they're schizoids on crack until they open their mouths."

"Bojangles didn't look nuts enough for you?" I asked as she pulled a scarf from her bag and blotted at my back.

"At least back home the glue sniffers are straight up." She threw her arms in the air. "What's the goddamn point? Soon the shelters will be shut down and these people will be thrown into state-of-the-art penitentiaries." She pushed through the hardware store doors. "Now, I was thinking periwinkle for the den and mint julep for the bedroom. Thoughts?"

A nymphish, dark-featured girl grazed against me as I entered the store. She wore platform sandals and was sucking on a Popsicle, her skin thick with goosebumps in her cut-offs and T-shirt. Before disappearing back into the streets, she gave me a penetrating stare and blood rushed to my ears. There was something familiar about her, aside from the scabs and track marks. She pushed a cart piled high with her possessions. A colourless, sullied version of the cart Viv had filled with Henry's inventory from the garage when we were kids.

"Damn, that chick looked like you," Raven said in a hushed tone. "I'd say you just met your doppelgänger."

My sister was essentially one of these down-and-outs now. But it could have just as easily been me. And this made me feel guilty, like I owed her.

I WAS ALREADY settled behind my desk in the viewing room when De Buuter slogged in after his lunch break. Raven had given me a spare top to wear, but it was too big and billowed in odd places.

"That's a tremendous blouse."

"Thank you," I replied, rolling up my pirate sleeves. "Where do you eat lunch, Dr. de Buuter?"

"Your cafeteria. I like the view—the hill and that metal ribbon. It's quiet."

"That's because the food's terrible," I told him as he signed the register. "How do you pronounce your name?" I asked. "Like *butter*?"

"*Bu*—like the French *u*. It means pedlar." His breath caught, forcing a halt in his speech. "My family came from a line of merchants."

"Dr. de Buuter, if you need anything—"

"Please. Call me Theo." He made his way to the back of the room where I'd already laid out his file. I wanted to continue our conversation.

Maud and Arnold were the only other ones there. Arnold sat at the opposite end of Maud's table. Although she didn't acknowledge his presence, her face wasn't as grave as she reviewed her father's drawings.

No one needed me, so I pulled out my book. I read through the afternoon about how the unicorn's annihilation came when scientists discovered that a cloven-hoofed animal couldn't grow a single horn in the middle of its forehead, because the skull bones of such a breed would be divided.

In the 1930s, biologists figured out how to surgically alter the horn buds of calves, kids, and baby deer so that they'd fuse together and grow as a single horn. Farmers caught on and did the same, selling their hybrids to county fairs until word got out that these weren't actual unicorns.

You could no more turn an animal into something it wasn't than turn a human being into someone they were not.

People don't change, Constance always said.

THIRY-FOUR

WHEN VIV LEFT THE hospital, she went back to her dingy basement apartment and I visited her regularly there, as did Dr. Black on his house call rounds.

She'd kept her job with the phone company and had the medical paperwork to call in sick when she wanted. She mainly stayed home, resting on the twin bed I'd bought from IKEA, which took me two days to assemble.

She was given strict orders not to consume alcohol for six months before the surgery or the procedure would be cancelled. "And believe me, they have ways of knowing," Dr. Black threatened. "They'll ship you straight home and you'll have to start from scratch."

During this time, I went through several weeks of rush medical testing. I passed the evaluation and was deemed a suitable donor so long as Viv's condition didn't deteriorate, making her too ill to withstand the surgery. Dr. Black agreed to "recommend us" — he said it like we were auditioning for a stage production — since we needed his authorization and signature to get onto any list.

The transplant centre was in Bangalore. I assembled paperwork on both of us, adding to the binders each day as though I was filing keepsakes outlining our life accomplishments. For a brief while this scrapbooking became my vocation.

The surgery was the last thing I could do for her. When I'd first announced my decision to Viv, her response was, no way.

"You're out of options, Vee," I told her. "Suck it up."

"It's not what I want. I can't pay."

"Calm down," I said. "Just stick to your new and improved healthy routine like you promised."

"I'm not letting you do this, Edith."

"It's practically minor surgery. Don't be a wimp."

Thoughts of what could go wrong terrorized me. Ten percent of recipients died soon after the operation due to infection, bleeding, rejection, other organ failure, or cardiac issues. Viv could not wake up. I could not wake up—five percent of donors had complications leading to serious infection, blood clotting, bile leaks, and bleeding.

"I'm not doing it to save you," I added. "My motives are selfish. I want to get you back painting so I can make money off your art and profit from your creative genius."

My sister's detoxifying body smelled of mothballs. Her appearance had marginally improved since leaving the hospital. I brought her food and drawing pads and pencils she didn't touch.

Eventually she stopped arguing with me. Her face changed as if she'd reached a decision, but she wouldn't share it. Instead she became complacent and lethargic.

"Mom tells me you won't return her calls from Florida,"

I prodded, "and that the packages she mails you get sent back to her."

"If it were up to the Con, I'd die." Her mouth turned downward and her eyes moistened.

"That's not true," I said too quickly, adding, "I thought we could visit the country after you recuperate. I'll look into some tours."

"Great."

"Temples, maybe a yoga retreat?"

"Sounds like a plan."

ALONG WITH WHAT little savings I had, I obtained a bank loan and a line of credit. I maxed my Visa and signed up with MasterCard and American Express. I pawned the medallion from Omar, which I'd worn around my neck until then like an amulet. It still wasn't enough for the flights and the three months we'd need to stay in India for the pre-evaluation, the surgery, and the follow-up monitoring period. Not to mention the deposit for the actual transplant, which would then allow for payments by instalment on the outstanding balance.

Constance wouldn't budge when I phoned her.

"I'll pay you back within the year."

"*Non.*"

"She'll die."

"*N'importe quoi.* The liver is a miracle organ. It will regenerate when she sorts herself out. What you are doing is a band-aid solution, *ma fille.* A dangerous mistake."

"You're in shock, Mom. You're not thinking clearly."

"*Non,*" she repeated, outraged, before her cell clicked off.

OFTEN I VISITED Monet's cliffs at Pourville on my breaks. It reminded me of Henry's canvases—his frigid flowers and snow people and outcrops of ice formed by the wind.

Rain, Pourville was an oil painting in a misty palette from 1896. It resided permanently in Impressionist Room C213. Although his eyesight hadn't yet begun to fail, in the hazy details and waning shapes it was as though Monet had foreshadowed his own blindness on this canvas, and the years when he'd use only the memory of colour to paint.

He toiled away in ferocious tempests to test his fortitude and his vision. You had to be five paces back to make out the cliffs and the windblown rain slamming down over everything inside the thick gilded frame.

I visualized the artist setting up his easel on treacherous slopes of the Normandy Coast. Braving winter gales to capture seascapes of mauves and greys where rocks jutted out of the choppy waters.

The painting was in crisis. It had cracks, many of them as long as the lines on the palm of my hand. Up close a red splotch on the right side of the painting became visible, in the middle of the stormy sea.

Like the generic yellow candy bar wrapper at the grocery store checkout—I couldn't pass the rack without seeing it—my eye was always drawn to that red mark on Monet's painting.

It struck me then that the dark spot in a family's tree didn't necessarily originate at the root but could germinate later on down the timeline. Who was to say some disorder didn't stem inside my sister's leaf? Viv was that tree in the park that looked from afar as if it was thriving—the yellows and greens, the golden glow—until you got closer and saw the fluorescent *X* spray-painted on the trunk.

I was ten thousand dollars short. I thought about going to the casino or learning the stock market, or finding a cheaper, illegal hospital that offered the same procedure. I thought about stealing from my own mother but couldn't figure out the logistics. I'd have asked Raven, but she was in debt. I couldn't ask Liam because I was frightened he'd fall back in with Viv. I also couldn't ask Liam because I didn't know where he was.

A visitor nearby dropped her change purse. Coins scattered, clinking like the bells on my sister's old costumes. The hard discs shone at my feet. In that moment, I knew where I had to go.

THIRTY-FIVE

HEADING TO MECHANICSVILLE, I turned down our old street. A warm summer wind lifted the hawthorn branches I passed under. Our house seemed tiny now, a brick dollhouse with strangers inside.

I stood there for a bit. Holograms of the four of us sprang from the lawn like nettles. Peeking through a crack in the tall pine fence around back, I saw a sky-blue hot tub where the painting shed once stood.

The signage was new at Ye Olde Coin Shoppe: Best GOLD Prices—Guaranteed! Get CASH Today.

Through the decrepit storefront, I made out a figure with headphones leaning over the counter, flipping through a magazine. The door was barred. I rang a buzzer that hadn't been there during Omar and Serena's time.

Alerted to my presence, the person sauntered over. A flat, low-pitched voice came through an intercom: "State the nature of your business."

"Are you Grigg?"

"Who's asking?"

"Edith Walker, a friend of Omar's. I used to work here."

The person unbolted the door, and a dark set of eyes narrowed on me then widened. With expert speed a head poked out and looked up and down the road. The door opened further and a hand grabbed me by the upper arm and pulled me inside.

Omar slammed the door and bolted it and squeezed me against his chest. I pushed away to face the taller, broader version of the boy I once knew.

The thick eyeglasses were gone and his hair went past his shoulders. The curls were scraggly now. And although it was late afternoon, Omar wore what appeared to be women's fuzzy slippers and pyjama bottoms.

"You're still here," I said, and maybe deep down I knew he would be. I was genuinely pleased to see him, and hadn't realized how much I'd missed him.

"You!" He moved in to hug me again. His muscular arms stifled my upper body and the hooks of my bra dug into my back where his hand pressed against me.

Then he released me and, chewing on his bottom lip, turned almost nervously toward the cruddy window, as if to make sure no one was watching us.

The last time I'd seen Omar was at my father's funeral, three and a half years prior. He'd retained his olive complexion, but his profile was leaner now, nearly harsh-looking, like an imperial portrait on a Roman coin.

Omar grinned. He walked a circle around me as he wiped the oily beads of perspiration from his forehead. A musky smell came off his body.

I knew sweat stains were visible under my arms, through my blouse. So far the summer had been one long heat wave, and based on the oven-like feel of the shop, Omar and Serena hadn't invested in central air.

"Looking good, songbird."

"What happened to you?" I asked.

"Thanks a lot."

"I mean, I thought you moved to Omaha," I added.

"Life happened. Or didn't, in my case."

I followed his ill-at-ease gaze around the room. Nothing in the small shop had changed. It was like stepping into a painting. The old school desk where I'd cleaned hundreds of coins was still in place, as were Serena's tins and receipt stacks on the back counter. A scrub brush and bucket looked as though they hadn't moved in years from the spot they occupied on the floor.

There was a fine layer of dust over the entire scene.

Only the light inside the Coin Shoppe seemed diminished somehow. Though the place had always been dark, it had lost its romantic Rembrandt quality and was all shadows. Like my parents' bedroom when my dying father occupied it.

Approaching the display cases, I saw that they were mostly empty. Some contained a few coins, but they looked new and valueless. The ancient pieces were all gone.

"Grigg didn't want the shop," Omar said, offering me a stool and pulling another one up next to mine. He took a bowl of cereal from the counter and slurped from it. I found myself looking up at the ceiling and listening for Serena's footsteps.

"Nobody wanted it," he went on, sucking back the last of the soggy flakes before putting the bowl down. "Mom left for Omaha two years ago, but I stayed. And here I still am."

"You look well," I said, even though he didn't seem all that healthy.

"Nice try." A fly buzzed around us and landed on his hand. He studied it without moving.

"So your mom's in Omaha with your aunt?" I asked, relieved.

"Yep. Residing there unlawfully, with her pills and her disillusionment." He smacked the fly and wiped the insect's body on his pyjamas before looking at me, expressionless. "But it's good she left. It was excruciating to live with someone that depressed. Not to bring it up, but she had a real thing for your dad. She was never the same after that fiasco."

I'd long ago figured out that Serena, and her come-hither home-wrecking ways, wasn't the destructive force behind my parents' marriage. Serena was an unessential ingredient in my parents' unhappiness, but their broken relationship predated her. Even so, I'd never stopped to consider that she might have actually loved my father.

"On the bright side, I grew out of my epilepsy." Omar pepped up.

"That's great," I said with false enthusiasm, my thoughts still on Serena.

"So tell me, Miss Edith. What brings you to the 'hood?"

He reached out to touch my hair. The gesture, though meant to be affectionate, was off-putting. I tried to calm myself down enough to make my crass request. "You'd mentioned if I ever needed anything, that Grigg..."

"You need money." His voice fell flat.

"My sister's sick."

"How much?"

"Ten grand. I have a steady job at the Gallery," I told him, "so I can pay you back within the year."

"I know."

"Know what?"

"I've kept tabs. I know you work there."

"That's creepy," I said, glancing toward the door.

But then he gave me a reassuring smile. "You're in the online directory, that's all."

"And you never stopped in to say hi?"

"I thought about it. A lot." He blinked. His eyelashes were still so long.

I reverted to small talk. "So what have you been up to aside from running the store? Did you go to university?" Omar had been one of the smartest teenagers I knew.

"This is it. My kingdom." He opened his arms wide around the lightless room. "You know what's funny?"

"What?"

"I had the biggest crush on you."

I shook my head and averted my gaze without responding. Omar still had a way of unsteadying me. I sensed him watching me intently, in an almost predatory way.

"Know what else is funny?" he asked, as he balanced on the back two legs of his stool. "Sometimes, I think, had the circumstances of our meeting been different—like, in another life—you'd have fallen in mad love with me."

"That's sweet," I told him, unsure of what else to say. "Anyway, I'll sign a contract or whatever paperwork," I added. We were getting off topic.

He folded his arms and sighed as the stool's front legs hammered the floor. "What's wrong with your sister?"

"I'm taking her to India. For a liver transplant," I explained.

Omar burst out laughing. "You gotta be shitting me."

I looked away.

"You can't bullshit a bullshitter, cupcake. Straight up, what do you need it for?"

"For my sister," I reiterated. "I'm giving her part of my liver."

He started laughing again, shaking his head. He laughed so hard he had to wipe tears from his eyes.

"You don't have to be cruel." I stood to go. "I came here because you're my last resort. Forget it."

"Wait." Omar moved ahead of me to the door, serious again. "It's just—you might want to change your story. It's too far-fetched."

"Will you give me the money or not?" I entreated, taking hold of his hand. I was desperate.

He looked at me skeptically. Then he disarmed me by reaching for my other hand, stepping in close as if he wanted to kiss me. He looked out the window again. It was nerve-racking how much he checked that window. "Come back in a week."

"Really?"

"For old times' sake." He hugged me, his chin reaching my forehead. He was that much taller than me.

"I'll repay you fast, I swear."

"You don't have to pay it back."

"I don't?" His body heat was affecting my thinking.

"Nah." Omar had a teasing, devious glint in his eyes. "You can return the favour some other way."

"Like how?"

He touched my waist before leaning against the door, his hand on the deadbolt. "I'm going to make it easy for you. Sex or art theft. Your choice."

THREE

THIRTY-SIX

I CONTINUED TO DROP in on Viv regularly. There were protein shakes all over the counter, and syringes for her vitamin injections. Cups lined with cigarette butts and too many pill bottles to count. When she ate—if she ate—she poured sugar on everything: on her pasta, vegetables, toast, and ice cream.

She wasn't faring so well. Her hair was thinned out and knotted, extending from her Technicolor toque. The eyeshadow and blush she applied to her cheeks to give her face colour looked garish. She pulled spasmodically at her eyebrows and eyelashes until there were hardly any left. Her palms were red, her nails were split, and she scratched at her skin as though there was an itchiness there that she couldn't get rid of.

There were times I was suspicious she might still be drinking or doing drugs. Like when her cell rang and she didn't answer, telling me it was cold callers as "Blocked" flashed on the screen. I wondered about her clean garbage too. Why had she suddenly started emptying it? When I checked the bins outside by the fence on my way out, I found the usual trash.

Mostly when I showed up she'd be knitting or reading the self-help books I brought her. She winced when she moved but insisted she wasn't in pain. Typically she lay on her side. She reminded me of a Magritte painting. The one of a woman resting on a daybed, only the woman was a wooden burial box.

"I'm chilled through my bones. Like one of Dad's winterscapes." She wore a shapeless knit sweater that had one arm shorter than the other.

A white, handmade scarf and mitts had been placed discreetly on the card table. She picked the scarf up and wound it several times around my neck, fumbling with the tassels. "For when the cold arrives," she told me.

It was early August and the hottest summer in a decade. While most of us survived it by moving from one air-conditioned space to another, I knew Viv turned her AC unit off after every one of my visits.

I thanked her and hesitated, asking, "If you can knit, why can't you hold a brush?"

Viv yanked the scarf tight around my neck then crossed her arms. "The knitting needles are gigantic, in case you hadn't noticed. I'm doing this to keep occupied."

She stood in front of the notepads and charcoal pencils stacked beside boxes of noodles on the microwave. "Two months down, four to go. Seems like an eternity." She gave me a vanquished look, full of doubt.

"You'll paint again, Vee. There's a way out of this," I coerced.

"I can't make amends. You have no idea. The people I've

hurt. I never told you about my — I thought the Con was a bad mother, but I'm the one —" Her eyes went big and glossy as if she was having a vision.

I tried to focus on the positive. "Before long we'll be riding elephants and visiting ashrams." I took the game of Scrabble from the kitchen cupboard and set it up on the bed.

"I wish I could have been like you."

The letters fell on the board, scrambled. *You could have,* I felt like saying.

I'd once heard this theory. That when you die, you'll be measured up against all the yous you could have been, in which case my sister would find versions of herself as a notable artist, wife, teetotaller. But I couldn't imagine her as me. She was too special to be me.

I got up again and poured us some lemonade, taking a puff off my Ventolin.

"I thought coming home would erase what happened in between," she said, her voice barely audible.

I wanted to bring her back to life. But when I approached and put my arm around her, she pulled away.

THAT NIGHT, I made fish and chips for supper. I thought about the rogue wave drawing I'd wrecked. I thought about Theo and his leaking eyes and the trust he had in some mysterious bird that kept him going.

I washed my dishes and called Raven. "What are you doing?"

"Reading Rumi. Although I find with poetry you don't get as much bang for the buck. Too few words, you know?"

"Mhmm."

"What's wrong?"

"Nothing."

"You sound manic."

I listened to her inhaling her Friday night joint, holding the smoke in, blowing it out. "If you had to steal art or have sex with someone for money, which would you choose?"

I heard her close a door. "Buzzkill. What are *you* reading?"

"Never mind."

"Your sister in some kind of sordid clusterfuck again? I hope you've changed your mind about that preposterous surgery."

"No. She's okay."

"Don't let her pull one over you, Edith. Addicts are untrustworthy liars."

I regretted mentioning anything. "I damaged a drawing."

"Jesus, who cares. By the time anyone catches on, we'll be dead." She had a coughing fit then added, "Steal."

"What?"

She cleared her throat. "I'd choose stealing over sex. It's more dignified."

After we hung up, I extracted the old janiform head from my jewellery box. Back when Serena had given it to me I didn't understand the meaning of Janus and I wasn't interested. But now I knew all about the god of gates, of entrances and exits, of doors opening and closing, of time and endings. I'd studied him inside out and backwards, this two-faced deity symbolizing youth and age and the transition from one condition to another. I often thought I was like a janiform bust, straining for what lay ahead with one face yet unable to look away from the past with the other.

When I flipped the coin, the nail of my thumb hit it sharply and it emitted a sustained ringing sound as it turned in the air. It landed on the hardwood floor, rolled on its edge, and spun faster and faster before coming to an abrupt stop.

LESS THAN A week later, I heard from Omar. He specified that I return to the Coin Shoppe in the evening, after regular business hours. Judging from his shifty manner and the lack of coins in the store, I suspected he conducted plenty of business there at night.

I walked over at dusk. Thin white clouds marked the darkening sky like brushstrokes on water. I wanted to get this ordeal over with, and I told myself I was doing it to save my sister. In truth, I wanted to take care of the situation to disentangle Viv from my life in case Liam came back. I knew he probably wouldn't. Yet I couldn't stop with the wishful thinking. I was no better than those women standing at windows in paintings throughout history. Holding a handkerchief, looking out at cows and castles, bracing myself for what would not happen.

"I NEED TO see the money," I told Omar.

He opened one of the display cases and pulled up a false bottom, handing me a thick wad of cash. From where I stood, I could see Serena's sawed-off shotgun, still in its same spot under the counter.

"You'll be awarded the rest when we're through, M'lady," he bowed.

"How did you get this?"

"I'm a sniper, can't you tell?" He raised an arm in the air and flexed. His muscles popped under his black T-shirt. I was still having trouble associating this suave guy with the gangly kid I once knew.

I unrolled the wad and flipped through the bills. "Prove it's real," I said, unflinching.

Omar frowned. Then he led me to the back room, where he switched on a metal tower that buzzed and shot out blue lasers. He told me to pick any bill.

"Flatten it under the light," he ordered. The counterfeit machine gave a green flash with each hundred I ran beneath it. "I'm a man of my word. Don't insult me."

I dropped the roll of cash into my backpack. Then Omar directed me to the staircase.

In his room, the Star Wars wallpaper curled off the walls. The windowsill where we used to sit was cracked and mud-spattered, the carpet scummy.

"Your place is a dump," I told him.

Omar turned on a floor fan and aimed the current of air at us. Then he made for the mattress and patted the spot beside him as he kicked off his boots. I sat next to him and he nudged my arm and tucked my hair behind my ears. "Let's lie down. Hang a bit."

He unzipped his pants and pulled off his T-shirt. Then he lay back and stretched out, watching me.

I knew I owed him. When I undressed, Omar whistled. The sheets smelled fresh, which surprised me. Crossing my arms over myself, I focused on the clean sheets. Then I zoned in on a water stain on the ceiling as Omar climbed on top of me and tore open a condom. The banana-flavoured smell triggered my gag reflexes.

"So amazing...baby...so...hot..." His voice cleaved the air as he bashed his body against mine.

My insides clicked and locked.

I pictured *The Child's Dream*—the tank appearing smaller each time I saw it, and the animal constricted inside it. Viv's destitute face flashed through my mind. Briefly, I even thought of Serena. I thought, this is the start of something horrible.

Minutes later, Omar's invigorated body slackened and he pushed himself off me.

"You weren't into it. You could've at least pretended," he said, perturbed. "I hate to break it to you, but you and your family are just as bad, the way you use people. It's all business to you."

I felt cheap and vulgar enough as it was. And here Omar was rebuking me, making himself out to be the victim. There was no purity left in either of us.

I moved away, sat up, and pulled my knees to my chest. Omar put his boxers on and lifted some weights in the corner of the room, grunting and pumping them to his shoulders.

"You're disgusted by me," he went on, his mouth ajar. "Your feelings haven't changed." He made noises from the back of his throat, swallowing repeatedly. The nervous tic from childhood was still there.

I watched his chest rise and fall. There was a long scar across his rib cage. "What happened there?" I asked.

"I'm the kind of guy that violence follows. Like Hercules." He looked at me, bleary-eyed. Then, resigning himself to the fact this was the first and last time anything would happen between us, he picked up my clothes and sat back down on the mattress, handing them to me. "Did you ever get that dude you were chasing after? Lismer? Mesmer?"

"Liam."

"Right."

"Not really."

"I didn't get the girl either." He flopped backwards, lying down again. "She came back briefly, but she only wanted me for my money and my body. Speaking of briefs, can I keep these?"

I grabbed my underwear and started getting dressed.

"So what's the story with your sister?"

"I already told you."

"As if. Why a transplant?" His nicotine-stained fingers made quotation marks in the air around the word *transplant*.

"Booze."

At this, he sat upright again. "That's whacked—your sister? Didn't she become a famous artist?"

"Almost."

"Man. Oh, man. Tragic." He shook his head, dumbfounded. "I remember when you stole those Baggies of snort from her, though. So I guess it's been a long time coming." He ran a hand through his hair over and over, as though it helped him to think. "My dad's Spaniard blood combusted with it too. Big time. Bourbon in his veins, Mom said. Douche bag. Watching him battle the bottle was more entertaining than watching a dogfight."

Apparently everyone had a drinker in their family.

We heard an explosion, then another, as firecrackers and sparklers went off in nearby yards—a common sound on summer weekends.

"At least there are fireworks somewhere tonight," Omar said, this time without malice. He went over to his dresser drawer, came back, and dropped two thick rolls of cash into my hands.

I sensed the colour rising in my cheeks. "I have to go," I told him. I shoved the money into the backpack and descended the staircase.

Omar followed me. "So this is adios, songbird. Deuces."

"I'll see you," I said.

"Chances are you won't. I've been holed up here long enough. I'm telling you, so you don't die of a broken heart or anything."

"Where are you going?"

"Not sure. Gotta bounce, though."

Omar seemed lost to me and his life, aimless. I hoped he'd abandon his dodgy ways. I knew I was hypocritical to think that, as I walked off with his money. There was some truth in what he had said. I was like a mercenary motivated by private gain, using whomever I had to to accomplish my final task.

He unlocked the deadbolts and I was outside again. He looked up and down the sidewalk, then the door shut quickly and the lights went out. Then it reopened a crack.

"Last chance, songbird—marry me?" he called out.

Omar's voice plummeted through the streets as I ran from the old neighbourhood into the darkness.

THIRTY-SEVEN

By MID-SEPTEMBER, THE AIR cooled drastically, and the days turned unstable and cloudy.

Viv told me that she'd decided to go on a medically authorized ten-day mindfulness retreat. I took it as a positive sign that she was finally making an effort, and wanted to meet people who were in a similar situation to hers, whom she could relate to and share with. It was encouraging that she had enough energy to leave the basement. I thought the group sessions would be good for her and I was glad to get a break from seeing her.

Meanwhile, I continued finalizing our travel arrangements. Sometimes I pulled the rolls of money Omar had given me from my sock drawer. The bills stank, but it was reassuring to flatten them and spread them across the table. Then one day, after touching the filthy cash and overanalyzing the transplant surgery, I ran to the bathroom and threw up. The violent spasms went on until I was sweating and dry heaving. Even in the shower under the hot flow of water, I couldn't get rid of my shakes.

Thinking about my sister—what I'd done with Omar and how I was going to be gutted, risking my health for hers, which she'd flushed down the toilet—an acidic residue developed at the back of my throat like the aftertaste of a cigarette. I started retching again. No matter how many times I brushed my teeth and rinsed with mouthwash, the sensation wouldn't go away.

THE NEXT AFTERNOON at the Gallery, the wind started up and an inhospitable rain pounded against the viewing room's panes.

We all put down our work. Maud tightened her shawl around her shoulders. Arnold had come in with her and sat beside her, studying the telegram relaying Tom Thomson's death. From his spot in the back, Theo looked up too. Even Dorothy stopped examining her etchings long enough to evaluate the sky and shudder.

I watched Theo struggle to button his blazer with his large arthritic hands. I realized our jobs weren't that different—what he did with hidden animals and what I did with collections, uncovering works locked away in storage, which remained unseen until I recorded their existence in Avalon, treating each one like a rediscovered species.

I prepared for closing. Everyone filed out except Theo. When he approached the desk, he leaned on his cane to steady his uncertain gait and asked if I'd join him for tea. Not wanting to be home alone anyway, I said yes and locked up.

We slowly made our way to the cafeteria. Theo lumbered beside me, his breathing laboured. In my peripheral vision all I could see was an immense, dark mass, as if I were accompanying a costumed bear.

I led him through back passageways to a restricted door entering directly onto the Veronese gallery—a ritzy, vaulted room with deep-red walls. He paused at the altarpiece of a dead Christ supported by cherubs. Before continuing on, I asked if he'd seen *The Child's Dream*.

"Indeed," he replied.

"And?"

"The artist should have used a larger horse." He struck the ground with his cane twice to seal his judgement.

"Ever track down a unicorn in your line of work?"

"Along with sphinxes?" He raised his thick grey eyebrows, his forehead transforming into a series of deep folds. "It is possible. There are many uncharted territories where they could be dwelling."

"Uh-huh." I was half listening, trying to make conversation.

We sat at the window with a panorama on *One Hundred Foot Line*. The sky lit up and there was thunder. From inside the glass and granite building, the steel sculpture shimmered.

"It's lightning proof," I told Theo.

"It resembles an alicorn."

I imagined the rest of the animal buried under the hill. "Actually, it's just a line."

He stared, waiting for further commentary. "What does a thing like that cost?"

"A million bucks."

We watched for the violet glow of lightning to strike the sculpture as it would the mast of a ship or a church spire. But the storm began weakening as we drank our tea.

Theo's cane leaned against the chair. The handle was carved into the head of an animal.

"What's that on your stick?" I asked.

"The okapi." He picked up the cane, turning it from side to side.

"Looks like a giraffe."

"The okapi is smaller with a shorter neck, a dark rust body, and zebra-like markings on its legs. And they have longer, blue tongues to strip leaves from trees, extending from your elbow to here." He pointed to his elbow and then to his knuckly hand. "Tongues that touch their eyelids."

"Where do they live?"

"In secluded forests of the Congo and western Uganda. They're not social."

"Endangered?"

"Even in some wildlife reserves, they have only been spied once in fifty years."

Raven walked by with a coffee and a bag of chips. She did a double take and gave an exaggerated wave before moving on.

Theo told me about the animals he'd been searching for over the years, which he called his cryptids. Many were being wiped out by deforestation, poaching, and civil wars. He went on about how parts of Africa and interior Australia and South America hadn't yet been inhabited by humans. Even though they were mapped out, cartographers had identified these ecosystems only from airplanes. In some far-flung places, Theo said, explorers chronicled descriptions in their logbooks of creatures so fantastical that they were considered insane.

"Are Bigfoot and Nessie part of your research?"

"I denounce hoaxes. You may have heard of the pygmy hippo or the giant panda?" I nodded. He dabbed his eyes again. They were silvery in the changing light. "The Indian tapir, the giant squid, or the Komodo dragon?"

"Of course."

"These used to be monsters of folklore."

The rain was pounding down again. I offered him a ride home and he declined, saying he'd arranged for a driver. Then he told me he wouldn't be in this climate much longer.

"Where are you going?"

"Somewhere far and warm."

My thoughts jumped to Liam on his hot continent, sun-tanned and surrounded by gems and minerals like a conquistador. For the rest of my conversation with Theo, my mind was elsewhere.

IN THE EVENING, Raven called.

"Who's your friend?"

"Theo."

"He's too old for you."

"I'm hanging up."

"What's he doing in an art gallery?"

"Long story."

"I bought a Rothko."

"Poster?"

"No."

"Print."

"Nope. Authentic replica from China. They paint them in seven days, exactly like the original."

"I heard about those factories on TV."

"Child labour?"

"Apparently."

"Fuck. It's a no-refund policy."

"Which one did you order?"

"*White Over Red*. Blood-red, I guess."

I told Raven about the nausea. I wanted to make sense of

my sister and her sickness, the way Theo wanted to make sense of the natural world.

"That's stress," Raven said. "When I'm stressed, my hair falls out in clumps. Like your mom's dog."

After hanging up with her, I had a flashback of me, Viv, and Henry in Bella Coola. On that trip—our last trip with our father before he died—we visited a fish hatchery. It wasn't one of my favourite memories, which would explain why I'd blocked it out.

At some stage of the hatchery tour, the guide led us through riverbeds of salmon battling their way upstream. The smell of festering flesh made me queasy and I wanted to go back to the station wagon, to where Henry was fishing on a nearby lake. But Viv's stamina was boundless that day, although she knew there were no bears to see there—the guide had said as much.

She told me to be a trooper and insisted we push on. She told me to get a grip and not to surrender to my anxiety, and that she'd buy me an ice cream if I kept going. So for the next two hours, in uncomfortable, hard rubber boots that tore my skin up under my socks, we trudged by half-dead carcasses, some still flailing, until Viv stopped in her tracks and turned to the guide with, "We can go back now." Just like that.

I didn't get my ice cream. And I never understood what it was my sister was seeking on that gruesome and pointless expedition. It was almost as if she put herself through these hardships on purpose, to test herself.

The part of me willing to undergo the surgery understood that this illness wasn't Viv's fault. Yet my sister had formidable willpower. I still struggled to accept her condition as something she had no control over.

THIRTY-EIGHT

WHEN I DIDN'T HEAR from Viv after two weeks, I began to feel uneasy. I'd left messages for her, but she hadn't returned my calls.

Eventually I walked over to her place after work. It was raining, the sky a sheet of pallid ink like the white linens Constance washed with dark colours. The leaves were skipping their usual fiery transformation, going from green to brown then falling, creating a thick paste on the ground. I held on to the railing to avoid slipping on the mulch-covered steps. Two men across the street looked on spiritlessly, drinking beer.

The screen came off its hinge when I pulled the door open. There was masking tape across the bell, so I knocked. A dog barked on the other side of the door, but no one answered.

I went around to the back entrance. As I fiddled with the padlock on the outer door, someone came out on the deck above, charging down the stairs. A bald man in gunmetal track pants slowed when he saw me.

He tugged at his crotch. His hard stomach bulged beneath his hockey jersey. "Hey darlin', what can I do you for?"

"Is Vivienne Walker here?"

"She moved out." He extracted a flattened pack of cigarettes from his pocket, offering me one then tapping his own on the railing. Smoking, he leaned over and retrieved a key from the Velcro pouch of his Adidas, passing by me more closely than was required to remove the lock.

"Didn't want no squatters." There was a whistle in his speech. His smile revealed a gap where his bottom front teeth were missing.

I followed him down the stairway, bowing my head to accommodate the low ceiling. When he pulled a cord and the light came on, a mouse scurried along the baseboard, vanishing under the stove. The unit smelled of industrial chemicals.

"Wife sterilized it for the next renter," he said, stubbing his cigarette in the sink. "So's you know, guy across the hall says she sold him her furniture before she took off." He turned the tap, discarding the butt down the drain. The water gushed out brown. "Motherfucker," he mumbled, appraising me. "Here's her things. Hadn't got around to chucking 'em." He pushed the two sagging cardboard boxes on the kitchen counter toward me then made his way back up the stairs with, "Door catches. Pull hard when you go."

One box contained her clothes. I sat on the floor in the area off the kitchen where Viv's bed and table used to be, going through scruffy jean and shirt pockets. At the bottom of the pile was her knit sweater. There was paint on it and a cuff was unravelling. I smelled it; its oiliness reminded me of our father's shed.

The second box was almost empty. I questioned what the landlord had kept for himself. What remained was Viv's Swiss Army knife with her name engraved on it. Henry had given each of us one, growing up. Viv used the knife for scraping canvas. I opened the compartments. The blades were rusty.

There was also a picture of Viv in a magnetized frame, meant for a fridge. She was smiling and the sun lit her hair, giving her an angelic appearance. There were large trees and a park behind her, likely Stanley Park. In Viv's eyes Liam was reflected, holding the camera.

Then there was the AA Big Book, with Viv's plastic chips taped inside the cover. When I flipped through it, a lacklustre Serenity Prayer page marker fell out, with a phone number written on it.

I looked for some clue as to where Viv had gone. I opened the cupboards and pulled back the shower curtain and lifted the lid of the toilet tank. All I found were mice droppings.

On the way out, I noticed another box near the trash bins. A box so big it came up to my waist. I walked through the mud and opened the wet flaps. It was filled with synthetic corks and screw caps, hundreds of them, maybe more.

I dragged the box back down the steps leading into the basement. I turned it upside down and a dank smell invaded the room as the bottle stoppers rolled out, covering the floor. Among them was one of the notepads I'd given her. It contained sketches of a boat made entirely from corks.

"What retreat?" Dr. Black asked when he returned the call I'd made to his answering service. "She knew I was going on holidays—my replacement informed me this morning that he couldn't get through to her by phone or by house call."

I barely maintained the control in my voice. "She'll get it together, I'm sure it's nothing. I'll keep you posted."

"Edith." Dr. Black's bedside manner usually kicked in when he addressed me by my first name. "Vivienne was not making satisfactory progress. She was almost too ill for the surgery."

"But she was passing the weekly tests," I protested.

"Her urine came back clean, yes. But it's easy to buy urine. She had refused her last two rounds of blood work, violating the drug testing component of this process. Even if you had made it to Bangalore, once they re-evaluated her, they would have sent you both home."

I SWALLOWED A couple of sleeping pills I'd taken from Con's before she moved, and slept for thirteen hours. The next morning, I called in sick and phoned Viv's manager. "She hasn't shown since last month. I don't want to be a dick, but the deal was she had to check in weekly. If you see her, tell her she's fired," he said.

I called the number on the Serenity Prayer marker. A raspy female voice answered. "Dial-a-Bottle, please hold." I hung up.

At eleven in the morning, I went to Viv's hangout, the Laff. The Château Lafayette was older than the Parliament Buildings. It was older than the Château Laurier and it was older than the city.

There were social bars and there were drinking bars. In a drinking bar, no one talked. Drinkers drank in solitude, not wanting to be disturbed. Mostly they stared into their glasses, devoted to the pursuit of dying. The Lafayette was such a bar. In the mornings the only ones in there were the addicts, the homeless, and the welfare recipients.

Dusty evergreen garlands were permanently fastened across the wrought iron railing, as was the artificial holiday wreath on the door. Festive, chiming bells sounded when I pulled the handle. Inside, a filmy ray of sun came through the window, hitting the worn chairs, the scuffed tables, and the brown-black wood floor. I went up to the bar where a few men were sitting with their backs to me.

An alarmingly skinny girl with a red bob, wearing a tank top that showed her belly button and a child-sized miniskirt, stood by the jukebox. She flipped through the song charts, jerking her hips back and forth even though there was no music playing. In a series of convulsive steps, she made her way over, in a walk similar to the one I'd seen in crack users over by the mission whenever Raven dragged me there. At the bar, I took in her smudged makeup and her dry, bleeding lips. Her face was covered in boils.

"Gimme another, Daddy!" She draped her arm around the grizzled man beside her, stooped over his drink. The man didn't budge from his stool or look at her, reaching into his pocket and handing her a crumpled bill. She stopped biting her nails long enough to grab it and slip it into her bra, doing a little twirl and bow. Barefoot, she went skittering out of the bar.

The bartender put his book down. "Help you?"

I'd seen broken bottles outside. "She's going to cut her feet," I said. "She'll freeze."

"She won't feel a thing."

I gripped the thick wood surface for a minute. I hadn't eaten since the night before and was dizzy. "Has my sister Vivienne been around?" I showed him the grainy picture from our camping trip, of Viv standing by the lake, her figure wavering in a halo of ruddy light.

The bartender was surly. "Haven't seen that one in ages."

"That one?"

"That hooker."

"She's not a prostitute."

"Suit yourself."

"What's your definition of 'ages'—hours?" My chest was tightening.

"Weeks."

As the patrons emptied their pints, he took the glasses, refilling the tap beer mechanically without being asked. Then he rubbed his beard and yawned, returning to his novel.

I wrote my name and number down on a napkin. When I put it on top of his book to get his attention, he stared back up at me, I thought to tell me off. Instead, he said, "There was a guy. Used to check in on her here. She called him Angel."

There were a lot of Angels and Jesuses in the underground world. Probably a pimp or a pusher with a name like that.

A minute later, it hit me.

The men lined the length of the bar as if they were tied to a train track. I wondered if they would get up if they heard the dark haul of a locomotive approaching. If they would look up and notice its black iron face about to plough them down. Or maybe that's what they were waiting there for.

IT WASN'T HARD to find him. An online search listed seven Nick Angels living in the city. Only one of them worked at the Department of National Defence. It had to be him.

When I phoned, he agreed to meet me at the Starbucks by the downtown library the next night.

He was there when I arrived, sitting at a table stacked high with children's books. When I tapped him, he regarded me thoughtfully. I sat down across from him. Fine lines extended from his blue eyes.

"Edith. It's been a long time. You've cut your hair since we were kids. It suits you."

I ran a hand down the back of my head. I'd chopped my hair off into a pageboy after Liam left and my neck still felt too bare; I hadn't got used to it the way Raven vowed I would.

"I thought of contacting you in the past. About your sister, I mean."

"You haven't seen her, then."

"Not since she was in that centre last year. She got day passes. We'd meet up." Through the noise of the coffee grinders, the steaming and hissing of the espresso machines, I tried to interpret this as Nick went on. "We had an argument. I didn't see her after that."

"About what?"

"Same as always. She said she was better, but she rarely lasted more than a few months. I moved to Vancouver for her—she didn't tell you that, did she? I moved back here for her too, to keep an eye on her. We weren't together anymore. Things seemed good with her. But then there was that Christmas potluck with the telemarketing co-workers."

"I hadn't realized you were back in touch."

"We weren't ever out of touch. Even after my dad shipped me off to the academy, I'd call her late at night. We never stopped."

How could I have missed the signs? All those midnight conversations I thought she was having with Liam as a teenager, while I eavesdropped against the bedroom wall.

Later, her lack of interest with Liam even when they lived together in Vancouver. Then her uncaring reaction when I expressed my own feelings for Liam, over the campfire in Algonquin Park. It was Nick Angel all along. Even Liam had suspected it.

Yet I couldn't let my guard down with this guy. I still reproached him for Viv's ruin. "I wanted you dead," I told him.

Nick slouched further into his chair. "There was a time I wanted myself dead too. I was a confused teenager. I would've done anything for your sister. Did a lot of shameful shit, pardon my language. All that experimenting. Viv wanted to party and I went along for the ride. But then you grow out of it. Or most of us do. I never touched drugs again after the overdose. Tried to get her to quit too. Your sister stayed hard-core with the sauce, though. That's the one thing she couldn't lay off."

He drank from his paper cup. Customers filed in and out, letting in a cold draft.

"Anyway, there was a gift exchange at the potluck. I helped her choose a set of cookbooks, but she called me that night, crestfallen." He picked up his camo ball cap, studying it. "When I asked her what happened, she told me there was a game where each person unwrapped a present then stole another. She wound up with a liqueur concoction nobody wanted. She gave it away, but it kept landing back with her. She had the bottle on her desk all afternoon. Then she put it in her knapsack and threw it into a Dumpster somewhere along the way home."

He looked beat. "She white-knuckled it till spring, then it all started again. I couldn't keep bailing her out," he said, as if seeking forgiveness. He paused and squeezed his eyes shut. "She bragged about you constantly. Said you were the smart one who'd go places. I have no idea where she is, but I wouldn't concern myself too much if I were you. She'll turn up. And when she comes back, I can't get involved again. My wife's losing patience. We have kids, things are different."

He steadied his gaze on me with those clear, almost neon eyes that had immobilized me as a girl. Before me was a burly, cynical man fighting back tears. Blaming himself for what I now knew was no one's fault. I didn't see the point in upsetting him with Viv's current diagnosis.

He glanced through the doors that led to the library. "If it wasn't the potluck, it would have been something else. There was always one temptation or another around the corner with your sister." He reached for his coat. "How is your mother, by the way?"

"She won't talk about it."

"I never met her, but I sometimes got the sense that Vivienne worshipped her."

"What do you mean? She couldn't stand her."

And then he gave a defeated smile. "From what I heard about your mom, they seem alike, those two. Sad, unfulfilled. Haunted by God knows what."

THIRTY-NINE

ANOTHER WEEK PASSED WITH no news. I decided to file a missing persons report. Even though Constance said don't.

Grief was untidy. My mother wanted no part in its damage to her composure. She'd had shingles since my sister's hospitalization, although she didn't complain about the belt-like pattern of blisters erupting along the side of her chest, which I'd noticed on her last visit.

"*Heureusement* this prevents you girls from doing that outlandish surgery. She is a grown-up and must care for herself. She is *not* your responsibility, Édith."

I waited for her common sense to kick in. Neither Con nor Henry had siblings. I shouldn't have expected her to understand the enduring allegiance I felt toward my sister. How this fidelity transcended the ill will.

"It was an imbecilic plan," was all she kept saying from her condo in Florida. "She'll come home when she is ready."

But this time Viv's disappearance was a complete fade away.

I brought the camping picture with me to the police station. When the administrator stapled it to the form, the fastener ran across my sister's forehead. I filled out Viv's personal information and a physical description from when I'd last seen her.

"Be sure to include unique features. People always forget that," she said.

"Like skills?"

"Like a birthmark or scars. Dentures or a hearing aid. A missing limb, tattoos, a limp. Any attribute to help us identify her."

When I finished, she brought me to a desk where an officer was sitting at a computer, playing solitaire and eating a healthy-looking wrap. He gave me the once-over, flipping through the form attached to the clipboard.

"This photo's terrible."

"It's from an old camera."

"You sure she's not with relatives or friends?"

"I'm sure."

"Has she gone missing before?"

"Sometimes we don't hear from her for long periods."

Wiping his hands and making a sucking sound through his teeth, he said, "Visit the places where you've found her in the past. Call hospitals and shelters. They usually refuse to divulge anything, but there are exceptions. What was her state of mind?"

"She was coping. She's never been a happy person."

"Drugs?"

"I'm not sure."

"This isn't the time to hold back."

"Maybe prostitution."

"Drugs, then."

"She can't afford drugs."

"Meth's five bucks a hit. Cheaper than booze."

"I only ever saw her drink. And do ecstasy recreationally."

"They all go together. Users switch up." He checked the form again. "Says here last seen in September."

"We were getting ready to go to India. I was collecting the money we needed."

"You give her any?"

"Not much." Before she'd gone on her retreat, I'd ended up sliding an envelope containing a few hundred bucks under Viv's door, with a note telling her to dump the old duffle bag and get a new suitcase and some clothes for the trip.

He looked dubious. "Anything else?"

"She had marks. Behind her knees, even. She said they were old. And she had to use needles to inject vitamins, so it was probably just that."

"You can inject meth. And junk, and crack. But tracks are a myth unless you shoot in the same places. Most have plenty of fresh veins to choose from. Marks mean your sister scarred easily." He kept typing. "What else?"

"She used to be a painter."

"Houses?"

"Pictures. She has a paintbrush tattoo."

"Where?"

"Left shoulder blade."

"Alcohol and cigarette brands?"

"Anything she can get, I guess."

"Is she on meds?"

"For her liver."

"You note her doctor here?" He flipped the page. I nodded. He handed the form back to me. "I can't file this."

"Excuse me?"

"I'll do you a favour and put her in our registry, but I'm not filing your report." He could see I didn't follow. "Your sister's not *missing*, missing. She's just gone."

"That makes no sense."

"If facts indicated foul play, we'd investigate. That's not the case here."

"Of course she's missing. We can't *find* her! She could be in trouble, and you're not going to do anything?"

"We have about a hundred reports registered here every month, miss. Walking away without telling anyone isn't a crime. When you can prove otherwise, here's my number. The name's Quinn."

"That's it? What am I supposed to do?" My voice reverberated back at me, borderline hysterical, when he gave me his card.

"Secure her belongings. Conduct phone and Web searches. Was she active in a chat room or other social network, or did she leave behind her cell or written materials like a journal?"

I shook my head.

"If you feel the need to pursue it, hire a licensed PI." He stood up then, opening his office door for me to leave. "Give him contact details for her dentist. And if you have a toothbrush or a hairbrush, drop them off too."

IN THE GALLERY'S heart, through the trees and flowers of the garden court, hidden from view unless one really looked, lay the entranceway to the Rideau Chapel — a sanctuary saved from demolition by volunteers, and reconstructed piece by piece.

I walked by angels made from pine and stood under the

fan-vaulted ceiling. The sound sculpture *Forty-Part Motet* played there on a loop. Spotlights flooded in through stained glass windows in simulated sunlight, torching the altars and balcony, the marbled columns and stencilled walls.

The artist said she wanted to climb inside the music. So she put forty speakers on stands in a horseshoe, creating eight choirs. From each speaker there came a separately recorded voice, beginning with a single chant from the first set of sculptures. Others lolled in like an undercurrent, each voice eclipsing the previous one as the fugue traversed the chapel. Then all the voices rinsed together and split apart in a torrent of sound passing through me as the choirs belted a final, harrowing culmination. All at once the voices were snuffed out until the loop commenced again.

Some said *Forty-Part Motet* was a clearing in the woods and the speakers were trees around its perimeter. The empty space in the core of the forest meant the absence of God.

I thought about how being killed by a unicorn would be like being killed by an icicle or by alcohol. There would be no evidence afterwards. No weapon.

When the voices rose in unison, a shrill, piercing sound escaped me until my vocal chords burned. I dropped to the floor, as the singers carried on.

FORTY

A MONTH INTO MY sister's disappearance, I still slept with
my cell by the bed. One night it went off, a melodious ring
tone set to the sound of a harp. The caller ID was *Château
Lafayette.*

There was a lot of noise in the background. Rough
voices, glasses, and country music. "Viv?" I said, too loudly.

"Your sister was here."

"Who's this? Can you put her on?"

"Andy. Bartender. Hadn't seen her till tonight."

"Is she okay?" I sat up and switched on the lamp.

"I'm not a mind reader. It was busy."

"I'll be right there." I checked the clock. It was 1:49 a.m.

"Don't bother. She left."

"What? Where?" I opened the curtains and the window.
It was so stuffy in my room I could hardly breathe.

"Closing time soon. Just wanted you to know she was
here."

"Why didn't you call me right away?" I paced and returned

to the window. "You shouldn't have let her go."

"Listen, I can't babysit all these freaks. Fine by me if you don't want to hear —"

"Wait, don't hang up!" The sound of clanking glasses was deafening. "Please, she needs to be in a hospital."

"Don't we all. I told her you were looking for her. Said for you not to worry." He breathed in and out, slow and deep. "That's the only reason I'm calling."

"There must have been something else. What else?"

"Gimme a sec." I heard the till opening and closing, and coins being poured into a receptacle. A tray of glasses smashing to the ground, and Andy cursing before he came back on the line. "Nothing to tell. Had a rye. Said it was her last drink. That she was going home to paint the golden lights or something. The usual drivel."

"To paint gold? Is that what she said, to paint gold?" Beneath the shadow of the oak tree a bat shot past, then another.

Andy sounded more introspective. "That's it," he said, "exactly."

I bit a hangnail and pulled the skin with my teeth. "You're sure it was her?"

"It was her."

She'd been ten minutes away the whole time.

When I hung up, I couldn't loosen my grip on the phone. I sucked on my bleeding finger. Then I sped to the Market in my pyjamas, winding through the streets and alleys. Two patrol cars circulated nearby. The area was dead, everyone hiding in the neighbourhood's hovels and crack dens.

I parked across from the Laff and sat in the dark. When the cops came to my window with their flashlight, I showed them Viv's picture and asked if they'd seen her. The female officer's hair was pulled back in a pageant-tight bun. With tedium she said, "Hon, you don't belong here. Look for her in daylight."

Daylight didn't come. As I drove home in the blue hour—the hour of sweet light for artists, changing like the purples of a bruise—a fog was settling down over everything.

When I lay on the couch and closed my eyes, I heard my father's supplicating voice. *Find her, kiddo. It's on you.*

I showered and dressed for work. I made toast, spitting it out at the taste of rancid butter. There was no food in my fridge since she'd gone missing. I'd stopped keeping up with groceries and cleaning.

I walked in early, reaching the Gallery before the fog lifted, while the city was still muted. The taiga garden at the mouth of the parkade was breath-catching, like a painting evading clarity. Hardly anyone noticed it, but the rocky site—the dry undergrowth and stern trees, the neglected stretch of deep earth tones—was inspired by the Group of Seven's Canadian Shield imagery.

Through the dim air I heard a rhythmic clomping. Then Theo emerged from behind some stunted poplars. With his walking stick, he made small jumps on one leg, landing on the same foot and bending down now and again to scout the ground. I watched him a while longer then called out to him.

"What are you doing, Theo?"

"Investigating tracks," he said, breathless. "And the distances between them."

"What are they?"

"Possibly cougar."

"In the city?" I scaled the rock and approached the bog rosemary.

"Ecotone."

"What's that?"

"When two ecological worlds collide."

I bent to touch the tracks in the dirt, approximating those of a large dog. "These are dried up," I told him. "Whatever it was is long gone."

"That does not mean it will not return." Theo rubbed the imprints. "There is a saying: Absence of evidence is not evidence of absence. You see the space between the markings? A dog cannot leap like that."

I pictured an alien big cat stalking up the Gallery's glass ramp. Theo's mind was a bestiary. From what he told me, he hadn't actually found any of his animals. He'd spent his life trying to reverse extinction, yet it seemed to me his occupation of resurrecting lost species was a futile one.

He gestured toward the Great Hall dome, though we couldn't see it. "I keep hearing voices."

"That's the *Forty-Part Motet*."

He was still absorbed by his discovery. "Edith, you are living in an era of animal kingdom casualties," he said, staring down at the track. "In your lifetime, fauna once common will be eradicated. The whale, the elephant, the gorilla, the tiger. One day they will be illusory, like Gauguin's bird."

"How did he die again?"

"Hmmm?"

"Gauguin. I forget how he died."

"Inconclusive. Presumably arsenic and alcohol."

The fog was lifting. The savage plot unfurled itself before us.

"I have a sister who's dying like that," I blurted through some windswept pines. "Her name is Vivienne."

"Vivienne," he repeated with slowness, "derived from the Latin *vivus*, meaning 'alive.'" His look held compassion. "I hope for you she will be all right."

"She used to be a great painter too." I slid down from the rock and straightened my skirt. Sensing my throat tightening, I grappled with my inhaler, afterwards taking Theo's stick and offering him my arm. "The trees are different today."

"Yes." Theo nodded. "Shadows are cast through fog in three dimensions." Then he eyed the dome again. "Those voices," he said. "They drive me to despair."

FORTY-ONE

WHEN NOTHING CAME OF my random late night visits to the Laff or waiting across from the bar through my lunches, I hired a private investigator named Bruce, using most of Omar's money to cover the fee for services, which came to nearly seven hundred dollars a day.

Bruce was in his fifties and had a bleached blond buzz cut, a fake tan, and a small hoop in one ear. He smelled strongly of cologne and wore pants and pastel shirts that had a sheen to them, as if he'd been imbued with a high-gloss lacquer. A toothpick often stuck out of the corner of his mouth, a habit he took up after quitting smoking, he said. The toothpicks were flavoured. When he spoke, bursts of cinnamon, lemon, and spearmint came off him.

I told him about the sighting at the Laff and I mentioned Nick and Liam. At his instruction, we put up posters across the city, hundreds of them on phone poles and light posts and construction site barriers. In restaurants, gas stations, cafés, and bus terminals and any other public space that would let us use their bulletin boards. We set up a blog with a message board and a contact number. Bruce was the contact person, not me, and only he could log in to the messages because he said we'd get pranks and vile notes.

Bruce checked out all the Jane Does in jails and holding cells. Then he scoured the city's hospitals and clinics, parks and shelters. He got hold of Viv's cell records, but the phone hadn't been used since before she'd disappeared. He made calls to his friends on the force in Vancouver. He had access to confidential databases. He had people and connections. But he found no trace of my sister.

Who he did find was Liam, unlisted and living in the suburbs. Once he ruled out Liam's involvement with my sister's disappearance, he gave me the street address.

In a daze, I went to his house unannounced. He'd gone to the farthest outlying neighbourhood of the city, to a rocky place where no plants or trees grew. My body shook in my thin coat as I rang the doorbell. When he opened it, he showed no emotion at seeing me. He just stood there, slack-jawed.

He'd put on weight and his skin was the colour of clay, as though he didn't get out in the sun anymore.

"Edith. How are you?"

"You told me you were leaving the *country*!"

"I'm going in a few months."

He offered no further explanation. I waited for him to invite me inside.

And the longer I waited, the more pitiful he seemed to me. His feverish look was proof of his unremitting passion for my sister. Since the day he saw her in Lake Louise, all those years ago, nothing had changed.

It was irrelevant that I'd been similarly haunted by

Liam since that day. His feelings for Viv were unalterable. I wanted what he didn't have to give me. Mine was a one-sided child's dream.

"She never felt the same way. You wasted years on her."

"I know."

I took his hand in mine. "Did you ever love me?"

"I tried."

His words stung. I turned away from him on the steps, to stand under the sun's tireless, incurable light. It wanted something from us. I stared straight at it, thinking how I would have carved it out of the sky for him. That was how much I loved him.

Then I released his hand and said goodbye.

LATER IN THE day, I wandered purposelessly through endless rooms of paintings and sculptures, until I reached *Portrait of a Young Man*.

Liam no longer resembled the boy who'd left me speechless, like when I saw the great grey peaks of the Rockies for the first time. And now I saw that the young man in the painting was agitated, not pensive.

Two men walked by with ladders. The galleries were being revamped. The small oil on mahogany would soon be removed, leaving a pale emptiness on the wall.

In the vaults, I retrieved the unsalvageable wave drawing from the bottom of its box. I stood in a corner where the overhead camera couldn't see me, tearing the rectangle into even strips, pressing a ruler down over it and pulling in a lengthwise movement in the direction of the grain.

The strength of the sound was unexpected coming from so weightless and delicate a thing. The bunker-like room amplified the vibration of the fibres as they broke apart.

I swallowed each piece as though it was a thin slice of cake. The paper tasted of age and dust. Each bit stuck to the roof of my mouth like a Communion wafer.

I rubbed out the accession number pencilled on the mat board. Then I disposed of the board and the tissue paper, in a stack on the floor where faulty frames and glass panes were set aside for cleaning staff to clear away.

The dryness of the paper stayed with me, as I sat wrapped in my double layer of lab coats in the half-light on the cold stepping stool. My mouth and throat were parched, my tongue swollen. I wondered what it would be like to die of thirst.

FORTY-TWO

In a barn on the city's Experimental Farm, there lived two goats. These were no common goats. They were genetically modified silk-spinning goats.

Theo said I should see for myself, so I asked if he'd accompany me there on Saturday morning. I looked forward to our outing all week. Other than Raven, I had no friends. Yet in my serendipitous encounter with Theo, I'd made an ally of sorts, regardless of how few words we'd exchanged.

I drove past the arboretum and botanical greenhouses, parking along the road by a cornfield where farmers sold pumpkins and gourds, displaying stupefying oranges and deep yellows against a grey sky. I was early, so I walked around to where families sat at tables, scraping the thick shells in preparation for a carving contest. Children made a spectacle of scooping out the insides and throwing the muck onto newspapers.

The smell of fresh pumpkin reminded me of our damp

Mechanicsville basement, and I got wistful for the years when Henry would drive us to a patch outside the city limits, to pick out our Halloween lantern. The breeze carried the scent of burning leaves, and the pumpkins on the roadside — some whose flesh was broken to pieces in the gully — ignited a homesickness inside me. An ache for a distant time I couldn't get back.

The farmers gave out salted seeds. I sucked on them, running my hands along the cool, ribbed skin of the melons. I picked up a pumpkin and hugged it. Hold still, it seemed to tell me. Hold still and don't let go.

I bought a miniature pie and ate it and then I bought one for Theo before making my way onto the property. This farmland in the middle of the city was an anomaly. There was a sci-fi factor about an experimental place for agriculture and livestock. No one could say for sure what testing and studying went on there.

I found Theo leaning against a fence enclosing cows.

Each cow had a small round window in its side, like a window on a ship. Theo said the hole led straight to the cow's stomach, for scientists to poke into for research purposes.

I wasn't squeamish, but it was disquieting, watching those cows. "Show me these goats so I can call your bluff," I told Theo.

He thought this over and guffawed. "That's very good." He tipped his hat to me. Under his wool coat today he wore an umber bow tie, attuned to the season.

Theo parted the grass with his cane and I followed him to a barn. The musty, warm air of animals, manure, and hay engulfed us as we entered the Agriculture Museum. The supernatural goats were in the back. I took Theo's arm so he wouldn't get knocked over by the roving bands of hyperactive kids.

We walked through a petting zoo of pigs, sheep, horses, rabbits, and turkeys. At the last stall, a label much like the Gallery's art labels read: *Spider (Transgenic) Goats*. I ushered some rambunctious boys out of the way so that we could get up close.

They looked like regular little white goats. They bleated and butted and pushed against our hands for food. One balanced on a log while the other tested the fence.

"These are GM goats," Theo said.

"General Motors?"

"Genetically Modified. They were created with spider DNA in them. Engineered to produce spider silk in their milk."

"For health and science, the sign says."

"And for making military-grade textiles. This protein is ten times stronger than steel. There is great profit to be had in bulletproof vests and parachutes. Great profit in warfare."

I deliberated whether I might be stronger inside if I drank silk milk. Or ate cobwebs. Damien Hirst would pay a lot for such goats.

"I come here when I am trying to make sense of human nature."

"You visit an unnatural place with unnatural animals to do that?"

"Instead of preserving existing organisms, they try to make new ones." Theo coughed into his handkerchief.

Sugar and Spice were fighting for my hand, licking it and gearing up to chew. I pulled it back through the bars, wishing I'd brought sanitizer.

"There are tens of millions of living species on this

planet." He turned his back on the goats, despondent. "Most have yet to be catalogued. So many we will not find before they die out."

"I have the same problem at work. With Avalon."

He didn't seem to hear. I could tell he was lamenting his cryptids again. We petted the goats on the head one last time and left the barn.

I led Theo to the greenhouse for tea. We washed our hands and found a table by a bed of cacti. I pulled the small saran-wrapped pie from my purse and got a paper plate and a plastic fork at the concession. Theo feigned pleasure eating his dessert, but his large fingers were stiff today, moving with painstaking slowness.

Drinking his tea, he held his cup with effort. Then he asked after Viv, calling her by name. It meant something to me, that he remembered.

I told him how sick she was. How she had disappeared and there was no news. I admitted that at night I lay awake debating if this was her destiny or a calamity that would pass. Ultimately, my gifted and accomplished sister had been dealt the bad hand, not me, the mediocre and inept one. This twisted fluke devoured me.

Theo observed the people all around us. His response was so delayed I didn't think he'd say anything. Eventually his eyes rested on a cactus sprouting a tubular flower. I was counting the awl-like needles when he spoke.

"This week I had a light bulb go," he told me. "Then they all went out, one by one, in different rooms. Some were used much more than others, and there were various kinds—halogen, fluorescent. They all went out within days of one another."

Many would say he was another old man yammering

on. Yet I respected his philosophies and anecdotes. Even if I couldn't always decipher their meanings, like messages from a fortune teller.

"The question of what is fated, what is chance. You mustn't waste your youth as I did. Why, why, why. It brought me no repose."

I asked why there was no point asking why.

"I had a friend who collected turtles. She had no end of tribulations. But the turtles gladdened her."

"Should I collect silk-spinning goats, do you think?"

"Find what brings you pleasure to monopolize your mind and fill you." He nodded to the cactus. "Like water sustains that one in dry earth."

That was what Liam had done. Filled me up. I'd never get that feeling back.

I scolded Theo for comparing me to a barbed plant. "Pumpkins bring me pleasure. I'll grow pumpkins," I told him, even though I got what he was saying.

His crinkled lips formed a smile. "Like Cinderella, then. Do what you must to find sleep."

FORTY-THREE

Six weeks into my sister's disappearance, Constance came and went like a travelling performer, returning home for a day or two with an hour to spare or less, between finalizing the sale of her condo and packing.

She called for lunch or coffee, waiting for me outside Pierre's downtown high-rise, the image of a bygone age in her leopard print coat and her turban cap with a brooch fastened to its centre, her shapely legs off to one side and a faraway expression on her painted face. My mother's canvas of her costumed life: *Self-Portrait: Hat, Purse, Gloves*.

What I thought was her handbag turned out to be Mira beside her on the bench, in an aviator hat and goggles. The dog rested her head on her paws and didn't react when I approached.

"She needs a walk before we go to the restaurant," my mother said.

We made our way toward a park. Mira doddered along on the sidewalk, sniffing her surroundings every few metres.

When Con passed me the leash to remove her gloves, she eyed my dry, cracked hands.

"I have some lotion for that skin of yours. Mirabelle's doctor prescribed it." She opened her purse and held out a tube of ointment.

"You want me to use dog's cream?" I looked down at Mira's patchy coat. The four-pound dog was shivering. My mother scooped her up and tucked her under an arm.

"It's not for dogs. It's for udders," she replied, petting the dishevelled Mira. "I tried to bring you back some oranges," she continued, "but the customs boy wouldn't let them through."

"That's okay."

"He said the peels were the problem, not the oranges." I pulled the gate to the park open so she and Mira could enter.

"I peeled them in front of him with a lineup behind me, and I gave him the bag of peels."

"Way to show them."

"Then the oranges leaked all over so we had to eat them."

My mother unleashed Mira and the dog made her way to a tree. When a breeze came, the maples released a shower of helicopter seeds on us. Mira returned. My mother bent over and snapped her leash back on.

"Aren't you going to bag that?"

"*Bof.* Fertilizer," she said dismissively, heading toward the gate.

Mira ambled in front of us.

"Why's she limping?"

"Bad hip. You see"—and here she paused for effect—"I don't think she'll make it to Florida *encore*."

The dog stopped in a puddle, settling down to lick a bald patch on her flank.

"There is a discontinuation in her," she added.

"You mean her body's shutting down."

"It distresses her to travel."

"So drive."

"The climate is problematic there. It affects her bronchitis and her skin."

"Mom. I have asthma."

"*Mais non*, Édith. She is hypoallergenic!" With this proclamation, Mira sat upright, panting at us. My mother pulled a biscuit from her coat pocket.

"Those goggles are ridiculous."

"They protect her cataracts." Mira finished her treat and my mother picked her up again.

"She's mangy. Are you sure she doesn't have rabies?"

She kissed Mira on the nose and raised a muddy paw, waving it at me. "Feel her footpads, *feel* them! Feel how soft."

I poked at the padding with my finger. "She's not even barking anymore," I said.

"She has fatigue."

"So do I."

"She is loyal and protective. She would be a good friend for you."

My mother couldn't bear further witness to Mira's decline and wanted me to do the dirty work for her. "I'll think about it," I said, then, "I still can't find Viv."

"She will turn up."

"It's different this time."

"Nonsense, foolish girl." She dropped Mira, who went ahead with more trot in her step. "How?" she asked, her tone hardening.

"It just is."

FORTY-FOUR

THEO WAS AT THE viewing room doors a half-hour before I was to open them for the public. He sat on the lone chair by the elevator. In profile he appeared older than ever, smoothing down his wild hair with an unsteady hand. I'd get in trouble if I let him in early, but I could leave; I had nothing else to do.

I suggested a short walk. It was late October and one of the last warm days of autumn, which arrived like a gift between the cold fronts and the rain. I guided Theo up the hill, past *One Hundred Foot Line* to the open-air amphitheatre. We sat on the stone seats and Theo told me more about his bird.

He was assessing the possible survival of a flightless rail in French Polynesia, in the middle of the Pacific on one of the islands where Gauguin lived. A swamp hen that had outrun islanders and naturalists for close to a hundred years.

"What does it look like?"

"A hen with stumpy wings. It has purplish-blue plumage, a green head, and long yellow legs."

"What's it called?"

"The koao."

"It vanished?"

"After the last one was killed and eaten. But then Gauguin documented the bird in 1902 in *The Sorcerer of Hiva Oa*— the third-to-last painting he ever made. Are you familiar with it?"

"I don't think so."

"It's of a Marquesan man in a red cape and two women peering out from behind a tree. The koao is in the foreground in the mouth of a hunting dog."

A flight of geese passed above us in a wishbone formation, preparing for departure. Their loud, insistent calls briefly interrupted Theo. Then he continued, "Nobody knows the source of the model Gauguin used to paint the bird. He could have done it from memory. Or it was a crazed phantasm. The bird is almost the same size as the dog. He was sick by then."

"The bird's not extinct?"

"I've gone twice there to investigate. If a specimen is living, sooner or later I will find it."

"And the woodcut?" I nodded in the direction of the glass dome.

"Your print has the motif of the bird in the dog's mouth. I only found that bird in one other canvas, entitled *Nevermore*. The scene of a young Polynesian woman lying on her side, nude on a bed."

"Sounds like most of his paintings."

"This one is unorthodox. Despite the vivid colours, the mood is solemn. I am most certain the girl is a prostitute. Ill or spurned by her lover. The bird is there by her like an angel of death."

As we got up to go, Viv entered my mind. The last time I saw her, she was lying in her awful basement bed, nearly lifeless.

"Have I upset you?" Theo asked as we zigzagged down the hill's pathway.

I smiled and told him no.

When we reached the viewing room and I held the door open for him, I said, "I enjoy our conversations."

"I do as well. But my work here is finished."

"You could volunteer."

"I am not one for organized groups. And I am leaving for the island soon."

"You'll be back, though?"

"I am eighty-six, my dear girl. I do not plan ahead." Then he added, "You are welcome to visit me on Hiva Oa. Mind you, it is not easy to access and my accommodations are far from luxurious."

"That's not much of an invitation."

He chuckled and became serious again. "I want you to see something at the Museum of Nature. Go there and ask for Jonathan Cole. I told him that you would visit. He will show you a phenomenal thing."

"Sure. I'll do that."

Through the afternoon, Theo jotted things down in his notebook and examined his folder of prints with a magnifying glass. He took no interest in the living things surrounding him. He was like Don Quixote in his search for animals whose existence was questionable — dream-creatures arising from conjecture. While peaceful, he didn't strike me as someone at peace.

Then again, maybe in the end we were all cryptozoologists. Trekking around in our own black forests, getting hopeful on a trick of the light. Hunting down lost species that are always just out of reach.

FORTY-FIVE

WE LOST OUR SPOT on the transplant centre's list. They reimbursed my deposit and I poured the money back onto the line of credit and the credit cards.

Then I settled up with Bruce. He told me he was moving to Vancouver because business was better there. We met in the Gallery's charcoal-grey stone enclosure, where rows of deep-plum flowers with spiky leaves were planted like crosses.

"Keep an eye out for my sister."

"No problem."

"I'm thinking of submitting a complaint to the police."

Bruce disagreed. "Not worth the paperwork. That'll take years to process."

"What if she was kidnapped or murdered?"

"I didn't get that impression."

He'd completed his investigation on Viv in under two weeks. He told me he'd be stealing my money if he kept looking for her. It doesn't take long to figure out cases like your sister's, he had said.

"If I volunteered in a soup kitchen, I might find her."

"You wouldn't last an hour."

"I should try."

"I'd say get on with your life." There was disappointment in his gruff voice. He closed his notepad, preparing to leave.

"Do you think she went far?"

"Your sister was gone before her physical disappearance," he told me, offering me one of his toothpicks. "People always think there'll be a revelation at the end. Most times there isn't."

AFTER MY VIEWING room shift, I locked up and stopped in on *The Child's Dream*. From the corridor, I heard a school group. Sprightly children jumped around the vitrine, slapping the glass and pushing each other. The young teacher tried in vain to restore order, then ushered them away.

I wondered at the need to create such a creature out of the unknown. It was hard to believe that sightings of this little horned horse with no skeletal remains had caught the attention of historians, explorers, and scientists for thousands of years.

As for Damien Hirst and his formaldehyde menagerie — the calf, the sheep, the zebra, the shark, and the unicorn, to name a few — what were these but the theatrics of a billionaire terrified of death, as were his diamond-encrusted skulls and his "cabinet series" of cigarette butts and pills.

How maddening it must have been to Hirst that, despite his works of art assembled in factories, despite his industrial units and aircraft hangars manufacturing his creations made by hundreds of staff, despite his three-hundred-room Gothic mansion and his line of jeans costing four thousand dollars a pair, he would die and, at best, be preserved in formaldehyde like his beasts.

I walked to the Coin Shoppe at dawn the next day. Before me, a dull sun rose and washed out the stars, looking like Omar's pawned medallion in the sky.

From a block away, I saw the For Lease signs plastered on the storefront.

What had I expected, why had I gone back? I thought Omar and his felon friends could track my sister down if I returned what remained of his money.

I stepped up close to the barred door. The store looked as if someone had been through it with a baseball bat. There were holes in the walls and the display cases were smashed and tipped over, their antique legs broken. Serena's teapot was in pieces on the floor and her dragonfly tin lay upside down and emptied beside it.

Omar had skipped town. Maybe he would outfox whatever chased him. Reinvent himself in a new country, go to university, become successful and rich. Maybe not.

In a way, I was relieved he was gone, especially after our last encounter. What filled me with sorrow, though, was the defaced state of the shop. The place where I'd spent quiet moments as a kid, where stories lay in gold, silver, and bronze beneath layers of grit, was no more.

FORTY-SIX

By Remembrance Day, we had two feet of snow. The ploughs didn't come, but I put my boots on and went to Confederation Park anyway, to watch the old war vets receive their honours.

There was a children's event on at the arts centre. Cutting through the crowds, I saw him standing in line at the ticket booth. Even among hundreds of other identical poppy-adorned uniforms, it was unmistakably him.

"Nick!" I said, in the same instant seeing a child in a brown snowsuit attached to his arm.

He looked at me then at the child and back at me.

"How are you?" I asked, filling the dead air as he pulled a toque off the child's head, smoothing down her hair full of static electricity.

She was about five years old. I saw my sister's traits in her. The thick waviness and treacly colouring of her hair. Her inquisitive violet-blue eyes framed by remarkably long lashes and the straight-edged nose suited more to an adult than to a little girl. Had I compared her with a photo of Viv at that age, it would have been difficult to distinguish them. Like Viv, she had a calmness about her as she surveyed the other children entering the theatre.

An attractive, dark-skinned woman came up to Nick then, holding an infant boy in her arms. He was enveloped in a fluffy blue coat and had the same curls and caramel skin colouring as his mother.

"This is my wife, Nahlah. And these are our kids. Clair and Amir."

Clair. "Au clair de la lune," the only melody Viv ever asked Constance to sing to her.

He turned to Nahlah then. "This is Edith Walker. Vivienne's sister."

Nahlah gave a cautious nod. "Nice to meet you."

"You too." I could not take my eyes off the girl.

Clair leaned closer to Nick's leg and stared back at me as her father extracted a Kleenex from his sleeve to wipe her nose. Then she crouched down and clapped her hands on the ground, wet with melting snow and gravel.

"Not here, sweetie," Nick said as a pack of children passed by, almost trampling her.

Clair glimpsed up at Nahlah. Tremulously she queried, "Can we go, Momma?"

Nahlah moved toward the building's entrance with the kids, but Clair came back, tugging at her father's arm.

"Sorry," Nick said, removing his toque and rubbing his forehead as if he had a headache.

"I understand," I told him. But he didn't hear me. His back was already turned, being led away by his daughter.

Dr. Black would have known. Maybe he hadn't disclosed this because of a doctor–patient confidentiality agreement, when Viv and I went through all that medical testing. Then, in spite of Viv trying to tell me about Clair when she said she couldn't make amends, I hadn't probed her. All I would have had to do was ask, only I hadn't picked up on her lead. Instead, I'd cut her off with some pretentious feel-good crap.

When I got home and phoned him, he picked up immediately.

"What about Clair?" I asked.

"Your sister tried taking care of her. It didn't last."

"When was she born?"

"A few months after your dad died. I was in Vancouver then. We had her for a year together." His voice caught. "I was on training in Chilcotin when she left Clair in her crib and walked out the door." I heard the sound of children's laughter near him. "A neighbour found the baby a day later. Child services took her. I got her back two years ago."

"Did she see her again?"

"A few times. But with the incessant quitting, her DTs got so bad there were hallucinations. She thought things were crawling all over her. I couldn't bring Clair to visit anymore."

"I want to know her."

"Let me talk to Nahlah. I'll call you."

"Nick," I added before he hung up. "I haven't seen her in a long time. I have this sinking feeling. I don't know what to do."

"Been there done that," he said. "Unfortunately, I can't help you."

FORTY-SEVEN

I HADN'T REALIZED OUR walk up to *One Hundred Foot Line* would be my last visit with Theo. But the following week, when I looked through the glass doors, he wasn't there.

When Alejandro saw me, he waved me in impatiently before grabbing his leather coat adorned with multiple zippers.

"I like your kilt," I told him.

"Beethoven left those for you." He motioned to a bouquet and some books on the desk. "Said he had to catch a flight."

"He's gone?"

"Tell her 'until next time' is what he said. I offered to get you so he could say so himself, but I guess he didn't want to see you."

After Alejandro took off, I put my things down and unwrapped the paper cone. Ferns swayed like feathers when I lifted the bouquet from the desk. There was a single bird of paradise flower protruding from the middle like a lobster claw. I dumped my canister of gloves into a drawer and filled it at the water fountain, placing the arrangement beside my computer.

The books—*On the Track of Unknown Animals* and *The Book of Imaginary Beings*—had an antiquated feel to them. I flipped through the paperback volumes for a note, but found nothing but page after page about animals that were no longer, and animals that never were.

In the afternoon, an art history class from the university came through. I laid examples of works on paper out on the tables. I explained how light damages artifacts and I talked about climate control. Then I called Alejandro and asked him to take the students through storage.

Once the group was gone, I found *The Sorcerer of Hiva Oa* on the Internet. The man in the red cape and the women half hidden by the tree unsettled me. They had a secret they wouldn't reveal.

The bird in the bottom corner seemed almost an accidental detail. But Theo was right: it was the same bird as the one in our print.

I was analyzing *Nevermore* when Raven came charging in.

"You can't have flowers in here. What's this, Native porn?"

"Gauguin."

"Perv. He was into prepubescent girls, you know that?"

"Theo left today."

"You mean the old Jew?" She pulled up her leg warmers.

"He's Dutch."

"The Dutch can't be Jewish?"

"He's gone to the island where Gauguin lived. To find this bird." I pointed to the winged figure looming over the girl.

"Seriously? We see those everywhere when we go to Cuba. They're a nuisance."

The table Theo had occupied appeared ephemeral with the sun coming down on it through traces of airborne debris, minerals, skin cells.

The fern stems glistened. But the old man's absence cast a shadow through me. How much longer could I carry on in my glass rooms, locked between the wings of a revolving door with ghosts pushing it in a counter-clockwise direction? Theo would become another spectre in my collection, like my father, Liam, and Viv.

"What's up, paleface?"

"I'm tired."

"Ever check his arm?"

"Jesus, Raven."

"Actually, Jews don't believe in Jesus."

"He didn't discuss his personal history. What makes you think —"

"Trust me. Us minorities who hath suffered recognize one another."

IN LATE NOVEMBER, a warm wind like a coastal chinook blustered through the city, melting all the snow. Then there was an earthquake. It happened over lunch. Raven was showing me pictures of her renovations in the viewing room when it struck.

"Exterior's not so hot. We'll slap some ivy onto it. Ivy always improves buildings."

We paused at a rumbling that got noticeably louder as it gained momentum. The ground shook as though there was a subway beneath us. Baskets of pencils and magnifiers fell off the shelf above my desk. The glass panes made a squeaking, crunching sound.

Raven grabbed my arm, pulling me under the desk. Her

ankle socks glowed in the dark. The shaking went on for another minute.

"I think that was an earthquake," I said in the quiet seconds that followed.

"No shit."

We went over to the window. Below us, staff ran on the grass and up the hill, congregating around *One Hundred Foot Line*. Then came the sound of sirens.

"We should go."

"I'm not getting into any death-trap elevator. We're safer in here, the panes will fall toward the outside."

I worried about all the works I hadn't catalogued yet, that could be decimated without record. I worried about my sister.

THE NEXT DAY, I found out that the earthquake had caused structural shifting in some of the galleries. A couple of paintings fell from the walls. A fibreglass sculpture of a giant penis capsized. And during the night, the guard on duty informed his supervisor about a pungent odour coming from the room displaying *The Child's Dream*.

I was notified of the leak when I went there on my lunch break, hoping for a quiet half-hour. At the entranceway, I was hit by the strong smell of cat urine. Dwayne the security guard came up to me, pulling his respiratory mask onto his forehead and handing me one from his pocket, telling me the area was closed off for "disinfection."

I peered over his portly uniformed shoulders. At the end of the corridor, someone in a white spacesuit walked by, carrying vacuum tubing.

When I asked Dwayne what happened, he told me that the crack in the case went undetected at first. Like the systematic release from an IV drip, the embalming fluid left its chamber gradually, seeping beneath the floorboards. As the formaldehyde level went down inside the vitrine, the unicorn acquired the look of a drowning beast with its partially submerged head, and then, as the level of the liquid declined, that of a drenched, ghoulish creation.

The few visitors who entered the room left without delay, gasping and covering their mouths. The day guard assigned there was new. Being an art student himself and a great fan of Hirst, he had assumed the transformation of the work and the stench were a genius component of the installation.

He went home early, complaining of headache and nausea. It was closing time, so the control room didn't replace him. For three more hours the fractured case continued leaking, until no part of the animal could forestall decomposition. When the night guard came upon the grisly scene, he sounded the alarm.

"What will they do with the horse?" I asked Dwayne.

"Inseminate it," he said.

"Incinerate?"

"Yeah."

"How did you remove it?"

"Forklift."

"What about the gold?"

"Artist wants it back. He paid a contractor to saw off the hoofs and horn. They're in the cooler." He gestured a few feet away to a container sealed with a hazardous waste sticker. "You shoulda seen those people we played back on camera—man, were they trippin'."

Dwayne pulled his mask off, swinging it around on his index finger. "I have to ask you to please vacate, ma'am."

I went to the water court I'd visited with Henry as a teenager. A glass-bottomed pool lined with stone benches — an austere, minimalist space fitted with desolate statues. I sat on a slab, watching maintenance staff in orange work suits in the lower reception area passing back and forth like koi under a sheet of ice and coins.

Looking through the pool, I recalled my sister's extinction by degrees. The tremors, and her dilated pupils and clammy skin erupting into a rash as the poison left her body.

I wondered where Hirst got that pony. If wishes were horses, beggars would ride, our father used to say, meaning it's useless to wish. I wished for blackouts, for instance. A time when events could be sapped from my consciousness. How easy would it be to forget this whole mess for a while, with such episodes of amnesia at my disposition.

When would the past let up? Like the small bodies of birds Viv once drew, memories burrowed inside me without disintegrating. She existed in my mind as an abstraction now, as imprecise as her paintings and as lost to the present day as the unicorn. Like Theo's elusive cryptids, I thought I saw her vaguely, from distances, until I approached and realized it wasn't her.

FORTY-EIGHT

A FEW WEEKS BEFORE Christmas, Constance wanted to visit Rideau Hall. It was one of the only city parks she approved of, with its rich grounds and deviating pathways. Her favourite spot was the garden with a large, circular fountain and a trellis lane for roses.

Through the night, a pillowy snow had fallen, muffling sound. The streets were quiet. When I picked her up in the early morning, she had Mira under one arm. The dog wore a fuchsia cap with earflaps.

There was nobody else around as we passed through the groves, walking toward the Governor General's residence where, all those winters past, there had been a skating rink and sleigh rides. Now it was as if we were walking through one of my father's colourless canvases.

The building was closed. I wiped the snow off a picnic table and we sat in the open parkland. Mira pawed at my mother until she lifted her from the tabletop and tucked her under the hem of her coat, where she fell asleep.

"Remember your raccoon fur, Mom?" She'd given it to Goodwill when she emptied the closets of Henry's clothing, saying it was too heavy. "Viv wore it here once. She was like a queen in it."

Constance pulled up the collar of her parka. "It's been years. Why have you not spread your father's ashes?"

"I will." I'd kept the urn on my kitchen windowsill, with a view to the wild gardens of the back lane.

My mother rubbed her hands together to keep warm. "I'll email you *les numéros de téléphone*. Are you sure you won't come for a few days?"

"Raven and Zach invited me over."

I sensed her watching me, but I kept staring straight ahead. I knew what was coming. Take a holiday. Relax. Stop waiting. Viv had been missing for close to three months.

"She could be dead," I said. "She needed medical treatment."

"Don't be absurd."

"Unidentifiable bodies are always turning up."

"Just because she is not present does not mean anything."

"We'd have heard from her by now. For money."

"You can't prove it." Her reaction was like that of a child. "She's fine."

Con told me then that she allowed herself ten minutes at the start of each day to think about Viv. Ten minutes. No more. Every day. And one email per week, on Sundays. No matter where she was. Even if she was writing to an unused or terminated account.

Mira awoke and whimpered. She gave the dog a hard, heart-shaped biscuit, breaking it into bits that Mira licked from her hand. When I told her I'd take the little mongrel on a trial basis, she gave me one of her scintillating smiles.

The sky was the colour of my ageing mother's hair. Someone flew a red kite. As it soared and glided, I followed the invisible line downward, across the field where there should have been the runner. But there was no one. When I looked back up again, the bright form had vanished behind the clouds. It might not even have been there in the first place.

THE CALL CAME not long after Constance flew away for good.

It was a sunshiny Saturday morning and I sat at the kitchen table with the newspaper and coffee, Mira nuzzling my feet. Waxwings chirped and faint voices filled the air through my closed windows as families populated the streets, pulling children on toboggans, ornamenting their yards with snowmen.

I didn't recognize the caller ID. The man said he was Officer Quinn, but I couldn't place him.

"Did we meet? This is about my sister, right?"

"You completed a report with us."

"And you wouldn't file it. Did you find her?"

"You said she had a paintbrush tattoo on her left shoulder blade."

"Right."

"You should sit. Are you?"

"Yes."

"We have a body that fits the general description you gave us. We couldn't get a match through fingerprints or dentals."

"A dead body?" I'd played this scenario out a hundred times already. I should have been prepared, but I wasn't.

"It's up to you whether you want to come down. We can keep trying to ID her, but it might take time."

"I thought this just happened on TV."

"Afraid not. I'm here till six. Forensic Pathology Unit, general campus of the Ottawa Hospital. Need the address?"

"I know it. She's been there."

I hung up and readied myself at a snail-like pace, overcome by an inexplicable drowsiness. You're getting dressed up for your dead sister, I thought. If you think it's her, it won't be her; if you don't think it's her, it will be.

A PUG-FACED WOMAN with a beehive sat behind the Plexiglas entrance desk. She wore a bubble-gum-pink turtleneck that hurt my eyes. She buzzed me through and checked my belongings. Her tired, worn-out voice brought to mind the Dial-a-Bottle lady's voice. Maybe she had two jobs.

Officer Quinn appeared and shook my hand and led me into the fridge with its wall of steel units, not dissimilar to the shelving system we had for precious metals at work. A hospital morgue staff member greeted me with a subdued nod. He wore a white lab coat just like the one I put on every day at the Gallery. Probably his deep pockets were filled with prohibited snacks, too.

"She had no personal effects on her. There's only the tattoo."

It addled me, how swiftly the morgue employee opened the drawer then—not giving me any time to change my mind. It must have been a tried-and-tested method, pulling the body out fast like tearing an adhesive bandage off a wound.

She was in more decent shape than I'd expected. It was obvious she'd once been beautiful. Her seaweed-like hair was as blond as Viv's. Her waxy skin was almost transparent, but her nose was raw and red, as if she had a cold. Even through the Vaseline you could see the pipe burns on her lips. Under her nearly invisible eyebrows, her lids were closed. Quinn confirmed her eyes were an aqua blue.

The face wasn't Viv's and I told him so.

He touched my arm. "Take your time. People don't look the same in death."

"It's not her."

"You're sure? You haven't seen the tattoo." He pulled some photos from a folder, of a melted black flower on a bluish-white shoulder.

"That's a rose." *You fucking asshole.*

"Cheap tattoos are prone to smudging."

"It's not my sister." I glanced at the girl once more. She seemed bloated to me now, an obscene corpse.

"This is traumatic. Families misidentify."

"Vivienne has a squiggly scar on her cheekbone," I retaliated. "I forgot to put that on the form." I tugged on the skin of my cheek for good measure. Then I was at the door and he was behind me. "I could sue you for putting me through this," I told him. "Please don't call again unless you find her."

When I turned back to confront him, he was scribbling something in his idiotic notebook.

"What if no one claims her?" I added.

"She'll be moved to the PFPU — the Provincial Forensic Pathology Unit — for longer-term storage until she's ID'd and claimed for disposition."

"What if you can't identify her?"

"Depending on the circumstances of the death, the coroner might retain a decedent for years until we ID them."

"But what if no one claims her even then?"

"If no one comes forward to claim the body and no next of kin, neighbour, or friend is willing to accept financial responsibility to bury her, the municipality where she died would bury her."

"How did she die?"

"Toxicology found enough alcohol and methamphetamine in her system to kill a horse."

I pictured a horse galloping across her body. My brain wasn't working right.

"Where did you find her?"

"Snowbank."

I'd read somewhere that when dying of hypothermia, the last sensation was one of warmth. At least there was that.

As I FILLED out paperwork in the waiting area, the antiseptic smell of the body fridge wouldn't dissipate, as though it had leached into me.

I ran to the washrooms and locked myself in a stall, hyperventilating. My airway was closing off.

"Are you okay?" The receptionist knocked on the door.

I was unable to speak more than a short word. "Ffff-ine." I searched for my Ventolin. I couldn't find it. There was oxygen all around me, yet I couldn't get enough air. The muscles in my neck were stiffening. My fingertips and mouth started tingling. I was breathing too deeply, taking too long for an inhalation offering no air, no relief, a stunted exhale. The pain in my shoulders was acute.

"Are you having a panic attack?" the receptionist asked, unfazed.

"Nnn-nnn-nnno, asth-ma," I sputtered, pursing my lips and grabbing my throat before everything went black.

When I came to, my head was in her lap and the stall door was open. She'd crawled under and had my inhaler in her hand. She shook it and brought it to my mouth. I pushed it away. "Your lips aren't blue anymore," she told me. "But I'm taking you to the Emerg wing, it's not far."

"I'm fine," I said, sitting up.

"Are you sure?"

"This happens. I'm all right."

She assisted me with my coat and helped me to the lobby. Officer Quinn was already with another family. I thanked her and walked slowly across the icy parking lot to the old Buick.

I went home and lay down, feeling as if I'd been punched in the chest. Barely four-thirty, it was already dark outside.

What did it matter that the mermaid-like girl in the morgue wasn't Vivienne? She was the prelude to my sister's own death song, whether in one year or two. What other outcome could there be?

Old Vespers glowed on my nightstand. I picked up the chunk of moonstone, missing three of his four limbs from the times I'd dropped him through the years. The alligator still gave off an astonishing incandescence. I thought he would have an expiry date and decompose like plastic toys. It must be that something that sacred and ancient, made from solidified rays of moon, retained its afterglow.

FORTY-NINE

I WAITED FOR NICK to phone. I suspected he never would. Yet I couldn't shake this urgency to see Viv's daughter. The child's face would not leave my mind.

He didn't answer my calls, so I sent texts. I emailed and messaged him on Facebook, cyberstalking him until he got back to me, reluctantly suggesting I could find them the following Sunday at Magnolia Park, where the kids liked to go sledding.

On the day of our meeting, I stopped off at Mrs. Tiggy Winkle's, thoughtlessly plucking a stuffed wallaby from a shelf for Amir. Then I agonized over a gift for Clair, finally settling on a Winnie-the-Pooh bear along with A. A. Milne's collected works.

I reached the downtown park as bells rang out from a nearby church tower, playing "Ave Maria."

"Jesus Christ is born!" a cadaverous man in a Repent to Christ sandwich board shouted at passersby. "Only Jesus can save you from damnation!"

Walking down a lane of twisting, grey-barked trees, I spotted them by an open-topped fort — Clair in the same brown snowsuit, darting in and out of the whiteness, and Nick in an army parka, punching his gloved hands together to keep warm before pressing more snow onto the walls. As I approached, he saw me and jogged over.

"Listen, Edith," he said after greeting me. He removed his sunglasses, holding back as though he was thinking twice about something. Fine-spun ice filaments extended from his eyebrows and eyelashes. "Nahlah thinks you'll get attached."

"And if I do?"

"I move around with work. There's no telling how long we'll be here."

"I'll hop on a plane, then." I took off my toque and headed in Clair's direction.

"Hold up a sec." He rushed to step in front of me with his imploring oceanic eyes. "She's also worried you'll say something."

"She doesn't know about Viv, then." I was confirming more than asking.

"She has no memory of her and we haven't told her. She's too young."

We watched Clair somersaulting in the snow. I could hear his teeth clattering. "I won't say anything. But how can you be sure she can't remember her own mother?"

"She gets attached fast."

"She's my family too."

He decompressed a bit then. "You're right. I apologize."

I went over to where Clair now sat on a snow seat at a snow table, making snow cups from a miniature beach bucket. She huffed with concentration.

"Hi," I said, stepping into her line of sight. She took stock of me, undisturbed, and continued with her enterprise. "Can I sit with you?"

"It's Edith, sweetie." Nick came up beside us, but she ignored him.

"Can you pass the scooper?" she asked in a small, hoarse voice, looking up at me again without blinking.

I knelt for a yellow shovel, placing it in her outstretched mitten. "This is a super-funky fort."

"It's going to melt," she replied.

"Not for a while, though, right?"

She patted the snow cup and dropped the shovel, sniffling. Then, with a mischievous grin, she pushed herself up, ran a circle around the fort, and gave my leg a punch. "You're it!"

I chased leisurely after her, letting myself slip and fall. When I opened my eyes, she was bent over my face, her gold ropes of hair brushing my cheeks.

I raised myself onto my elbows. "So, Clair Angel, can you make snow angels?"

She gave a dry, crackling squeal as she dropped down beside me and fanned out her arms and legs. "This one's Amir." She rolled over to an unspoiled snow patch. "This one's Momma!"

Of course she remembered her mother. If only in an indiscernible way. Like a fresco preserved deep in the ground, the memories were surely there, waiting to be unearthed.

She pulled me up by my coat, leading me back to the snow table. I sat with her while Nick crossed the park for hot chocolate and Beaver Tails.

"I brought you something," I said, retrieving the bear and the book from my bag.

"Pooh!" she trilled.

"You like him?"

"I like Piglet better." She stationed the animal in her lap, placing his paws on the table, before she flipped through the pages with her red-mittened hands. Chewing on a hood string, she slid over to me and scampered onto my knee. "Read!" she cried, repositioning the bear.

I slipped my arm around her waist to hold her warm little body in place. Through her snowsuit, I could feel her belly moving in and out, in and out. She was so small. So trusting. I wanted to protect her. Even in her whirr of activity there was a serene aspect about Clair that allayed my fears.

I dragged the book over and she dropped a mitt onto an illustration of Winnie-the-Pooh in a green bed. A whopping tusked elephant with a pot of honey floated above the sleeping bear. I went to the start of the story and read.

IN WHICH PIGLET MEETS A HEFFALUMP

One day, when Christopher Robin and Winnie-the-Pooh and Piglet were all talking together, Christopher Robin finished the mouthful he was eating and said carelessly: "I saw a Heffalump today, Piglet."

"What was it doing?" asked Piglet.

"Just lumping along," said Christopher Robin. "I don't think it saw me."

"I saw one once," said Piglet. "At least, I think I did," he said. "Only perhaps it wasn't."

"So did I," said Pooh, wondering what a Heffalump was like.

"You don't often see them," said Christopher Robin carelessly.

"Not now," said Piglet.

"Not at this time of year," said Pooh.

Then they all talked about something else, until it was time for Pooh and Piglet to go home together.

Clair listened attentively, resting her head on my chest and kicking her boots back and forth between my legs. Nick returned with our hot drinks and the steaming, flat doughnuts coated in sugar and cinnamon. After a bite and a gulp she was off again, the heavy book sliding from the slick table onto the ground as she scooted back into the fort.

"I should know better than to bring a book. My dad drowned me in books when we were kids. It stressed me out," I told Nick.

"Riiiiiight. Your sister found that a riot. Wasn't your furniture made from books?"

"I had a book chair and book steps up to my bed."

"Gotta give your dad points for originality." Nick brushed some of the topping off his doughnut before taking a bite, his knees practically to his chin on the snow chair.

"How did you and Nahlah meet?" I asked.

"Pilates."

I laughed at the thought of Nick Angel doing Pilates.

"What's so funny?" He looked amused. "I can hold the plank longer than anyone. Still can't sit cross-legged, but I'm working on it."

I was glad for him. He deserved a redo.

"She's a health nut," he added. "Into all that holistic mumbo-jumbo." He wiped his sugary fingers on his jeans. "How about you?"

"There was someone, but . . ." I still couldn't articulate about Liam.

"The right guy will find you," he said, patting my knee.

I hadn't thought of it like that before. I believed I was the one who'd eternally be searching.

I pulled the red-necked wallaby from my bag. "For Amir," I said.

He thanked me, stuffing it down the front of his coat so that the wallaby's head stuck out.

"I need to spend time with her. It's important."

"We'll sort something out," he said, thumping his combat boots together to get his circulation going. "She has a lot of problems," he added.

"Like what?"

"She had breathing and feeding issues when she was born. Now it's her digestion. She's already had two operations. She gets chronic pain. Sometimes she's scared to eat. I gave her a pill today so she could have a treat with you."

Clair whirled around the white walls, oblivious to us. This living part of my sister. My elfin niece humming and chattering to herself.

"She has learning disabilities. You're seeing her on a good day. She hasn't got the alphabet down yet. She can't read or write. She wets her bed and has to wear diapers."

"But once she feels better, this will all happen, like, presto, right?"

"Out of nowhere she'll hit and punch us. She can't tie her shoes or do up buttons or zippers. Some things may not develop. She was in foster care for two years and your sister wasn't in top form when she was pregnant. But it's pointless to torture myself over what caused this."

The church bells started ringing once more. Through the magnolia branches was the great sledding slope. Bodies coasted down on black inner tubes, their screams of delight travelling through the music of the bells.

When Nick waved to Clair, she skipped over to us. He leaned forward so she could squeeze the wallaby's face. "Roo Roo," she cooed, adding, "Daddy, let's go sliding!" She jumped around and yanked on his sleeve.

"Let me take her," I told him as we stood up.

Clair wrapped herself around my leg and Nick studied his daughter. "This is rare. She's not usually keen on strangers."

He knelt down, kissing Clair on her rosy cheek. He zipped her coat up to her neck, rewrapped her scarf, and adjusted her toque and mittens. "You two go ahead," he said, patting the walls of the fort. "I'll keep vigil from our stronghold."

I took my niece's hand in mine and we started for the hill.

FIFTY

THE GALLERY'S SPECTACULAR CHRISTMAS fir went up again.

Each year the colossal tree reached its destination like an emerald animal on an altar, and the Gallery made a big production of the unveiling. I walked in as it arrived on its flatbed truck, bound by thick cords. Traffic cops held back rush-hour streams while the driver went over the curb and onto the plaza, the boughs brushing snow from *Maman's* legs where a crew waited to drag the old conifer in on its side, up the ramp and into the Great Hall dome.

It took a day to hoist it up with wires and clamps. Overnight, workers climbed ladders, decorating it with nooses of glittering lights and opaline balls larger than human heads. I imagined lumberjacks hunting nearby townships for the oldest, most majestic balsam fir, piercing the heart with a spike. It would be taken down the morning after New Year's Day to be disposed of in a landfill, dragged out of the glass dome and down the ramp, leaving a trail of flat green needles behind.

During the lighting ceremony, musicians wearing Santa Claus hats played carols, signalling the holidays. I went up close to the giant fir, expecting my lungs to open. But the tree had no scent.

I drank eggnog and watched Raven beaming with Zach, her belly growing beneath her spangled dress. She hadn't said a word until just before the party, even though for the last month I'd suspected. I wasn't upset that my closest friend hadn't let me in on her news earlier. For all her no-nonsense ways, Raven was superstitious about things going wrong. Afflictions and maladies, or worse.

When she motioned me over, for a moment I pictured Liam and me standing with them, the four of us in our prime. *Beatific Couples*, the painting would be called.

Soon after, I left the party.

Over my vacation, I took nightly strolls in the snow, dragging an unresponsive Mira along on my outings. Often I put her in the hood of my anorak. From the sidewalk we observed festive families around tables, their door-ways framed in twinkling bulbs, their houses lit up like cathedrals.

I nailed a wreath to the wall to perk up my interior and broiled delicacies including fish cheeks. The scent of paperwhites infused the apartment. I spent time reading and standing at the window. The family across the alley had moved away and the rooms were gloomy and bare.

On Christmas Day, I visited Raven and Zach. They gave me a replica of a Pantin salamander—an 1870s paperweight from a glassworks in Pantin, near Paris. There were only twelve known originals in the world. Recently, one had sold at a UK auction for $66,000. Within its glass dome, the bottle-green amphibian rested on sandy ground near a desert flower. Its skin pattern filigreed with gold entranced me. According to mythology, the salamander was associated with fire and resided in the glass-blower's furnace. It travelled back and forth to the flaming underworld, returning unscathed.

I brought Raven and Zach a yule log and a Jolly Jumper. Their euphoria drained me and I went home early, wishing an avalanche would clear my mind of all its debris. Just before Christmas I'd received a polite postcard from Chile, wishing me happy holidays. One last tangible trace of Liam. I inhaled deeply from it but, like the fir at the Gallery, the paper smelled of nothing.

In the early New Year, I recalled Theo telling me to go to the Museum of Nature. Ask for Jonathan in ichthyology, he'd said. For lack of anything better to do, I made an appointment.

When I spoke to Jonathan by phone, he recommended I wait in the main entranceway of the building. Children ran everywhere, their shouts resounding around me. I distanced myself from them, examining a moose mosaic on the floor, thinking back to that day with Henry at the Royal Ontario Museum, when we stood beneath the heavenly dome. How I was merrily ignorant then, not knowing there would come a time when I wouldn't revere and champion my father.

I'd gone rigid with these thoughts when Jonathan appeared, seemingly out of nowhere. He was maybe a few years older than me. He wore high-top sneakers and a T-shirt with a *Tyrannosaurus rex* on it. His face was bristly and his thick brown hair uncombed, as if he had better things to do with his time.

He shook my hand enthusiastically. "You must be Edith. I see you've met Ted." He pointed to the moose. "Sorry to keep you waiting, right this way." He offered me a Visitor sticker and led me through a double set of doors marked Staff Only.

We entered a clean, sterile lab. He tossed some papers on a desk covered in binders and cups, with rubber dinosaurs glued along the top of the computer monitor.

"You're here for the coelacanth, right?"

"I'm not sure."

"No worries, right this way. I know what he wants you to see." He patted his pockets for a swipe card. We walked down a hospital-like hallway and entered another lab marked Wet Specimens. "Most of our collections are off-site. Lucky for you, this critter was recently on display."

In the lab, some students sat around a counter covered in jars of dead mammals, deep in discussion. Jonathan steered me toward a stainless steel tank on wheels. He pulled back the thick cloth that was covering the front, revealing a window to the gargantuan fish inside.

"Ta-dah! Presenting the darling of cryptozoology." He slapped the tank. "This is one of the oldest fish in the world. A living fossil from the Devonian period. More specifically, a coelacanth in an ethanol bath."

"Devonian," I muttered, transfixed by the mammoth creature. "When was that?"

"Three hundred and fifty million years ago. Way before dinosaurs. He's their ancestor, like a great-great-grandfather."

The *seelakanth* was a primeval-looking fish from marshy lore. It was at least five feet long and looked to weigh a couple of hundred pounds. Rather than the soft exterior of fish I knew, it had an armour-plated outside consisting of shale-like scales as large as guitar picks, speckled with silver flecks. Its fins were more like arms and legs, and it had a big, wary eye. Its mouth was agape, revealing sharp teeth.

"Is it real?" I asked.

Jonathan nodded. "Extinct and eluding us for sixty-five million years, until a fisherman trawled one off the coast of South Africa in 1938." He knelt so that he was level with the fish.

"How many are there?" I leaned in closer to the peculiar fins.

"Less than five hundred. After lasting millions of years, they're headed for the abyss of mass extinction again," he said, his voice thickening. As I stared into the milky-white marble eye, Jonathan added, "They need constant water pressure around them. When they're brought to the surface, they die, turning from indigo to slate grey."

It was a bewitching fish extricated from primitive art. A mirage.

Jonathan took a cloth from the counter, wiping his fingerprints off the glass. Then he asked if I wanted to get a coffee.

We went by the gift shop. In the window a pyramid of sea monkeys was displayed, each kit stamped with the Instant Life! insignia. I hadn't seen any in ages.

"My sister and I used to buy these," I told him.

"Same here. Retro, hey? They're a big hit."

"What were they, tadpoles?"

"Brine shrimp in a state of suspended animation."

"Ours didn't live long."

"Ours neither."

Still, the aquarium pets were magical to me back then, so I entered the shop to buy one for Clair. Although they were spending the holidays with Nahlah's family in Montreal, I was already planning another visit with my niece.

The coffee in the canteen poured brownish clear. We sat at a table near some lively camps of children. Jonathan watched them with a mirthful look on his face.

"They're here for the planetarium show," he explained.

"Do you always work over the holidays?" I asked.

He nodded. "It's fun to tour the kids around this time of year. I don't get much accomplished." With his guileless brown eyes, he was like a big kid himself.

I noticed he had dry, chapped hands. "I have the perfect cream for that," I told him.

"Yeah? I've tried everything." He laced his fingers together, then asked, "How do you know Theo, anyway?"

"I work in the National Gallery's viewing room. He came in to study some prints. You?"

"He advised me for my thesis on the thylacine. Did he tell you about it?"

"I don't think so."

"Check out the archival footage on YouTube. Type in 'last Tasmanian tiger, thylacine, 1933.' It died of exposure in the zoo three years after that film."

"So Theo was your professor?"

He looked up at the ceiling as though he was trying to determine how much information to disclose. "And I worked with his wife here. Saskia. She was our librarian."

"Theo didn't mention her."

"She passed away a few years ago. Brain tumour. I owe them both a lot."

"Did they have children?"

"No, no." He paused before going on. "His family was in the Amsterdam diamond trade." There was a malaise in his voice as he spoke.

"He said they were merchants of some sort," I told him.

"He didn't speak of it. But he would get in these moods. It was hard on Saskia."

"Was he —"

"Not him, his family. All of them. His parents, two sisters, a brother. He went out to buy bread, and when he came home, the door to the house was open. A chair was overturned. The rest was exactly the same, except everyone was gone. The neighbours — a doctor and his wife — hid him. Not for long, the war was almost over. He slept on a slab of cement in the attic, in case soldiers fired at the ceiling. Never saw them again."

"I wish I'd known."

"Better you didn't. He wouldn't have wanted you to."

"I hope he's doing well on that island."

Jonathan seemed puzzled.

"Where he went to find his bird," I went on. "Hiva Oa."

"The koao? Funding for that was cut. Grant committees said his work was founded on too much circumstantial evidence."

"I guess he went on his own dime," I said. "He told me goodbye in November."

Jonathan shook his head. "Theo's travels ended years ago. He had bypass surgery in November. There was a stroke. He's in a home now."

AFTER MY VISIT with Jonathan, I stayed up past midnight, reading about Theo on the Web. Dated Internet biographies stated that he was a renowned zoologist who conducted research in the most inaccessible habitats of Vietnam, Africa, and South America. The only personal information I found was that he'd emigrated from Holland in the 1960s with his wife, and that he taught zoology at the University of Toronto, where he lived for many years.

There was just one picture of him. In it, he looked to be in his early thirties. He wore a narrow suit and thin tie. His hands were in his pockets and he leaned against the bars of a cage with a pipe sticking out of his mouth. Behind him to the left was the okapi, with its long, tapered face and butterfly ears. Like Theo's, its enormous eyes were on the camera. Theo's furrowed brow, his untamed hair and intense gaze gave him the presence of a brooding artist. The younger Theo had been what Constance called *un beau laid*—a person of ugly beauty whose disproportioned features made him alluring.

Online there were dozens of articles with his name on them, about quests for exterminated species and species discovered over the last fifty years. Then I came across Bernard Heuvelmans, who wrote one of the books Theo had given me. Heuvelmans was a Belgian-French zoologist who became known as the father of cryptozoology. I wondered if he'd mentored Theo; Holland being adjacent to Belgium, where Heuvelmans had studied.

On the Track of Unknown Animals was reputed to be one of the most influential works in the field. Like Theo, Heuvelmans had searched the world's oceans and forests for animals known to local people but unknown to science. Skeptics called his belief in cryptids outrageous, but he held to his convictions until he died.

"Cryptozoological research should be actuated by two major forces," Heuvelmans said, "patience and passion." He founded the International Society of Cryptozoology in Washington, DC. But it was now defunct.

"There are lost worlds everywhere," Heuvelmans also said.

I CHECKED MY email. There were no messages. I scanned the weather forecasts for Ovalle, Hiva Oa, and Florida. All were hot and sunny.

I envisioned myself following Liam all my life, leagues behind him, unnoticed, floundering for him inside his vast landscapes studded with crevices and meandering rivers. I envisioned seeing Viv in his eyes.

I resisted writing to tell him that the open-air amphitheatre where we used to meet had been roped off and would be dug up in the spring—the grass and trees, the curved stone seats with a view onto the bluffs. Since the earthquake, the entire area was deemed unsafe. Even *One Hundred Foot Line* would be moved once the ground thawed.

Before going to sleep I googled the thylacine. Jonathan had described it as wolflike with a straight, stiff tail and a pouch opening to the rear of its body. What the choppy footage showed was a graceful and otherworldly animal with the facial traits of a small kangaroo and the stripes of a tiger on its back and hind legs.

When the black-and-white film opened, the thylacine gave a dramatic, toothy yawn. For an instant its jaw seemed to come unhinged, so concealed was its face by its gaping mouth. The animal paced in its cramped concrete and wire enclosure. It held a piece of meat down with its paws, tearing at it. It rested in the sun, lying atop a crack extending the length of the ground, and did more pacing, momentarily looking like a plain old dog, almost smiling.

The image of the last living thylacine that died from neglect in the zoo stayed with me, replaying in my head as if on a reel, like the voices in *Forty-Part Motet*.

The film was too exposed—the animal and its surroundings at times whited out completely in some areas, erased then reappearing and disappearing altogether.

FIFTY-ONE

VIV FLOATED THROUGH MY sleep in a birchbark canoe, all decked out in a glitz dress. I swam up to her, but she peeled my fingers off the rim of the vessel. When she smiled and said *Don't worry, little one*, I saw a hole in her throat. Then she rose and danced the cancan. A monstrous snake emerged from the water, a hairy, toothy serpent with red eyes. It bit Viv's head off and spat it out. Her white plaster-cast death mask bobbed up and down like a buoy in the black waves, singing *Que sera, sera* while I drowned.

Something smacked against the window with a *kowww kowww*, startling me from the nightmare. I opened the curtains. A crow lay in the snow, stunned but breathing.

As the sun crept across the blanketed yards, the snow stole colour from its light sources like a Vermeer—purplish off the clouds, intermingled with streaks of yellow and red from the mountain ash berries. The crow flew off, leaving an indentation of feathers.

It was my first day back at work and I went in early.

Passing the taiga garden, I asked a security guard for a cigarette. I sat on a powdery ledge and smoked it in requiem for Theo. All morning I felt seasick from the cigarette and the dream.

There was a stack of botanical studies to get through. With precision, I noted details—accession number, object name, maker, title, date, culture, materials, and measurements—in the vaults. Then I entered what was outstanding at my desk: legal status, home location, current location, valuation, activities, authorities, and on and on. But I just didn't care anymore, about dandelions and bramble. In the grand scheme, their insignificance was blatant.

The librarian had loaned me a tape player. I'd had it on my desk for weeks. I fished through my bag for the cassette Con had given me, and inserted it into the slot. When I hit Play, the machine's mechanisms squeaked and there was a granular hissing.

The quality of sound wasn't great. But I made out the muffled voices of my young parents right away. *"Grand sourire, ma fille!"* and "Attagirl!"

Then came a pitter-patter of feet and a little voice—mine. "Reeeeee…fffeeeee…rrreeeeee…fffeeeeee…" in quick succession.

"Elbow, elbow, wrist, wrist," Con instructed.

"Say it slower, Edith." Henry spoke over our mother. "Like this: *Preee-sennn-tiiinnng…Vivieeennnne!*"

"Prrreee fffeee prrreee fffeeeee preeeee fffveee ffvvvee fvvveeeee vvveeee Veeee!"

"Maman, put the wings on me," Viv demanded.

"Vivienne, don't pull your sister's arm so hard."

"C'mere, sis, watch this. I'll flutter away flut flutter awayyy…"

I could hear Viv skipping around barefoot. Then a jingling—our father playing a tambourine. Dropping the musical instrument to tickle us. Viv and I shrieking like crazy.

"Henri, enough!"

"Fffffeeee bye-bye ffffffffveeee bye-bye fvvveeeee Vvvvveeeee!" I started up again. I guessed I was maybe two. It was all I kept saying till someone pressed the Stop button, probably Con.

I pulled the cassette out of the machine. I didn't want the player to eat the tape. I had no recollection of us that small, or of me enunciating some of my first words with my sister. The black plastic rectangle was my memento. If I took proper care of the artifact, it would outlive us like a heart in a reliquary.

I PACED THE office halls. Alejandro and Raven were off for another week, and the staff quarters were empty. I continued feeling sorry for myself through lunch, eating a spongy ham sandwich until a *ding dong* notification alerted me to an email from Jonathan Cole. *Just wanted to see how you're doing,* the message read. It was invasive to have someone inquire after me like that. Even though we'd exchanged contact information, I hadn't expected to hear from him again.

On a whim, in my bleak mood, I responded. *Fine thanks. I'd like to see Theo.*

Jonathan's reply was instantaneous. He'd be going to Theo's later in the afternoon and I could accompany him then. It crossed my mind that he was instigating the visit for my sake, which further aggravated me.

He pulled up at the Gallery in a Smurf-blue Smart car.

When I squeezed into it, he had a coffee waiting for me.

On the drive to Sunnybrook Lodge, he updated me on Theo's condition, assuring me that he was making progress. He could sit in a wheelchair and move his right arm and leg. He wasn't speaking, but he was writing. That Theo had lost his speech didn't deter Jonathan. His grandmother had two good years after her stroke, he told me.

"I watched the thylacine on YouTube last night," I said as we parked. "What happens when you catch your species?"

"It's not a cryptid once it's scientifically accepted."

"And the animal?"

"It becomes a conservation problem nobody wants to deal with." He reached into the back for his gloves. "But I didn't have that issue. Neither did Theo." His face was uncomfortably close to mine in the cartoon car. I made the move to open my door when he added, "Because we never found what we were trailing."

Despite its upbeat name, Sunnybrook wasn't much different from Mechanicsville's low-income housing. The roof was in disrepair, windows were cracked, and paint peeled off the building's exterior. Inside, the air was oppressive and damp. We signed in for visiting hour that went until five o'clock. After that, meals were served, Jonathan said. Most residents were in bed by eight.

Theo was in the high-needs wing. We passed through a light green hall jazzed up with motivational posters. A kitten dangling by its claw hooked into a branch: *Hang In There!* A beaver resting on a log: *I'm not procrastinating, I'm waiting for divine inspiration.* A snapshot of the sky with *I am not afraid, I was born to do this* scrawled across it.

There were no seniors milling about. Other than the sound coming from TVs in rooms where doors were open a crack, the atmosphere was glum.

I tried not to breathe in the sickly-sweet odour of decaying flowers and apple juice mixed with stale smoke and diapers. Where doors were open, nurses smiled at us. We seemed to be the only visitors.

"It's busier on weekends," Jonathan told me. "Most folks can't get away from work this early." The last person I'd heard use the word *folks* was my father. There was something hokey about Jonathan, as if he came from the olden days.

I stopped him before the common area. "He doesn't need to know I'm here," I said, taking a chair against the back wall when we entered the room. I respected Theo's dignity too much. I wanted to see him without disconcerting him.

"Fair enough. Maybe next time," he said affably before leaving me there.

Someone had already wheeled Theo in. He sat by the bay window above the river pathway where joggers ran with dogs and strollers on a salted path of packed-down snow. Even with a thick wool sweater over his shoulders, he didn't look so big anymore. I didn't like seeing him confined in this ghastly place — and it was ghastly, however much Jonathan raved about the staff.

I hardly knew a thing about him, other than that he studied animals people thought were extinct. Yet believing he'd been out there on his island had brought me peace of mind. At that point, I understood my attachment to Theo, who, on blind faith, brought the dead back to life by seeking proof of their existence out in a lonely and far-off wilderness. He'd given me what nobody else had: hope. So what if it was delusional or unrealistic? Theo was the firefly in the pitch-dark lairs where I searched for Viv. How many people like this did we come across in a lifetime?

Jonathan sat by him in an easygoing, natural way. I only half made out his words as he gave him news on recent discoveries in the animal kingdom. Not once did Theo's head move. But Jonathan touched his arm frequently, and made a point of laughing. Sometimes he pulled a tissue from his pocket and dabbed at Theo's eyes.

Later, the nurse came over. She spoke to Jonathan like they were friends. Jonathan gave her the *National Geographic* he'd been reading from.

Then he walked over to me and extended a hand for me to stand, as though we were in a dance hall or something. "A round of chess?" he asked.

"I'd like to go," I told him as I watched Theo. The nurse sat beside him now, chit-chatting. "Where did they put his okapi cane?"

"It's hanging on his door. He just sees this as a setback," Jonathan said. "Thinks he'll walk out of here and resume tracking die-offs."

Jonathan drove me home with more stories of the thylacine and his voyages to the Australian outback. Then—I sensed he added this bit of information for my benefit—he told me he was a homebody, and was relieved to be done with fieldwork.

"Not me. I want to travel," I said, realizing it was true.

Theo had privileged me with a picture of the greater world, the journeys and expeditions that were possible.

FIFTY-TWO

WITHIN A FEW DAYS, Jonathan phoned to ask me out for dinner.

"Like a date?"

"Affirmative. Or an un-date if you fancy."

"Why not," I told him, feeling neutral about it.

When the designated night came, I didn't primp. Had it been Liam, the beautifying rituals would have taken hours. With Jonathan, I put on a fresh sweater and jeans just before he got there, washing my face, combing my hair, and doing up my eyes in under five minutes. I was engrossed in a reality TV show and was cranky that I couldn't stay in and watch with a box of strawberry Passion Flakies, especially on such a cold night. Seeing the farcical Smart car pull up through a crack in the curtains, I cursed myself for having said yes.

When I opened the door, Mira went wild. She jumped onto Jonathan's leg and fell, rolling over and repeating her attack a dozen times, yipping and growling.

Under his coat I could see he'd dressed up for the occasion. He wore jeans but had on a canary yellow shirt and a matching tie.

"You should harness her into wind energy." Jonathan blocked Mira with his slushy sneaker as he proffered a complicated bouquet of pine cones and evergreen interspersed with carnations and a sprig of mistletoe. Christmas was over. He'd probably got them on clearance.

"I had that one special made. To prolong the best time of year," he said, pleased with himself.

I grabbed the water jug from the fridge and tossed the arrangement into it, hastily zipping up my coat and leaving Mira there whining as I rushed us out.

He moved ahead of me to open my door first. The car tottered along until we pulled into the lot of a downtown restaurant covered with parrots, sombreros, and palm trees, called Maria Guadalupe's Cantina. The windows were boarded up with plywood, but the lot was full. Passing it vacant in the daytime, I'd always assumed the place was out of business.

He rushed around to open my door again, bending his arm for me to slide my hand through it. I did so only because the ground was icy.

The restaurant was loud and crowded and colourful, as if a rainbow had detonated inside. After spending the holiday in isolation, the fiesta was daunting.

Jonathan was helping me with my coat when a woman resembling Frida Kahlo accosted us. We followed her swooshing, richly dyed skirt to a reserved table by a tile fountain. He ordered margaritas while I studied the mural behind him, struggling to make small talk.

"How did you get into cryptozoology?" I asked over the

sound of mariachis tuning up nearby.

"My dad's an entomologist. He found a new bee species in the nineties, but it died out within a year." He dumped some salt onto his fruity drink before tilting it toward mine. "He taught me to see beyond what's there." His smile was frank. It bewildered me that he didn't give off a fraught vibe. I decided his face was artless. "So, Edith Walker, what led you to the world of art?"

"My dad." I didn't elaborate, rubbing at the embroidered flowers on the tablecloth.

He sat back and rolled up his sleeves like he was thinking this through. "Tell me about your hobbies."

"I don't have any."

"Everyone's got hobbies." His laughter was confoundingly free of deceit.

What was missing in Jonathan, which was engrained in myself and everyone I knew, was bitterness. Only Clair was like that. I couldn't stay annoyed with him. Even so, I wished he'd back off.

"How do you spend your free time?" He looked at me expectantly.

I searched for my sister. What else was there to do?

"We need to get you a hobby," he continued as I pressed my hands on my forehead to fight the margarita brain-freeze.

When our shared platter arrived, it smelled delicious. I was famished, as though I'd been deprived of real food for months. I turned my attention to the mariachis while we ate.

"I've always wanted to bake pies," I finally told him between songs.

"Now we're talking. What kind?"

"Coconut cream, rhubarb. Pumpkin. And I want to play

the piano," I added, finishing my third taco and moving on to the enchiladas.

Through the trees in adobe planters, I saw a moving flash of colour. The mariachis were making their way around the tables. Couples stood and danced. I was ready to go home.

"IS THAT A toucan?" I asked Jonathan when we walked out.

"It is indeed," he said, discreetly sliding an arm around my waist as he led me into the cold. The arm didn't feel so bad there.

I invited him in. If only to have him enter the silent space between my routine thoughts, so my mind couldn't stir up unwanted memories. Being with Jonathan was simple and straightforward. Maybe I needed this for a while.

Once inside, I plugged in the lights dressing the living room window frame. The pegs livened up the dull space. It was the first time I had experienced their effect since stringing them up the month before.

Wearing herself out with barking, Mira manoeuvred her way onto Jonathan's lap as soon as he sat down. He patted her head and spoke directly to her. Then he picked up *On the Track of Unknown Animals* from a stack on the floor. "This one's a keeper," he said, flipping through it. "It's hard to find, no pun intended." The book had that out-of-print, musty smell to it. I'd read parts of it, but the stories of extinct animals were so disheartening I couldn't finish.

I made espresso on the stovetop. When it was ready, I emptied the grinds from the funnel filter as Liam had shown me how to do. The grinds left a hard, dark puck in the sink. I regretted Jonathan's presence again.

I carried the small cups and box of dessert over on a tray.

Jonathan's eyes were the same colour as the coffee. I offered him a Flakie, still in plastic.

"I can see why you want to bake pies," he said after a bite. "On the upside, if there's ever a nuclear disaster, I bet the shelf life of these bad boys would save us." He rearranged Mira so they both viewed me. "So. Tell us about yourself."

I couldn't say what possessed me. It was that mellow face of his, all sincerity.

"I have a sister. Vivienne." As if by mentioning her I'd keep her existence going, like an occult spell where you invoked a person's name aloud to conjure them up once more.

Then I ate some Flakie and started blubbering. I poured everything out to Jonathan. About Viv's pageantry and the scraps between her and Con, and how Con was still in denial over Viv.

I told him how Viv was missing four months now. How she wreaked havoc wherever she went. Or was it misfortune persecuting her from the get-go, was she damned? I said there were times I wished her dead.

And I told him about the hospital and our plans for a transplant in India. I told him about the morgue. But other events I didn't mention. Those surrounding Henry's betrayal. Or what happened with Liam, whose name I wouldn't say aloud ever again. I left out the part about Omar. The history I shared with him and what we took from each other.

But in releasing the rest to Jonathan, I processed those events also, laying them down in separate, hard-to-reach spaces like the compartments in Henry's paperweight boxes. The weights I wouldn't think about anymore. The weights I'd close the lid on. This was my bereavement for those parts of myself I'd squandered.

Afterwards, I was spent. I'd gone through half a box of Kleenex. Since Mira was scratching at the door, Jonathan suggested we walk.

We put on our coats and went around the block, Mira leading the way like an invalid reindeer. Moonglow permeated through the clouds. The snow sparkled like tinsel. The air had warmed up and a fresh snowfall gave the neighbourhood the feel of a new bar of soap.

We passed through the quiet streets without talking. In giving me this gift of silence, Jonathan went up again in my esteem.

Back at the door, I saw something reliable in his open face that warmed me. Briefly, I considered a kiss. Instead, I only asked him a question. "I read about this healing river, inland in Florida. Where unicorns supposedly dip their horns. Do you believe it's there? I mean, can you take sick people there, hypothetically?"

His eyebrows lowered with concern. "Does it matter what I think?" He said it with something like tenderness. "If you want, we can try to find it," he added.

"Someday, maybe."

Whether or not the place was mythical would probably be unclear to me for the rest of my life.

FIFTY-THREE

Spring came anyway. Just before her due date, Raven begged me to be the godparent.

"I'm not Christian," I told her.

"Me neither, I'm doing this to shut my mom up," she said. "Besides, this kid needs all the protection it can get."

Most days she looked terrified. Maybe she didn't want a child in case it was predisposed with the gene that skipped generations like hair and eye colour. Like cancer.

My cell still rang, but it wasn't about Viv anymore.

Sometimes, on my breaks, I'd find a bench in the Great Hall dome and call Constance in Florida. I suppose I missed her. Everyone in my family was gone.

Through the dome's glass wall, I watched the last of the winter's snow fall on *Maman's* spiralling body and her long, arched legs. Groups of schoolchildren ran beneath the giant spider, launching snowballs at her cage-like sac of eggs.

I asked Con if she got the books I sent on emphysema and she thanked me, all the while puffing away on her cigarettes

327

at the other end of the line, probing when I was going to fly out.

She asked after Mira but didn't mention Viv. Most likely she tricked herself into thinking Viv would snap out of her suspended animation and resurface—Instant Life!—as she once was: intact, youthful, alive.

I told her about Clair. The few visits I'd had with her, and how I'd grown fond of Nick and Nahlah. "I will come to meet the little one *bientôt, je viendrai*," Con repeated.

So far she hadn't shown up.

I introduced Jonathan to Clair after I stopped putting off his advances. So enraptured was he with my niece's games that he forgot I was even with him. I saw then what a good father he'd make, though I gave myself no illusions—he didn't spark my insides the way Liam did. But I'd been through that fiery passion. Maybe I was more the type for a painless intimacy that grew casually, shaped by the years.

Peng gave me roots and remedies, telling me I was spiritually empty. I also brought Mira to him. He cleared up her infections with kelp and garlic, saying she'd live forever if I gave her five drops of ginseng root a day. Her bronchitis went away and her eyes became clean and shining. The more I exercised her, the less she limped. I asked Peng if there was a cure for her licking and he said no, so I plugged my nose and tolerated it. The only thing that fascinated her equally was the salamander paperweight. She pawed at it and rolled it around on the floor like a chew toy. Give it up, it's in there for good, I told her. Locked in its own patina. Lustrous and untouchable, like some higher power.

When it came to Viv, I had a hard time sequencing events. I tried to arrange them as frames of a film strip, but they scattered on the floor like the fake pearls off one of her tiaras, falling through heating ducts, rolling behind furniture. Pieces of my sister, in disarray and impossible to refabricate.

Occasionally I still walked past the Laff and thought I saw her in there, sketching, sipping on a sparkling ale. I told myself, cork *floats*. It's buoyant and impermeable. I saw what wasn't there.

I took over Raven's job in the streets. I included my sister's picture in every bag of food I handed out. I got used to people telling me they'd seen her, their eagerness faltering when I asked for proof.

Girls with teased hair sat rigid against derelict buildings, their once-virginal skin gone flaky, their once-full lips razor-thin. *You're so ghetto,* the one mainlining meth told the one shooting up Wellbutrin, a pharmaceutical prescribed for depression. It was the new cheap alternative to a blast of rock. It burned through the veins and ate the skin down to the bone, carving abscesses like shark bites into the body.

The novelty of seeing me wore off quickly. This one offered me an injection. That one told me for five bucks I could take her picture. *Hey! I used to be a majorette, jelly bean!* On sedate days she pointed out how I could improve my pies. On grandiose days she antagonized me and hurled the food back in my face with a myriad of profanities, because I didn't have any idea. I really had no idea.

With these girls, I stood alongside enlightenment. It was right there and I renounced it, even though they prepared me, as the morgue had prepared me.

But I couldn't believe Viv curled up and died like an animal in a skeleton den. I read that cirrhosis had become reversible, what with advances in medicine. She could have been in good health somewhere warm. Eating salads and painting.

If Con and I were patient, she'd call for cash or a place to stay and we'd have a good laugh about how she worried us. "You shouldn't stress so much, Worm," Viv would say.

I had it figured out. I'd get her fixed up and stick by her until she was better. Do what I didn't the first time around. While she rested in bed, I'd comb her flaxen hair and tell stories. Starting with the time, as girls, we sat in a patch of clover and found a hummingbird there in our own backyard, iridescent and no larger than our palms. Viv drew it in all its stillness and gave me the picture, before Henry put the body in a shoebox of grass.

He told us the next morning that it had flown away.

DRIFTING THROUGH GALLERY spaces, I thought of Theo often. Mostly I pondered his lifelong obsession with the remnants of lost worlds, and his pilgrimages through pristine and unravaged lands. And I thought about how we were all caught up by unreachables: those lost to us that we couldn't get back, who beckoned from a place off the radar, beyond our grasp.

Against logic, I imagined Theo recovering. The day he'd no longer be wheeled to the window like a corpse, I'd go with him to Hiva Oa. I pictured us in the lush, humid jungle with sketches, maps, binoculars, and nets, looking for that splendid phantom bird. Trekking inland past high-class resorts on the sea, past huts and villagers and roosters crowing through the night, with the koao in our hearts.

The purple-plumed cryptid was always ahead of us, dashing into mudholes, digging tunnels beneath the ground we walked on as we made our way through the mist.

Winged souls moved inside the landscape unseen. We tripped over a clue. Caught sight of something, held our breath. In the pre-dawn, we waited for a reappearance.

It didn't materialize again.

EPILOGUE

I STAND WITH STRANGERS in the shuttle parking lot. It's the middle of June, but the thin mountain air is still cool enough to give me goosebumps this early in the morning.

For over a year, I added to and removed from the suitcase, planning more than one itinerary in my mind.

Viv's scarf and mitts keep me warm.

When the yellow bus finally comes hurtling around the bend, we pile into it like criminals. I slide into a seat near the front and put on Liam's scuffed-up aviators. The vehicle is packed—everyone reserved months ago.

Voices hush down as we climb the rugged spine of dirt road, everyone's face glued to the windows as meadows sprinkled with burgeoning wildflowers, soft pine forests, and snow-capped peaks emerge before us like a fairy tale.

The little motel along the highway is gone. On an impulse I booked a room at the Château Lake Louise, where we dropped Constance off and where she spent her days while we went hiking.

Last night, I wandered the shore of the ice-cold lake. I sat on a log at twilight, looking across the emerald water and the glacier rising above it, until the scenery turned into a whitish-blue ghost of itself, changing to a shade Henry would have found challenging if not impossible to recapture on canvas.

My hiking boots pinch at the ankles. By the time these two months are up, the leather will be broken in. When I told Jonathan where I was going, he insisted I borrow his bear bell and his walking sticks. He brought me to MEC to buy pants with legs that unzip at the knee to make shorts. Henry would have got a kick out of these. He gave me a container filled with granola and beef jerky. He drove me to the airport and kissed me before I went through Departures. Whether we'll stay together, I don't know.

The bell chimes as I step down from the bus and put on my backpack. The tourist hut is a miniature of what I recall. Inside, I buy a few postcards. One for Clair, one for Con, one for Jonathan and Theo, one for Raven and Wren.

"Won't she get pestered with a name like that?" I asked Raven when she was born. But now I see the name suits her, with her shiny black hair and her small, powerful fists. At fourteen months, Wren is conspicuous with a loud, complex song.

Wren and Raven adore Mira so much they've adopted her while I travel. I miss that tiny mutt. We got used to one another this past year, during which time we took walks with Jonathan and his shepherd Darwin.

I pick a card with a hoary marmot basking in the sun. I'll send it to their new address at Body Poets, which had its grand opening last month and where Raven says I have a job in the front spa if I want one. Yet I already miss the viewing room. My few regulars there, and the quiet light after mornings in storage. I even miss Alejandro's antics.

For Clair, I choose the card with the yearling deer. On Viv's birthday this past May, I picked her up and we went to Magnolia Park, just the two of us. The trees were in bloom, these cups aimed skyward and falling like eggshells into the grass around us, as if we were in some kind of Shangri-La. I don't spend as much time with Clair as I'd like. But I see Magnolia Day becoming a tradition between us.

I can't hear my father anymore, telling me I've given up too soon, too easily. In the dead of winter, his voice dissolved and I began to feel my sister's presence beside me. Sometimes I can almost smell her sweet, sisterly essence from childhood.

Over time, my idea of happiness has changed.

Viv's erasure took away the possibility for profound joy, scarring like a clear-cut so vast it can be seen from outer space. Nothing grows back there.

THE SPRUCE AND larch forest around Lake O'Hara yields to ridges, cliffs, and stream beds of lichen. I climb in solitude through the fragile alpine terrain.

I go by brooks and lakes, each one a different blue-green unlike any man-made hue.

I pass hanging valleys and boulder fields as I gain elevation. Then I reach the rock slide and the roaring waterfall bursting forth, and the hillside.

The slope is patchier than I remembered. Eroding and worn out from the trampling of goats who probably moved on to more abundant pastures long ago.

Still, the unicorn could exist. In a remote place we haven't yet been.

I keep climbing. Eventually I crest the peak and a breath-taking chain of Rockies comes into view, this immense crown of snow and stone, and lakes strewn below like gems.

Briefly, I see us all together, When We Were: Constance with her cherry lips and polka-dot bikini, sunbathing by the kidney-shaped motel pool. Henry at his easel, painting the mountain with me clinging to his side. Viv cannonballs off the diving board, splashing us. Liam is on the periphery, collecting fossils. My mother's honeyed laughter erupts, we're all laughing, and then the memory is gone.

Here I spread his ashes — what didn't go in the Gatineau Hills and the little I put in Con's suitcase, unknown to her — to mix with cloud and glacial silt.

I could stay for hours, finding solace in the tundra, the plays of grey and pink. But it's time to head northward, to the place they both wanted to see. Up the Alaska Highway to Whitehorse — *white horse* — where daylight doesn't end at this time of year.

Above the treeline I inhale, exhale, breathing clearly. The world slows down around me.

Then, out of the corner of my eye, this brilliance.

ACKNOWLEDGEMENTS

One character in this novel was inspired by someone real. My great uncle, Theo Kunke, was a psychologist, world traveler, and art lover. His Amsterdam home resembled a museum. He was a passionate, loud, generous, and eccentric person. I wish I knew him longer before he died.

I would like to thank my wonderful agents, Samantha Haywood and Stephanie Sinclair, for their enthusiastic belief in my writing. I am also grateful to my editor, Janice Zawerbny, who took a chance on me, and whose invaluable suggestions greatly improved the story. Thank you to John Sweet for his masterful copyediting. And heartfelt thanks to the entire House of Anansi team, who made it all come true.

I am indebted to my family: Hans, Denise, and Nadine Berkhout, and Farhad Kazemzadeh (*dooset daram azizam*), for reading the first and last draft, and for their unfailing support. Thanks to Shawna Lemay, Ruth Linka, Tom Mack, and Joanne Reaves, who read the manuscript in its earliest form, and offered encouragement, too. And thank you to the National Gallery and its extraordinary collection that illuminates my every day.

There exist few scholarly publications on cryptozoology or unicorns. I would have been lost without the writings of Chad Arment, Loren Coleman, Bernard Heuvelmans, Chris Lavers, Willy Ley, Odell Shepard, Karl Shuker, and Scott Weidensaul. I am also appreciative of the advice received from the following experts: Dr. Kaiser Raja of BGS Global Hospitals; Debbie Dunn and Reina Fuller of Ontario Parks; Cheryl Mahyr of OFPS; and Judy Stilwell of Shepherds of Good Hope Foundation.

Finally, my deepest gratitude to R., most especially Brooke, Lyn, Paula, Ron, Shelley, Teri, and Wolf. I will never be able to properly communicate everything you have done for me. This book wouldn't exist without you.

ABOUT THE AUTHOR

NINA BERKHOUT is the author of five poetry collections, most recently *Elseworlds*, which won the 2013 Archibald Lampman Award. Originally from Calgary, Alberta, she now resides in Ottawa, Ontario, where she works at the National Gallery of Canada. This is her first novel.